JUST A LITTLE TEMPTATION

MERRY FARMER

JUST A LITTLE TEMPTATION

Cover design by Erin Dameron-Hill (the miracle-worker)

ASIN: B085F2CZ5D

Paperback ISBN: 9798639272516

Click here for a complete list of other works by Merry Farmer.

If you'd like to be the first to learn about when the next books in the series come out and more, please sign up for my newsletter here: http://eepurl.com/RQ-KX

Created with Vellum

CHAPTER 1

LONDON – APRIL, 1890

Stephen Siddel had his hands full. More than full.

"Sir! Fanny is hogging all the biscuits!"

"I can't find my other shoe, sir!"

"Jane dipped my braid in ink!"

"No I didn't!"

"Sir, it isn't fair!"

The second Stephen stepped into the great hall of his orphanage, chaos erupted. Without fail. It was no wonder. Two dozen girls between the ages of five and fifteen ran mad in the spacious room, finishing up their breakfasts, attempting to complete last-minute schoolwork, playing with ragged dolls or roughly-carved wooden animals, chattering up a storm, and generally behaving the way all spritely and contented children did. The pandemonium always made Stephen smile, in spite of the exhaustion it inevitably brought with it.

"Jane, the only things that should be dipped in ink are pens," he said, adjusting his spectacles and walking down the center aisle between two long tables and resting a hand on the shoulder of a ten-year-old with freckles and hair that was still cropped short after an unfortunate bout of lice. "Your hair will grow back in no time, so there's no reason to be envious."

"Yes, sir," the girl said with a sigh, glancing adoringly up at him.

"And Katie, let's work on your tattling, shall we?" he grinned at the girl with the end of her braid blackened.

"She shouldn't have done it," Katie protested. Stephen gave her a frank look and her shoulders sagged. "Yes, sir."

Stephen walked on, "Fanny, one biscuit only until you finish your maths." He plucked the mostly empty bowl of biscuits from the end of the table as he reached a plump eleven-year-old and her coterie of studious friends.

"I was sharing them," Fanny reassured him, peering up at him with moon eyes.

"I know, sweetheart." He rested a hand on her head before carrying the bowl on to the head table.

"Sir, can you help me find my shoe?" a small girl named Ivy asked, tugging on the tails of his coat.

Stephen turned to find he'd developed a small

entourage of girls. They looked to him as though he held the answers to every question in the universe in his hands. "When was the last time you had two shoes?" he asked Ivy in a kind voice.

"I don't know." Ivy shrugged.

Her younger sister, Lori, slipped a sticky hand into Stephen's and leaned against him for no apparent reason. The gesture lifted his heart, making him smile in spite of the chaos that still ruled.

"Did you check under the stairs?" he asked. "I've no idea why, but missing things always seem to show up under the stairs."

"We didn't check there," Ivy admitted, filling with energy. "Come on," she said to her friends, turning and dashing off down the aisle between tables.

"No running," Stephen called after them, though he might as well have been telling them not to be young.

A game of tag had popped up on one side of the room, under the windows that beamed with morning sunshine. The sun illuminated the sad state of the great hall. It was large and bright, but half the wallpaper had peeled away months ago, leaving grubby plaster exposed. The wainscoting needed a thorough scrub, and perhaps a coat of paint. The floor was scuffed and worn. It most certainly could have used a polish. The curtains that hung from the windows—or what was left of them after the moths had had their way—were in desperate need of laundering. The entire orphanage had a run-down, drab feel to it. At least, in appearance. Stephen was fiercely proud of the fact that, underneath the wear and tear, his home, the home he'd provided for the unfortunate girls who had been cast off by an uncaring society, was filled with joy and love.

Hard on the heels of that blissful thought came a sigh from Mrs. Ross, who was seated at the head table, several ledgers spread in front of her.

"It's no use, Mr. Siddel," she said, shaking her head and rubbing her temples. "There's far more going out than there is coming in. At this rate, we might have to shut our doors by the end of the year."

"We're not going to shut our doors," Stephen told her, still maintaining his smile. "These girls have nowhere to go and no one to care for them if not us."

As if to emphasize his point, a thin, tow-head girl skipped over to him, silently handing him a drawing of a bird that she'd just finished. Stephen took it, adjusted his spectacles as he glanced at it, and exaggerated his delight as he studied the drawing.

"This is beautiful, Ginny," he told her resting a hand on her head. "You've the makings of a brilliant artist."

Ginny smiled up at him, her two front teeth missing, then wheeled around and darted back to her place at one of the tables.

Mrs. Ross humphed. "The way you let them waste paper is a sin. Are you aware of how much paper costs?"

"It's a price I'm willing to pay to foster creativity," Stephen said, placing Ginny's drawing on the table.

Mrs. Ross glanced at it with a fairly impressed look,

and Mrs. Ross wasn't generally free with her praise. She had seen more than most people in her fifty years, which was reflected in her grey hair—which she still managed to style fashionably—and the lines on her face. Stephen had been lucky to find Mrs. Ross, and her daughter, Annie, when he'd inherited the building that housed the orphanage ten years ago, at the tender age of twenty. Few people would even consider hiring a former prostitute and her illegitimate daughter, especially to run an establishment meant to care for children, but Stephen had recognized the older woman's sharp mind and savvy business sense right from the start.

She had recognized a few key things about him as well. Things he desperately needed to keep hidden if he was to maintain his place in what passed for society in East London. She had been willing to keep his secrets right from the beginning, and he had been quick to give her a secure living and a roof over her head.

"You'd better hope the concert at the Bardess Mansion next week brings in a flood of donations," Mrs. Ross warned him. "We're living hand-to-mouth as it is."

"We'll be fine, Mrs. Ross," Stephen told her with a wink. "Something always comes along to rescue us just before we're thrown into the fire."

Mrs. Ross hummed doubtfully, then pulled the largest ledger closer to her. She did have a point, though. They needed to perform outstandingly at the Bardess Mansion concert so that the high and mighty of society opened their purses. The wallpaper and curtains depended on it. Although, if the concert proved to be a disappointment, Stephen had other places to turn for help. He'd already appealed to The Brotherhood and had faith that the organization would come through for him.

Until that happened, God helped those who helped themselves.

"Girls!" He clapped his hands, doing his best to snag the attention of the noisy, busy room. "Girls, it's time for song practice."

Several of his young charges erupted into shouts of excitement. A few raced from one end of the hall to the piano in the front corner. Fanny and her group closed up their schoolbooks, stacking them neatly on the corner of the table. Katie and Jane appeared to be bickering and hadn't paid attention to his announcement. Stephen started toward them, dodging pigtails, skirts, and giggles as the girls made their way toward the piano, where Annie Ross already sat, playing the first notes of a simple hymn. The piano was badly out of tune, but the music of a dozen young voices breaking into song was like heaven.

That slice of heaven burst into the full glow of paradise as Stephen glanced to the doorway and spotted the most handsome gentleman he'd ever seen. He stood a little straighter and touched his spectacles to make certain he was seeing right. The man was clearly a part of the aristocracy. His clothes said as much. They were of fine fabrics and fit exquisitely, though Stephen knew he shouldn't be studying the man's trim waist and broad shoulders. His thoughts refused to settle as he took in the man's dark, curly hair, sparkling, hazel eyes, and shapely lips. If he didn't replace thought with action, he'd be in trouble before he could say "boo".

"Can I help you?" he asked, striding up the aisle between the tables to meet the man.

"Yes, I'm looking for Mr. Stephen Siddel," the gentleman said.

Stephen's heart flipped in his chest. *Thank you, Lord.* Aloud, he said, "I'm Stephen Siddel," and extended a hand.

The gentleman took it with a pleased grin. "Lord Maxwell Hillsboro," he introduced himself.

"My lord." Stephen nodded respectfully.

"Oh, none of that," Lord Hillsboro laughed. "I'm barely a lord at all. Only by default. I'm a younger son, and it was only a stroke of luck that my father had a subsidiary title left over to give me the honorific. In truth, I'm desperate to get as far away from all that as possible." He was rambling, and a charming flush splashed his cheeks.

"I see." Stephen smiled in spite of the voice in his head that told him to behave. Lord Hillsboro's hand felt strong and warm in his as they shook, which made good sense hard to hold onto. The man really did have the most fetching eyes. He hadn't had such a strong reaction to a stranger in years. "How can I help you, Lord Hillsboro?" he managed to ask.

"Actually, I was hoping I could help you," Lord Hillsboro said.

Stephen's brow inched up. The music from the other side of the room grew louder as the majority of the girls gathered around the piano to practice. Stephen glanced over his shoulder, spotting Katie and Jane still squabbling at their table.

"Excuse me for just one moment, Lord Hillsboro. Then we can find a quieter place to speak." Stephen held up a finger, then headed over to Katie and Jane. "Girls, it's time for song practice," he reminded them.

"My hair is turning black," Katie said with an indignant frown.

"At least you have hair," Jane huffed.

"Song practice," Stephen reminded them, tapping their shoulders to get them to stand.

The two girls rose reluctantly from their bench, glaring at each other. Stephen escorted them away from the table and over to the piano. He checked on Lord Hillsboro, sending him an apologetic look as he did. But Lord Hillsboro looked utterly charmed by the scene. That fact did nothing to stop the pulsating feeling in his heart...and lower. He'd been around young girls too long and had grown a sentimental heart, just like them. Other parts of him were far more grown up. Parts he needed to bring in line. Lord Hillsboro would probably be appalled if he could read Stephen's mind.

"Sorry about that," he apologized as he returned to the man and gestured for him to follow him down the hall to his office. "Things tend to be a bit chaotic around here in the morning." He paused, glancing over his shoulder to the gorgeous man as he turned the corner into his shabby office. He laughed. "Things tend to be chaotic around here in the afternoon and evening too."

"I imagine so with a houseful of children," Lord Hillsboro said good-naturedly. "Which is why I'm here today."

"Oh?" Stephen gestured for him to sit on one of the mismatched chairs in front of his desk. He would much rather have sat in a chair beside him, but protocol dictated that he hide behind the desk. Which was probably for the best, considering what just the sight of the handsome nobleman was doing to him. He straightened his glasses, then folded his hands on the top of the desk. "How can I help you?"

"As I mentioned," Lord Hillsboro said, sitting on the edge of his chair and leaning toward Stephen, "I am but a humble younger son of a noble family. And as such, no one has ever expected much from me."

"I doubt that," Stephen smiled. Good Lord, he was flirting.

Lord Hillsboro laughed. "Believe me. Neither my family nor anyone else has ever expected anything from me. But I expect things of myself."

"Oh?" Stephen was intrigued by the decisiveness in the man's eyes.

"Yes. I want nothing more than to create a life for myself outside of the pervue of my family, even my class, if you can believe that. I intend to use a portion of my inheritance, such as it is, to cause real good in this world,"

Lord Hillsboro explained. "I want to contribute to society, not just benefit from it. I want to build something instead of just enjoying the fruits of someone else's labor."

His energy was contagious. "A very admirable goal," Stephen said, leaning in as if drawn toward him.

"Your orphanage was suggested to me by...a friend, as a potential outlet for my charitable impulses."

A rush of joy filled Stephen. Suggested by a friend? Could that friend be The Brotherhood? The timing of Lord Hillsboro's arrival coincided with his request for help. And if The Brotherhood had sent the man, it was highly likely he shared Stephen's tastes. The possibility thrilled him. And filled him with anxiety.

"We could certainly use help," he said, smiling far more than he should have, but inching back as though Lord Hillsboro were fire and if he got too close he would burn. "The orphanage is home to twenty-five girls between the ages of five and fifteen. It's quite a stretch to keep them all fed, clothed, and educated. We do our best, though."

"The girls I saw seem quite happy." Lord Hillsboro grinned at him just as openly as Stephen was grinning.

The idea that they were flirting as outrageously as any other coquettes left Stephen with a surreal feeling. "I do my best to provide a loving home for them," he explained. "With the help of Mrs. Ross and her daughter, Annie."

"How long have you been running this establishment?" Lord Hillsboro asked.

"Just over ten years. I inherited the building from an uncle. It was a boarding school before, but had closed a year or so before my uncle's death. I intended—"

His explanation was cut short as a small boy in a starched, navy blue uniform wandered into the room. He ignored Lord Hillsboro as he walked around the desk and hopped up onto Stephen's lap. Once there, he rested his head against Stephen's shoulder and poked his thumb into his mouth.

"Hello, Jerry," Stephen laughed, writhing awkwardly. His mood had shot into an entirely inappropriate direction as he talked with Lord Hillsboro. He desperately needed to pull himself together. Anything that split his focus away from his responsibilities to the children was dangerous, even if it was tempting. "Tired of the sisters today, are we?" he asked.

Jerry nodded and continued sucking his thumb.

"The sisters?" Lord Hillsboro asked.

"The Sisters from Our Lady of Perpetual Sorrow up the street," Stephen explained. "They run an orphanage too. Very different from ours."

"I see." Lord Hillsboro waved at Jerry with a friendly smile.

"We have a bit of a rivalry," Stephen went on. "Mostly because my methods of childrearing are quite different from those of the nuns."

"I can imagine," Lord Hillsboro laughed.

"Jerry here likes a bit of respite from the rigors of the nuns now and then." Stephen ruffled the young boy's hair.

"I can imagine we all would." Lord Hillsboro beamed, glancing up and meeting Stephen's eyes. The mirth in those eyes was exactly what he didn't need with a child sitting on his lap.

"Why don't I give you a tour of the orphanage so you can see the sorts of needs we have?" he asked, rising and setting Jerry on his feet. He had other sorts of needs he wagered Lord Hillsboro could satisfy as well. Needs he hadn't even considered for ages. It was sheer madness for him to consider them now. He took Jerry's hand, hoping the infusion of innocence would keep him on the straight and narrow.

He stepped around the desk, gesturing for Lord Hillsboro to precede him out of the room. The sound of the girls practicing in the great hall filled the entire school.

"I love music," Lord Hillsboro said as Stephen accompanied him upstairs to show him some of the dormitories. "I always have."

It was another point in the man's favor.

"The girls are practicing for a concert next week," Stephen said, stopping at the top of the stairs. "We're hoping to raise funds for some essential repairs. These are the dormitories."

He proceeded to give Lord Hillsboro a full tour of the upstairs, explaining how what little discipline his girls had was maintained and where most of them had come from. There were far too many orphans in that section of London, and because of the reputation for kindness that his orphanage had, there were always more girls in need of homes than Stephen had room to house.

After touring the upstairs, they moved to the ground floor and the kitchen and laundry. Jerry held Stephen's hand the entire time, perfectly content to tag along in silence.

"Everyone takes a turn with cooking and chores," he explained. "Even me."

"You cook?" Lord Hillsboro asked, seemingly charmed.

"And do laundry," Stephen added with a bashful laugh. "If everyone didn't chip in, nothing would ever get done."

They made their way back to the great hall, where song practice had hit some sort of a lull.

"Oh, Mr. Siddel." Annie jumped up from the piano bench and dodged through the girls surrounding the piano—most of whom had continued to sing even after Annie stopped playing, though not necessarily the same song. "Mr. Siddel, something must be done."

Annie reached him, clasping his arm and staring up at him with the same moony look that the younger girls wore.

Stephen squirmed inwardly even more than he usually did, highly conscious of Lord Hillsboro standing beside him. "What's wrong now, Annie?"

"It's the piano, Mr. Siddel. Something must be done

about it," Annie said, standing far too close. "It's out of tune, and I'm afraid one of the strings just snapped. Middle C at that."

"Oh, dear," Stephen sighed.

"We need the piano," Annie appealed to him, batting her eyelashes. "How could we possibly fulfill your vision for an angelic girls' choir without it?"

Heat rose up Stephen's neck. He peeked sideways at an amused Lord Hillsboro, then cleared his throat. "I'll see what I can do. For now, let's continue with rehearsal. The concert is next week."

"Yes, Mr. Siddel," Annie said. She hesitated for one moment, gazing up at him, before scurrying back through the girls to the piano.

As soon as she started playing again, Lord Hillsboro asked in a teasing voice, "Is she your wife?"

Stephen burst out with embarrassed laughter. "No, not at all." He faced Lord Hillsboro more fully and said with careful deliberateness, "I'm not the marrying type."

Recognition lit in Lord Hillsboro's eyes, followed by an interest and warmth that sent Stephen's pulse racing. "Is that so?" he asked. His lips twitched and his gaze dropped to Stephen's mouth. "I would be more than happy to pay to have the piano repaired," he said. "Or replaced entirely. In fact, I believe I would like to finance a great many repairs that I can see your establishment needs."

"Did The Brotherhood send you?" Stephen asked quietly.

Before Lord Hillsboro could answer, there was a commotion in the front hallway, followed by a woman bellowing, "All right. Where is he?"

Stephen and Lord Hillsboro turned almost in unison as a tall nun in a drab, black habit stormed into the room.

CHAPTER 2

Stephen Siddel was the most adorable creation Max had ever laid eyes on. Everything about the man exuded charm and sweetness, from his relaxed posture to his threadbare suit to the spectacles that framed his arresting, blue eyes. The way he interacted with the orphaned girls and Jerry warmed Max's heart. It was clear that the children adored him, and with good reason. Stephen's round face and gentle features made him seem younger than Max suspected he was.

Stephen. He couldn't possibly think of the man as Mr. Siddel or plain Siddel, like he would any other acquaintance. There was too much familiarity about the man, as if he were an instant friend to everyone he met. Or so Max thought until the nun charged into the great hall.

"There you are," the nun snapped, standing tall and looking down her long nose at tiny Jerry—who now pressed close to Stephen's side as if hiding. "You are a wicked child for running away from your lessons."

Max's brow flew up as the nun marched over to Stephen and grabbed one of Jerry's hands. Jerry made a sound of protest as he was pulled away, but Stephen did nothing to stop the nun. Max considered intervening, but there was just enough kindness in the older woman's pinched features to hold him back.

"Sister Constance," Stephen addressed the nun in a conciliatory tone. "You know that Jerry is welcome here whenever he wants to visit. The girls enjoy his company, as do I."

"I like Jerry," one of the older girls interjected, inching closer to the confrontation.

"We all do," an older woman in plain clothes and an elaborate hairstyle added, stepping up to Stephen's side. She crossed her arms and stared at Sister Constance with narrowed eyes.

Max subtly shifted a hand to cover his mouth, as he was sorely tempted to laugh, or at least grin, at the scene. There was clearly no love lost between the older woman, who had taken sides with Stephen, and the nun.

Sister Constance proved his suspicion by tilting her head up and sniffing. "I absolutely forbid any of the young souls in my charge to sully their souls by spending even a minute under the same roof as a woman like you, Mrs. Ross."

Mrs. Ross didn't look impressed by the insult. "It's a damn sight better than them being stuffed and starched and forced to stand in rows or kneel on stones to say fruitless prayers by the likes of you."

"Ungodly abomination," Sister Constance hissed, pressing a hand to her heart.

"Uptight bitch," Mrs. Ross sneered in return.

Several of the girls who had gathered around gasped at Mrs. Ross's expletive and burst into giggles. Max had a hard time containing his mirth. Particularly since Stephen seemed to be enjoying the exchange on some level. He, too, had covered his mouth with one hand to hide an obvious grin. His eyes sparkled with humor behind his spectacles. Best of all, he shot a glance Max's way that made him feel as though they were watching the comedy together. That moment of connection sent Max's head spinning and his blood pulsing.

"Mr. Siddel, will you stand here and allow your employees to speak to a servant of God in this way?" Sister Constance boomed, turning to Stephen.

"Don't you go waving your god at me," Mrs. Ross countered before Stephen could answer. "What has He done for me lately? What has He done for any of these girls but set them down in a world that sees them as animals, simply because they are poor and female?"

Max lowered his hand and stared at Mrs. Ross in surprise. She had a good point—one that hit rather close to home, when all was said and done. How many times had he wondered about God's purpose in making him the way he was?

"The poor will be with us always," Sister Constance

said, standing taller. "And womankind is made to atone for Eve's sin."

"Balderdash," Mrs. Ross huffed. "You should know better."

"I know that salvation comes through the Lord, not your arrogant insistence on your own superiority," Sister Constance flung back at her.

Mrs. Ross let out a sharp laugh and crossed her arms. "You think I'm the one who has always thought herself superior?"

"Aren't you?" Sister Constance fired back.

Max glanced back and forth between the women as though watching a tennis match.

"You've been a pain in my arse since we were girls," Mrs. Ross sneered.

"You only think that because Mama loved me more."

Max nearly choked on the sudden revelation, or rather, on the laughter the revelation sparked in him. No wonder Stephen looked so amused by the confrontation. "The two of you are sisters?" Max asked.

"We *were* sisters," Sister Constance said, her superior manner growing even more pronounced. "The only sisters I have now are my sisters in Christ."

"And I wouldn't lay claim to sharing blood with her for all the tea in China," Mrs. Ross said.

Max was at a loss for words. He'd been told that Stephen Siddel's orphanage was unique by the agent in The Brotherhood who had recommended the place as something he could invest his charitable inclinations in, but he'd had no idea he'd take to the place so instantly.

Stephen cleared his throat, taking charge of the situation. "Again, Sister Constance, I apologize for luring Jerry away from his studies."

Max arched an eyebrow. As far as he could see, Stephen had no reason to apologize, nor had he lured anyone. The fact that he was willing to take the high road only raised Max's estimation of his character.

"You and the Sisters are doing important work," Stephen went on.

"Work which you are seeking to undermine, sir," Sister Constance snarled.

Stephen flinched in surprise, the expression making him look even younger. "I beg your pardon?" Hints of steel resolve were suddenly visible under the kindness of his outward expression. Hints that made Max grin all over again. Apparently, kindness was only one facet of Stephen Siddel's character.

"The Sisters of Perpetual Sorrow depend on the Bardess Mansion concert every year to raise funds," Sister Constance went on, swaying closer to Stephen as if she could intimidate him. Indeed, Max suddenly realized that the nun was just as tall as Stephen, and Stephen was a few inches taller than him. "You and your ragamuffins have swept in and stole our potential funding."

Understanding seemed to dawn in Stephen's expression and he relaxed by a hair. "My girls were invited to participate in the concert, Sister. I can assure you, I did not seek the event out from any malicious intent."

"I seriously doubt that," Sister Constance said with a humorless laugh. "It would be just like her to try to undermine me at every turn." She sent a seething glance to Mrs. Ross.

"I know the Bardess family," Max said, wary about cutting into the conversation, but eager to defend Stephen in every way. "They have buckets of money to give, as do their friends. I'm certain there is enough for everyone."

Sister Constance glanced to him as if noticing him for the first time. "And who, pray tell, are you?"

"This is Lord Maxwell Hillsboro," Stephen said, gesturing toward Max with a smile that made Max feel like the angel atop a Christmas tree. "He has come to investigate the orphanage as a potential donor."

Sister Constance studied Max as though he were an escapee from Bedlam. "You wish to give money to this den of misconduct?" she asked, incredulous.

"In fact, I do." Max glanced sideways at Stephen as though they were comrades on the same team sharing an old joke. He certainly felt like he'd known Stephen for years, even though they'd only just met. That feeling came as a surprise and a delight, and Max intended to grab hold of it and not let go. It was a rare and precious thing for him to feel so relaxed around anyone, let alone a stranger.

Sister Constance huffed and shook her head. "Be it

on your head then, my lord. But you should know that Mr. Siddel runs this establishment with appalling laxity. There isn't a shred of discipline among his charges. They are wild and wicked, and none of them will ever amount to any good."

Around the edges of the confrontation, the girls who had gathered to watch the encounter gaped and squeaked in indignation, folding their arms and, in a few cases, stamping their feet or sticking their tongues out at the nun.

"You see?" Sister Constance gestured to one of the girls sticking out her tongue—whose braid was black with ink on the end—as proof of her claims. "Wild beasts, all of them. And who is to blame for that?" She sent a pointed look to Stephen before turning it on Mrs. Ross.

"The girls in my care are happy and healthy," Stephen said, once again projecting kindness over iron-hard resolve. "My methods may be different than yours—"

"To say the least," Sister Constance snorted.

"—but they are effective." Stephen turned to Max. "I've been running this orphanage for ten years, and in all that time, every one of the girls who has reached an age where she can set out on her own has managed to find gainful employment, to stay honest and true, and to make more of herself than the lot that life handed to her."

"I'd say that's a glowing sign of success," Max said. He had a feeling anyone that spent more than a few minutes under Stephen's care would come out wanting to make the world a better place, if only for him. Max himself already felt a deep compulsion to create a world of happiness worthy of the goodness that radiated from Stephen.

Sister Constance shook her head. "Men," she huffed. "You know nothing about raising children. They need discipline and God."

"Like we had?" Mrs. Ross drawled.

"If we had been reared with rules and a respect for God, you wouldn't have ended up making a living on your back," Sister Constance hissed.

"What does making a living on your back mean?" one of the girls asked.

Stephen's face went bright red, which did nothing to help Max keep his composure. Sister Constance seemed to remember that they had an audience. She, too, flushed and looked ashamed.

"Never you mind, Betsy," Mrs. Ross said. "It's not something you're going to do in any case."

"I'll tell you later," one of the older girls whispered to Betsy. The others instantly looked at her like she was their leader.

"You will not," Stephen said with firmness and affection. "In fact, I think after our lessons this afternoon we'll all sit down and remind ourselves about good behavior and how we should be treating each other." He looked especially at a short-haired girl who stood next to the girl whose braid was black on the end.

Max spotted a pair of scissors in the short-haired girl's

hands. She raised them toward the other girl's braid. He cleared his throat and stepped closer to her, holding out his hand. The short-haired girl was stunned at having been caught and dutifully handed the scissors to him. At the same time, she seemed impressed that he had noticed her mischief.

"I think we've spent quite enough time here," Sister Constance said, tugging Jerry—who had watched the entire confrontation in silence, holding Sister Constance's hand with one hand and sucking his other thumb—closer and starting toward the door. "But don't think that things are resolved between us, Mr. Siddel. We will discuss the concert later."

Max watched the woman leave. As soon as she was gone, the girls who had gathered to watch the scene disbursed, taking seats at the long tables in the center of the room, returning to the piano, or running as though they'd been given leave to play.

"She always was a wet blanket," Mrs. Ross grumbled, turning back toward the front of the room. She paused as she turned, eyeing Max up and down. "You're a sight for these old eyes," she said with a saucy grin. "Back in my heyday, I'd have eaten you for breakfast."

Max choked on a laugh as she sauntered off to the head table. He had no doubt that she'd meant her words literally.

"My apologies for Mrs. Ross," Stephen said, his cheeks as pink and his expression as embarrassed as ever. "She speaks her mind."

"I'll say she does." Max grinned, closing the distance between the two of them. "I found it rather refreshing."

"You did?" Stephen's brow inched up in surprise. "People usually find Mrs. Ross to be a shock to the system."

Max shrugged. "Sometimes we need a shock to push us out of the ruts in our roads."

"And are you in a rut?" Stephen asked, a warmer quality entering his smile. "Is that why The Brotherhood directed you to our humble establishment?"

Max heard all the layers of Stephen's question and grinned. "To answer that, yes, The Brotherhood sent me. As I mentioned, I'm a boring, younger son intent on breaking away from an old, aristocratic family. I'm too low down on the list to end up with a seat in Lords, I'm not clever enough to enter the law, and I'm too wicked to consider the cloth."

Stephen's eyes lit up at the suggestion of wickedness.

Max went on with a shrug. "Neither am I the sort to be idle, though. Not like my brother, George. I must be active, and since I've had no luck at all finding a cause that interests me through the usual channels, I sought out the advice of The Brotherhood." He paused, almost certain he knew which way the wind was blowing, but eager to be absolutely sure, before asking, "I take it you're a member as well?"

"I am," Stephen answered with a smile that bored straight into Max's core. "I have been for years. They've been exceptionally helpful in enabling me to keep the doors of this place open, both in terms of donations and legal advice."

Max's smile widened. "Don't tell me you've actually had the pleasure of doing business with Dandie & Wirth."

Stephen met his smile as though they suddenly shared a commonality that tied them together even more closely. "I have. Though it was quite some time ago. I doubt they'd remember me."

"They're extraordinary, aren't they?"

"I've never met anyone like them," Stephen said. The light in his eyes shifted slightly and he lowered his head just a bit. "Well, until now."

Max's insides began to dance a jig. The last thing he'd expected to find himself doing when visiting an all-girls' orphanage was flirting shamelessly with its owner and headmaster. He certainly wasn't the type to engage in any sort of naughty behavior without thoroughly knowing a man, and only then in an absolutely private setting. But there was something about Stephen Siddel that tickled his fancy, and a few other things.

"Remind me to thank the bloke who gave me your name," he said, taking a risk and brushing Stephen's arm lightly. "I think this is just the sort of place I'd like to become more involved with." He raised his eyes to meet Stephen's, making it as clear as possible that he wanted to become more involved with him. And why not? Stephen was a delight, and if Max was right, he was interested.

"The orphanage could use whatever help you'd like

to give, my lord." Stephen's use of the title set Max's teeth on edge. So did the fact that he stepped back slightly. Had he read the signals wrong?

"My friends call me Max," he said.

"And am I your friend already?" The hope in Stephen's eyes was sweet and irresistible.

"I think we've been friends for ages without even knowing it," Max replied.

"It's good to have friends," Stephen said, then hesitated, glancing down to the floor. "Sometimes life feels very lonely."

There was no mistaking his meaning. Life could be lonely for men like them. Which was why he felt so willing and eager to rush into temptation, knowing the dangers it presented.

"I have to go now," he said, taking a reluctant step away. "But I'll return soon."

"You will?" Stephen looked both delighted and slightly wary at the prospect.

"Of course," Max said. "I don't intend simply to throw money at the orphanage. I'd like to be involved as well. I have two hands, after all, and they're perfectly capable of hanging wallpaper—" he nodded at the wall, "—or repairing furniture or polishing floors." They were good at a few other things as well, but time would tell whether he would get a chance to show those skills. "If you don't mind," he added quickly.

"Mind?" Stephen laughed. "I would be eternally grateful. We need all the help we can get."

Max grinned. "You have that help in me, then. Until tomorrow."

He winked, not trusting himself to reach out and shake Stephen's hand in that moment. He had a feeling that if he touched Stephen, he wouldn't be able to bring himself to leave. As it was, the temptation to rush headlong into Stephen Siddel's life and his world was almost irresistible.

CHAPTER 3

Stephen felt the effects of Lord Hillsboro's—or rather, Max's—visit almost immediately. The very next day, an astounding cheque was delivered to the orphanage from Max's bank along with a note: "*It isn't much, but it's a start.*"

In fact, it was more than a start. The orphanage hadn't seen that large a donation in years. Stephen took the cheque immediately to his bank for deposit. On the way home from his errand, he stopped by a bakery to purchase four dozen sweet rolls and the haberdasher to buy several spools of ribbon. The frivolous expense was worth it for the sight of Jane tying a ribbon in her cropped hair and staring at her reflection in one of the dirty windows with joy instead of despair.

Max had made it all possible. He had put smiles on the faces of Stephen's girls and ignited something far less innocent within Stephen. It was madness, but he couldn't stop thinking of the man. He couldn't get the memory of Max's mischievous eyes or his open nature out of his head. They barely knew each other. They hadn't spent more than an hour in each other's company. In spite of his protests, Max was of a higher station than Stephen could ever hope to be, though his own background was respectable enough. It was like Stephen had discovered for the first time how delightful it was to fancy someone.

Which terrified him. Having his head turned meant he wasn't keeping both eyes on his girls. They were his responsibility, his life. Woeful past experience had taught him that if he didn't pay single-minded attention to his charges, if he put himself first and indulged in a flirtation of his own, they could end up in danger. He would never be able to shake the memory of Alice who, at the tender age of fourteen, had found herself a beau while he was carrying on with a clerk who worked for a shipping company near the docks. Alice's flirting with the young man on the street had turned to sneaking out at night. Clandestine visits had resulted in Alice getting with child at too young an age. She and the baby had died in a horrific birth that still woke him up in the middle of the night in a cold sweat, even though it had happened eight years ago. He'd failed his girls once by putting himself first. He would never do it again.

Or so he'd thought until Maxwell Hillsboro had walked into his orphanage, all smiles and teasing, looking like Adonis reborn.

"You seem awfully sunny these days," Annie

commented as Stephen attempted to usher the girls from the great hall to the two classrooms at the back of the building for their daily lessons a few days after Max's initial visit. "I haven't seen you smile so much since that couple from Kent adopted Mary Louise." She dodged around two girls racing down the hall, swaying closer to Stephen.

"It's springtime," Stephen said, sighing happily. "The sun is shining, the garden is starting to bloom, and we have a chance of financial security for a change." Thanks to Max. Thanks to the orphanage's handsome, endearing patron. But Annie didn't need to know the real reason for his good mood.

Annie inched closer to him, batting her eyelashes as she glanced up at him. Her cheeks were pink and her brown eyes glowed with admiration. "I like to see you smile, Mr. Siddel. It does my heart good."

Prickles of awkward warning broke out down Stephen's back. He stepped away from Annie, pretending to be shooing the last of the girls coming out of the great hall along to the classrooms. "Life is better when we all smile," he told her. "And security is a certain recipe for happiness."

"I can think of other things that make people happy." Annie followed him down the hall. She stopped too close by his side as he peered into the first classroom to make certain Miss Brooks—a former resident who had gone on to teacher's college and who now worked for the orphanage as an instructor—had her class of younger students in hand.

Stephen's smile turned uncomfortable as he turned his head to study Annie. "That's the joyful thing about the world," he said. "There are so many things that can bring us happiness. We have but to seek them out with an open heart and they will come to us."

His mind and heart filled with Max—bringing joy and wariness—but right away he realized he'd said the wrong thing. Annie leaned closer to him, her eyes filling with stars as she pressed a hand to her heart.

"You're so right, Mr. Siddel," she said breathlessly.

Stephen cleared his throat and stepped away from her, ostensibly to check on the second classroom, where Mrs. Ross was settling the older girls into their lessons. It was his fault that Annie had the wrong end of the stick. He'd known almost from the start that she fancied him. Anyone with eyes could see it. It was also his fault that she persisted in her delusions that there could ever be anything between them. The practical voice in the back of Stephen's head told him that Annie could be a perfect escape if anyone ever seriously questioned his nature and therefore his fitness to own and operate an orphanage. She'd marry him in a heartbeat if he needed her to. But the very thought made him sick with guilt. She had no idea how uninterested he was and would always be. He was reasonably certain she didn't know men like him even existed.

"What do you have planned for this afternoon's

music lessons?" he asked, hoping to refocus her energy into something that would give her confidence instead of crushing her.

"Yes, I would like to know the same thing," said an unfamiliar woman's voice.

Stephen flinched and glanced down the hall to find a lady dressed to the nines in the latest fashions posed regally in the front hall. She looked utterly out of place in her butter yellow day dress, plumed hat, and diamond brooch as she stood between rows of ragged and threadbare coats hung on pegs on either side of the hall. Her haughty expression was at odds with the orphanage's humble appearance as well.

Stephen broke away from Annie, striding down the hall to greet the woman. "Hello," he said, feeling as awkward as he usually did when faced with a woman of the aristocracy. "I'm Stephen Siddel, owner of this establishment. And you are?"

"Lady Bardess," the woman said, holding out a gloved hand as though offering Stephen alms.

Stephen adjusted his presentation to something more in line with what the woman probably expected, though his mouth twitched into a wry grin as he did so. He'd never cared much for titles or protocol, but years of depending on the generosity of the high and mighty had taught him to play the part.

"Lady Bardess, you honor us with your presence today," he said, taking her hand and bowing over it.

Immediately, he wondered what Max would think of his nearly comical show of deference.

He straightened, pushing that thought aside. Indulging in fantasies was a horrible way to run what amounted to a business.

"I have been warned that your ragged orphan girls are not the sort of entertainment I should include in my upcoming concert, Mr. Siddel," Lady Bardess said, tilting her head up and sniffing at him. "I came to investigate whether that is true."

Stephen managed to keep his benign smile in place even as he clenched his jaw in frustration. He pushed his spectacles farther up his nose as he stood straighter. "I would be delighted to give you a tour of the place to reassure you that you have been misinformed," he said. Misinformed by Sister Constance, no doubt. Bless her, but the nun seemed intent on starting a war.

Lady Bardess tilted her chin up even higher. "Yes, I think a tour is necessary at this point. I am loath to bring dirty little urchins into my home."

Sour dislike filled Stephen's gut the way it did every time someone disparaged his girls. He had half a mind to cancel his girls' participation in the concert then and there. With Max's money, their needs were taken care of. But it would have been foolish to bite a hand he might need to feed his girls in the future.

"Right this way, my lady," he said, pretending good cheer and command as he escorted Lady Bardess down the hall toward the classrooms. "The girls have just begun their lessons."

Annie fell in by Stephen's side as he and Lady Bardess passed where she stood. Her eyes were round with admiration for the fine lady, which made a nice change from her adoration of him.

"We are home and family for twenty-five girls between the ages of five and fifteen," he explained, lowering his voice so as not to disturb the lessons. "Our establishment provides a home and education for those who have been cast off for various reasons. I am flattered to say that our reputation is such that small girls are often dropped at our doorstep in the middle of the night. And though we have limited facilities and cannot take them all in, we do our best to find homes for those we cannot keep and to take in as many as we are able to."

As he spoke, it dawned on Stephen that, with Max's donation, they might be able to purchase a few more beds and rescue a few more souls. That thought put a genuine smile on his face.

It stayed in place as Lady Bardess stepped into the classroom where Miss Brooks was teaching the youngest girls their letters. Lady Bardess paused inside the doorway, narrowing her eyes slightly as she studied the dozen or so girls seated in a circle on the floor with Miss Brooks at the front of the room.

"Why aren't they at desks?" she asked, not bothering to lower her voice.

Miss Brooks and the girls paused their lesson to stare

at Lady Bardess. The girls all gaped at Lady Bardess and her gown and hat.

Stephen cleared his throat, sending Miss Brooks a look that hinted for her to keep going as though they weren't there. "We've found that the younger girls are more engaged by this intimate approach," he said. "It is an educational experiment."

Lady Bardess made a non-committal sound. She continued to stare pointedly at the girls. There was something veiled and vaguely eerie in the way she watched them. It unsettled Stephen, but he couldn't tell why.

At last, Lady Bardess sniffed and turned to march into the hallway. "Just make certain they're cleaned up and ready to perform at my home next week."

She might have said more, but she was cut short as the front door opened and Max stumbled into the hall, arms laden with several paint cans. He had a canvas sack thrown over one shoulder from which the handles of paintbrushes stuck out.

"I knocked," he said, out of breath, as he moved farther into the hall, turning to shut the door with his foot. "But no one answered."

Stephen's heart flipped in his chest and other parts of him stood up and took notice. "Let me help you with that." He rushed forward, knowing full well he was grinning like a fool, and started taking paint cans from Max's arms. "What is all this?" The act of shifting paint cans from Max to him caused the two of them to brush up against each other and touch in a dozen intriguing ways.

"I said I wanted to help with repairs," Max said, helping to shift cans over to Stephen. Their eyes met for a moment and the air between them crackled with energy. For a heartbeat, neither moved, they simply gazed at each other. Then Max took another breath and launched into motion, stepping toward the entrance to the great hall. "I thought you would want to consult on wallpaper, but at least we could get started painting the wainscoting in here."

"Lord Hillsboro?" Lady Bardess interrupted Max's forward motion by stepping forward. Evidently, she startled him. Max jerked straight, nearly dropping the remaining paint cans in his arms. "I thought that was you," Lady Bardess went on. Her entire countenance had changed to a fetching smile.

Max twisted to face her with movements that were both clumsy and endearing. "Lady Bardess," he said, then attempted to bow graciously, in spite of his arms being full. "What a surprise to find you here."

"I was just thinking the same, my lord." Lady Bardess walked forward to meet Max with a sway in her steps that had the hair on the back of Stephen's neck standing up. He refused to call the sting that made his smile turn brittle jealousy, though.

"I, um, I am a patron of Mr. Siddel's brilliant establishment," Max explained, glancing to Stephen for a moment before focusing on Lady Bardess once more. He seemed to notice his hands were still full. "Oh." He glanced this way and that, finally pivoting toward the great hall and quickly setting the remaining paint cans and the canvas sack just inside the door.

Stephen marched past him, sending him a teasing smirk as he moved to set his paint cans against the wall with the others.

"I had no idea you were involved in the same sort of charities as I am." Lady Bardess took thorough charge of the scene, striding regally past Max and into the great hall. The look she sent over her shoulder to Max ordered him to follow her.

Max exchanged a look with Stephen as he strode into the great hall. "Yes, well," he fumbled. "I've no wish to simply sit on my inheritance and let it grow like grass under my feet."

Lady Bardess laughed as though he'd said something far cleverer than he had. "You always were a charmer, Lord Hillsboro. And how is your esteemed father, Lord Eastleigh, these days?"

"Quite well, my lady." Max clasped his hands behind his back. Stephen was impressed by the way he transformed from an approachable friend to a lord with as much of a stick up his arse as any other nob. Though the thought of anything up Max's arse sent his thoughts flying to all the places they shouldn't have been. "He's enjoying the season as usual. My sister is marrying Lord Tyson in June, and the entire family is preparing for that."

"So, your family will be connected to the Tysons now too?" Lady Bardess lit up, batting her eyelashes at Max.

She laughed, sending Max a flirtatious look. "I dare say your family is one of the most well-connected in all of England."

"Something that was certainly not my doing," Max answered modestly. He managed to appear confident and fiercely masculine while deferring to a woman, which sent Stephen's heart thumping.

Lady Bardess shifted her stance, stepping closer to Max. "I came here today to make certain Mr. Siddel's waifs are prepared to sing at a concert I am hosting at my late husband's mansion next week." She put emphasis on the word "late". "I do hope that you will be in attendance, my lord." The way she raked Max with a look made Stephen clench his hands into fists behind his back.

Then again, he was certain his jealousy was for nothing. Max was no more interested in Lady Bardess than he was in Annie. The quick, sideways look Max sent him said as much.

All the same, Max smiled and answered, "I wouldn't miss it for the world."

"Good." Lady Bardess grinned from ear to ear. "Now, if you will excuse me, I am a busy and important woman with many more errands to run this morning. Good day, my lord." She curtsied ever so slightly to Max before assuming her regal posture and walking out to the hall. The look she shot Stephen was as much an order for him to see her out as if it had been issued by a general.

Stephen strode forward, moving to hold the door for Lady Bardess. He said a gracious goodbye, which she more or less ignored as she marched to the carriage waiting just outside of the orphanage. As soon as she was gone, Stephen shut the door and shook his head, laughing.

"I had no idea you had a sweetheart," he told Max with a lopsided grin as he reentered the great hall.

Max laughed. "God forbid." He'd already turned and leaned over to pick up one of the paint cans. The movement gave Stephen a perfect view of the man's astoundingly perfect backside. He had to take a breath to steady his mounting desire. He couldn't afford to give in to madness.

"So. Painting the wainscoting, eh?" He forced himself to step away, to put as much distance as he could between Max and himself. It was like attempting to fight the pull of gravity.

"As I said the other day," Max started, removing his jacket and crossing to drape it across the end of the closest table, "I don't just want to throw money at a cause, I want to be involved."

Stephen's brow rose slowly as Max rolled up his shirtsleeves, revealing strong arms with the perfect amount of dark hair. He pushed his spectacles up his nose as if to get a better look. "Your lordship plans to paint wainscoting?" he asked, lips twitching into a grin.

"With your permission." Max bowed his head quickly.

"Well, I couldn't possibly let you do it alone."

Helping the man to paint wouldn't put his girls in

danger, or so Stephen told himself. He removed his own jacket, laying it on the table beside Max's and getting a ridiculous thrill at the sight of their clothes side by side. He rolled up his sleeves as well and was gratified by the look of interest Max gave him.

"I would never have expected a soft-hearted orphanage owner who wears spectacles to have such impressive biceps," Max said, his smile a little too wide, as he knelt to rummage through the canvas bag. He came up with a pair of paintbrushes and something to pry the paint cans open with.

"Carrying around small children all day and doing all the manual labor around this place does help keep one fit," he said, joining Max on the floor. He should back away, find something else to do. Alice's final, plaintive wails of pain echoed in his memory, but even they weren't enough to stop his heart from pounding as he smiled at Max.

As he took a paintbrush from him, their hands touched. They both lingered over the contact, meeting each other's eyes and getting lost there. Stephen tried to summon the will to be sensible and stoic, but without a hint of luck.

"Should we start here and see how far we can get?" Max asked in a low voice laced with deeper meaning.

Blood and heat pounded through Stephen. Never in his life had he lost his head over a man so fast. But Max didn't feel like a stranger, he felt like the limb Stephen didn't know he was missing. On top of that, their fingers still touched as Max hadn't let go of the paintbrush between them.

"I think that sounds delightful," Stephen said, his voice deeper than usual.

"Delightful," Max echoed. He leaned closer, his gaze dropping to Stephen's mouth.

Fear and the weight of responsibility screamed in Stephen's head, warning him to back away. But he couldn't move. All he could think about in that moment were Max's lips and the temptation they presented. Max was close enough for him to drink in the scent of his cologne and his skin. It felt as though he were falling into a bottomless pit and he couldn't stop.

They were a hair's breadth apart, so close Stephen could feel the heat pouring off of Max, so close blood pounded through him, hardening his cock, when Annie marched into the room.

"Is Lady Bardess staying for tea?" she asked.

Stephen and Max jerked apart so fast that Stephen nearly upset the can of paint by his side. The paintbrush between them clattered to the floor.

"Er, what? No." He leapt to his feet, adjusting his glasses. He cleared his throat, feeling heat flood his face. "She's already left."

"Oh." Annie's shoulders sagged. "I was hoping she'd stay and sample the scones I made this morning." Her expression turned moony again as she glanced up at Stephen, grinning. "I made your favorite, orange ginger."

"Thank you," Stephen said, still desperate to catch his breath.

Annie blinked, looking past him to Max, who was red-faced and furiously slapping white paint on the wainscoting closest to the doorway. "Oh, Lord Hillsboro." She managed a quick curtsy. "I didn't realize you were here. Would you like some tea?"

"Um, why, yes. That would be nice." Max smiled guiltily at her and continued painting, sloppily enough to drip white on the floor.

"I'll fetch it right away." Annie smiled, twirled toward the door, and skipped on her way.

As soon as she was gone, Max burst with laughter. "I can't believe she didn't see that." He sent Stephen the most adorable, guilty look.

Stephen cleared his throat and lowered himself carefully to his knees, picking up the fallen paintbrush. "I don't believe she would know what she was looking at even if she did see it," he said with a meaningful look.

"Thank God for innocence," Max agreed, attempting to be neater with his painting. "That and ignorance has kept more of us alive and safe than any measure we've taken ourselves, that's for sure," he added.

Stephen hummed in agreement, wondering how long Annie's innocence and ignorance would last if Max made good on his promise to devote himself to the orphanage. He wondered if he would be able to resist the man's charms or if disaster were about to strike again.

CHAPTER 4

Max took Stephen's comment about ignorance saving lives to heart. He was right. The vast majority of men like them that he knew were able to lead perfectly normal lives and to engage in society the same as anyone else by virtue of the fact that the world around them was ignorant to their true nature.

He wasn't ignorant about his attraction to Stephen in any way, though. The man was like catnip. His cheer and good nature were infectious. Max had been instantly enthralled by him. And when they had come within inches of kissing, he knew that he was gone. He wanted Stephen. He wanted to pull off his spectacles, tousle his hair, peel off his clothes, and explore every inch of the man's body. He wanted to hear the sounds of passion Stephen was bound to make and feel the release of tension in his body as he came. It didn't matter to him that they'd known each other for such a short time. If he had anything to do with it, they would know each other for a very long time to come.

But even the longest stretches of time started at the beginning.

"Are you certain you have time to pay this call with me?" Stephen asked him with genuine concern as the carriage Max hired to take them to Bardess Mansion pulled into the short drive in front of the townhouse.

Max laughed. "I thought I told you that I was an idle aristocrat with nothing better to do than throw himself into the affairs of a certain orphanage." He opened the carriage door without waiting for the driver to do it for them and hopped down, turning to offer Stephen a hand.

"I'm not keeping you from an afternoon of cards or shooting or whatever it is that the upper classes do to amuse themselves?" Stephen asked, taking Max's hand and stepping down.

Of course, he didn't need a hand getting out of the carriage at all. Max's assistance was all just an excuse for the two of them to make contact. He lingered with Stephen's hand in his for a moment, enjoying the heat that passed between them. Not a soul who witnessed the moment would think a thing of it. Ignorance was indeed bliss.

"I'm terrible at cards," Max chuckled as they fell into step together, heading from the drive to the impressive stairs that led to Bardess Mansion's front door. "And as unmanly as it makes me, I'm not particularly enamored of shooting helpless animals." He paused, tilting his head to the side. "Except, perhaps pheasants. There's nothing like a well-roasted pheasant with new potatoes and seasoned vegetables. And perhaps a good Yorkshire pudding to go with it."

"Stop," Stephen laughed. "I haven't had lunch yet. You're making me hungry." He sent Max a sideways look that hinted his appetite went far beyond excellent cooking.

Max's trousers went tight, particularly when Stephen walked ahead of him on the steps, giving him a perfect view of his excellent backside as he reached to ring the bell. It was all just so delicious—the titillation, the budding desire, the feeling of instant kinship—that Max couldn't wipe the smile from his face. He enjoyed the sensation of feeling unsettled in his own skin, and if he were honest with himself, he wasn't in any hurry to rush things to the next level. Not that he didn't imagine all the ways he could have his way with Stephen in every free second of his day and most of the ones where he was supposed to be paying attention to something else.

Stephen stepped back from the door, adjusting his glasses and glancing to Max. "What is that look for?" he asked, his cheeks going pink. There was just enough reserve in his manner to check Max and to leave him questioning whether Stephen was as open to wickedness as Max wanted him to be.

Max didn't have a chance to answer. The door opened and a dour-faced butler glared down his nose at them. "Can I help you?"

"Mr. Stephen Siddel and Lord Hillsboro, here to see Lady Bardess," Stephen said. In a flash, he switched from being hot and bothered and a bit sheepish to being a business owner in command of the situation in front of him. The transformation shot straight to Max's cock. He would be entertaining fantasies of Stephen having his way with him instead of vice versa for the rest of the day.

"You are expected," the butler said, standing aside with a formality that would have put the beefeaters at Buckingham Palace to shame.

Max followed Stephen into the house. He'd been there before for balls and social events. The Bardess family was wealthy to the point where they could flaunt it. The front hall alone was a masterpiece of marble and gilding, straight from the heart of the Georgian era. The paintings that surrounded the hall were of ancient men and women staring down on any new guests, judging them. Oriental carpets marked off areas where the guests should walk and places that were clearly out of bounds. The whisper of rules and elitism on all sides certainly had a way of putting people in their place. Max felt the deliberate intimidation, and he was the son of a duke.

Stephen marched through the hall as if he owned it. For a man who hadn't been born into the aristocracy, Stephen certainly did know how to carry himself. It made Max wonder exactly what the man's origins were. It was yet another thing to add to his list of topics for pillow talk, when the time came.

"Her ladyship is waiting for you in the conservatory,"

the butler said, leading them down a side hall and on to a huge room lined with tall windows on all sides. He stopped by the doorway, gesturing for Stephen and Max to go in.

"Thank you." Stephen nodded to the butler, even though the haughty old man all but ignored the two of them and turned to go about his business.

"Looks like you've made a new friend," Max joked in a low murmur as they stepped deeper into the room.

Stephen did his best to hide a laugh. The way his face pinched and his eyes sparkled made Max want to try to get him to laugh at inappropriate times more often.

"Ah. Mr. Siddel. There you are." Lady Bardess turned from where she stood supervising a small team of servants as they moved furnishings aside at one end of the room. Several large pieces of what looked like a platform rested against the wall, waiting to be constructed.

"Good morning, Lady Bardess." Stephen's mannerisms switched again as he approached the grand widow. Now he looked like a humble supplicant, come to pay homage. Max liked that character far less than powerful, confident Stephen, but he had to give the man credit for knowing how to play the situation.

Lady Bardess's no nonsense frown shifted to Max, and she smiled. "Lord Hillsboro. How delightful to see you here as well."

Max wasn't fooled for an instant. Lady Bardess wasn't the first society woman to take a shine to him, or rather, to his father's title and his family's position. "Lady

Bardess." He greeted her with a respectful nod, taking her outstretched hand as she approached and bowing over it with all the decorum that had been drilled into him by the finest nannies and tutors money could buy. "It is a pleasure to see you again."

"If I had known you would be accompanying Mr. Siddel, I would have arranged for tea," Lady Bardess said, flickering an eyebrow at him.

"You are too kind, my lady. But Mr. Siddel and I are here on business," Max said, deliberately glancing to Stephen as a hint that he was the one Lady Bardess truly should have been speaking to.

Lady Bardess didn't take the hint. "And how is your dear mother?" she asked.

"Quite well," Max answered as curtly as possible without being overtly rude. "She is enjoying her time in the country, assisting my sister in her confinement."

"How delightful." Lady Bardess batted her eyelashes provocatively. "You must miss them terribly."

Max shot a sideways glance to Stephen, his lips twitching in amusement. He expected to find Stephen glancing mischievously back at him, but something else had caught Stephen's attention. He was engaged in studying the room with a slight frown.

"I'm afraid my business in London takes up much of my time these days," Max said, keeping an eye on Stephen as he spoke to Lady Bardess. His bubbling good mood began to flatten as Stephen's expression turned graver. "I am chief patron to Mr. Siddel's orphanage now, and with this important concert just over a week away, I thought it was my duty to accompany Mr. Siddel so that we could see the arrangements and plan accordingly."

"Yes, I called you here today to explain the performance space to you and to make certain the rules I have set in place for the performers are understood." She spoke to Max as though he were the one in charge, ignoring Stephen completely.

Max's instinct to be offended by that was overruled by his sense that Stephen needed him to handle the interaction while he contemplated whatever had brought a frown to his face. "We are at your mercy, my lady," Max said, making a deferential gesture.

"Good." Lady Bardess turned away from him, marching back to the side of the room that the servants were preparing. Max nudged a distracted Stephen, and they both followed her. "The stage will be set here," she said without checking to confirm the two of them had followed her. "Prior to the performance, I want the children lined up here, so that my guests can get a good look at them." She indicated an area to one side of the room. "They should be lined up in single file, and I insist that they have all the dirt scrubbed from them. They should be dressed in their Sunday best and groomed."

"Yes, of course." Max took a page from Stephen's book and feigned complete deference to the woman, though he was irritated enough by her arrogance and obvious distaste for the very children she was inviting to perform in her home that what he really wanted to do was call her out for it.

"After the performance, I want the children removed to the parlor across the hall while I speak to those who have come to donate to the cause," Lady Bardess went on. "Some say that children should be seen and not heard, but I say they shouldn't be seen either. Not when their betters are speaking."

Stephen stood close enough to Max that Max felt his indignation at the comment.

"I'll have one or two of the maids keep the darling little ones quiet as we conduct our business," Lady Bardess went on with a sour sneer. "I trust this all meets with your approval, Lord Hillsboro?"

Max turned to Stephen. Stephen's expression had gone as dark as a thundercloud, but he did an admirable job of evening it out as he nodded to Lady Bardess. "I believe we can accommodate you, my lady."

"Good. Now, after the concert—" She was cut short as one of the footmen moving furniture dropped a small table. The sound of wood cracking made Max cringe. "What the devil are you doing, you ham-fisted lout?" Lady Bardess whipped away from Max and Stephen to deal with the footman.

"What are you thinking?" Max whispered quickly to Stephen, unsure how much time he had to discover the source of Stephen's frown.

"I don't like this place," Stephen murmured back, leaning closer to Max. "Something isn't right about it."

Max inched closer to him, enjoying the closeness, but more concerned with Stephen's observations. "I've been here several times before," he said, speaking out of the side of his mouth while keeping his eyes on Lady Bardess as she harangued the footman. "The Bardesses have always been stuck-up nobs. They're deeply proud of their own importance and not afraid to throw their influence around. Other than that, they're only skin deep."

"That may be," Stephen whispered in return, "but this isn't a house built for children."

"No, it's not." Max let out a humorless laugh. "You'll have to warn the girls not to touch anything."

Stephen looked directly at him. "It's not that. There's something else about the place. Something I can't put my finger on."

"Now you know why I wish to break away from this life," Max said, arching one eyebrow.

Stephen hummed as if he agreed with Max's intentions.

"Do you want to cancel the concert?" Max asked. "Or at least your girls' appearance in the concert?"

Stephen pressed his lips together and let out a breath through his nose. "I don't know," he said, brow furrowed. "We need the money."

"You have my money," Max told him, brushing his hand against Stephen's arm.

The uncertain smile that flittered across Stephen's lips as he glanced down to Max's hand filled Max's gut with butterflies. "Please don't misunderstand me,"

Stephen began, moving away, "but as deeply valued as your sudden patronage is, I must be circumspect about things. What is given today may be taken away tomorrow. I have to think of the girls and their security first and foremost."

Max's smile dropped. Was Stephen implying that he might change his mind, lose interest, and take his money elsewhere? Or was there something deeper? Was Stephen putting him off on a personal level? The guilt in Stephen's eyes seemed to hint at that. Max fought his burst of melancholy. He couldn't deny he had been extraordinarily forward with Stephen. Their friendship was barely a week old, and as magnificently as it had started, as much as Max felt he and Stephen had known each other forever, it was all new. Stephen was being practical. Which only endeared him to Max more.

"You're right," he sighed, trying to be practical. "If it helps, I can promise you that I have no intention of withdrawing my support. But logic and reason dictate the girls should have an alternative means of income."

"Thank you for understanding." Stephen's grateful smile was even more dazzling because of the way his expressive, blue eyes were framed by spectacles. He turned to face Lady Bardess, who was finishing up with the footman. "Is it my imagination or did she just fire that poor chap?"

The footman in question had been forced to remove his livery jacket and now slinked away to one of the doors at the far end of the room.

"I think he's just been sacked," Max agreed, shaking his shoulders as if chilled.

"We need the money," Stephen murmured as Lady Bardess headed back toward them, "but let's stay here as short a time as possible after the concert."

"Agreed," Max said, clearing his throat and straightening as Lady Bardess drew close enough for conversation. In spite of the discomfort of the situation, Max was acutely aware that Stephen had spoken of them as a unit. It fed the hope within him.

"It is impossible to find competent servants these days," Lady Bardess huffed, giving her full attention to Max and virtually ignoring Stephen. "Never mind, though. Let me show you the parlor where the children will be held."

Max shot Stephen a wary look as the two of them followed Lady Bardess out of the conservatory and across the hall. The tour was short and far more informative than Lady Bardess intended for it to be.

"Do you notice how none of the servants look happy?" Stephen whispered as Lady Bardess led them out of the parlor and back toward the front hall, clearly intending to see them on their way.

"I had noticed," Max said in return. "Never a good sign."

"I expect you and your rabble to be on time for the concert," Lady Bardess said with an air of finality as she stopped in the front hall, assuming a stance that was clearly meant to get them to leave.

"Begging your pardon, Lady Bardess," Stephen said, without the subservient mien he'd used before, "but my girls are not rabble. They are beautiful young children with bright futures ahead of them. I will not hear them spoken of dismissively."

Max's pulse quickened at the show of strength. Compassionate as he was, Stephen was definitely a man. A potent man.

Lady Bardess didn't share his appreciation. "Mr. Siddel, do you wish to reap the benefits of the connections I can provide for you or not?" she asked in clipped tones.

"I do," Stephen said with a crisp nod. "But I believe it is possible for my girls to benefit from your magnanimousness without being viewed as trash."

Lady Bardess's brow shot up and her mouth worked as though she didn't know how to reply.

Max's whole body thrilled at the clever way Stephen took charge.

"We will be on time," Stephen went on. He nodded, back to being deferential. "Good day, Lady Bardess."

He started for the door before Lady Bardess could give him leave to go. Max tried not to grin too widely at the shift in power. "Good day, my lady," he said, providing the respect that Lady Bardess would demand so that Stephen wouldn't have to give it. "I will be certain to give my mother your regards when next I see her."

"Yes, please do." Lady Bardess clumsily attempted to

flirt with him one last time before Max hurried out the door after Stephen.

Once they were out on the street, they both burst into laughter. Max leaned into Stephen, gripping his arm and hiding his face against Stephen's shoulder for a moment as though they were mischievous boys in a schoolroom instead of grown men on a fashionable street in London.

"We shouldn't," Stephen warned him, straightening and clearing his throat. "I shouldn't have defied Lady Bardess that way."

"I'm glad you did," Max said, letting go of Stephen's arm and slapping his back instead. "There's more fight in you than meets the eye."

"I have to fight," Stephen said, his expression hardening. "I have twenty-five helpless souls in my care to fight for."

"And I adore you for it."

Max didn't grasp the full implication of his words until Stephen turned to him with a look of utter, bashful surprise. The flush that came to his face was enough to make Max wish there were a dark and undisturbed alcove nearby where he could show Stephen just how deep his adoration went.

But Stephen cleared his throat, stepping away from Max. "The hired hack is gone. We'll have to find another."

"It shouldn't be hard to do," Max said, unable to wipe the smile from his face, even though he worried he'd crossed a line. A few beats went by as they walked toward a busier street where they would be more likely to find a carriage. "I'm glad you stood up to Lady Bardess. Our sort need standing up to more often."

Stephen sent him a look that was both grateful and wary. "I wish I was as convinced. I'm still deeply uncertain about letting any of my girls take part in that concert."

"What are you worried about?" Max asked, deliberately slowing his steps so that they could walk together for as long as possible.

Stephen winced and rolled his shoulders. "I don't know. Something about that house just seems off."

Max shrugged. "I'm not denying it, but I am used to houses like that."

Stephen glanced at him with a look of trust, but also with question, as if he craved Max's opinion. It did decidedly carnal things to Max to know that Stephen wanted any part of him.

"I'll tell you what," he said, grinning to put Stephen at ease. "Why don't we all take a trip out to the country to give ourselves time and space to think about it."

Stephen stopped on the curb and gaped at Max as though he'd gone mad. "A trip to the country? What in heaven's name does that mean?"

"My father has a massive estate in Hampshire," Max told him. "There's plenty of room for a passel of young girls and their pseudo-father to set up a camp for the weekend. There's a pond—though it's probably frigid at this time of year—pastures, meadows, animals, both wild and tame, and plenty of activities to be had."

Stephen's eyes grew wider. "You want to host the entire orphanage at your father's estate for a weekend trip?"

"Why not?" Max grinned. "I'm not even sure my father, or anyone else, is there. And how often do your girls get to enjoy fresh, country air?"

"Never," Stephen answered, adjusting his spectacles. "But are you certain you really want to take this on?"

"For the chance to spend a weekend in the country with you?" Max let his grin turn heated. "I'd be willing to risk anything."

Temptation filled Stephen's eyes. A devilish grin slowly spread across his face, matching the fire in his eyes. Within seconds, though, Stephen schooled his expression, like he was fighting what Max could clearly see he felt. "I'm intrigued by this idea," Stephen said, walking on as if to avoid his feelings.

"It's settled, then," Max said, caught between giving Stephen space and pushing him until he gave in to what they both wanted. "I'll make all the arrangements, purchase the necessary train tickets, and warn my father's staff that we're coming. I can guarantee that it'll be a weekend you won't soon forget."

At least, it would be if Max had anything to do with it.

CHAPTER 5

Making arrangements for twenty-five girls, Annie Ross, Stephen, and himself to take the train to Hampshire was a Herculean feat, but one that Max was able to manage. He knew about money and how to throw it around to get what he wanted. He knew about twisting arms and cajoling his way into the things he needed. It was relatively simple to secure an entire train car from London to Winchester.

What he was completely unprepared for was a two-hour train journey in what amounted to a sardine can with two dozen active, curious, incorrigible little hellions.

"Jane, give Lord Hillsboro those scissors," Stephen called across the din of chatter, laughter, and squeals as the train rocketed through the countryside. "I don't know how you managed to bring them to begin with. Minnie, pull Ursula back into the train. She shouldn't stick her head so far out the window anyhow. Hester, darling, why are you crying? It's a holiday. We're not taking you to the country to leave you there."

As Stephen marched down the aisle to take the weeping Hester into his arms, lifting her even though she was far too old and likely too heavy to be carried, Max rushed to the other end of the car to snatch the sinister-looking scissors from Jane's hands.

"What are your intentions for these scissors, madam?" he asked the spritely, short-haired girl, one eyebrow arched.

"Nothing." Jane handed over the scissors with a look of pretend innocence that fooled no one.

"She's trying to cut my hair off," the girl seated next to her declared indignantly. "She can't stand not having hair herself."

"I am not!" Jane shouted.

"Are too!"

"Am not!"

"Are too!"

Max kept smiling through the headache that was forming behind his temples. He had no idea how Stephen could maintain his sanity in such a storm.

"But you do have hair, Jane," he interrupted the argument. "Quite lovely hair too, if you ask me."

Jane snapped away from sticking her tongue out at the other girl and stared up at him with wide eyes. "But it was cut short because of the lice," she explained to him.

Max shrugged. "That may be, but it's delicious and curly." He scrubbed a hand through her messy hair, which, admittedly, needed a good washing. "Just like mine." He raked his free hand through his own, curly hair.

Jane blinked, and realization dawned in her eyes. "Your hair *is* curly," she said in an awed voice, touching her head. "We're exactly the same." Her eyes suddenly filled with stars.

Max laughed. It wasn't the first time he'd been compared to a girl. "We are ind—"

His words were cut off by a sharp scream. He snapped straight and turned to the center of the train just in time to see Stephen lunge across a row of seats—Hester still clinging to his side—to grab the back of Ursula's dress as she lost her footing and pitched forward through the open train window. Several of the girls screamed—and screamed and screamed and screamed—until Stephen yanked Ursula all the way back into her seat. Of course, the girl didn't stay seated. She twisted and launched herself into Stephen's arms.

"I ate a bug!" she wailed, burying her head against Stephen's shoulder.

Some of the screaming turned into weeping in solidarity along with Ursula. Stephen straightened, now carrying a girl in each arm, though both were years too old to be carried.

"You're all right, sweetheart," Stephen cooed to her. "I've got you. You're safe with me."

Max's insides turned into absolute mush at the sight and he mooned over Stephen as blatantly as Jane mooned over him. Never in a million years would he have thought a man with two awkward orphan girls clinging to him while he stood, surrounded by more laughing, crying, and chattering girls, could be so masculine. Never would he have imagined a man who wore his tender heart on his sleeve could be so devilishly arousing. Max's tastes had always tended toward obvious shows of strength and virility. But there was something about a man who could exude masculinity while surrounded by girls that fired every one of his senses and filled him with lust.

"I can take Ursula from you." Annie Ross rushed from the seat where she had been helping two of the older girls organize snacks to hand out to the younger children, and settled in at Stephen's side. "You have so many more important things to do."

Max grinned. He wasn't the only one utterly captivated by Stephen.

Stephen peeked down the length of the car, meeting Max's eyes with a look that seemed to reassure him that he had nothing to worry about where Annie was concerned. "It's no trouble at all," he said, though Ursula seemed more than willing to slip into Annie's arms. "We should be close to Winchester at any rate."

Max checked out the window. He'd made the journey to his father's country estate enough times to know they would be arriving in a matter of minutes. He only hoped the army of carriages he had asked his father's butler to have sent to the station would be there.

"Can I have my scissors back?" Jane asked, still

staring up at Max with adoration. "I promise not to use them for anything but paper dolls."

Max shook his thoughts away from Stephen—never an easy thing to do—and glanced down at Jane with a suspicious look. "I think it's best if I hold onto them for now, young lady."

Jane's shoulders sagged as she settled into a pout.

A few minutes later, after biscuits had been distributed to all the girls and the train whistle sounded, the train jerked and screeched its way into the Winchester station. Pandemonium erupted as the girls leapt from their seats, some gathering their belongings, others forgetting them entirely in their rush for the car's doors, the cases of extra clothing and nightgowns they'd brought with them were fetched from overhead racks, and chaos reigned as they prepared to disembark.

"If you would please form a line in the center aisle," Stephen called over the squirming, rushing, chattering din. "We will split into two lines when we exit the station, and we will all behave as we climb into Lord Hillsboro's carriages. Isn't that right?"

"Yes, Sir," rang a chorus of tiny, female voices.

It was one thing to issue the order, but they all had their hands full as they hurried to implement it before the train chugged on to its next stop. The conductors they met on the platform frowned impatiently as the full complement of the girls spilled out into the station. Max, Annie, and Stephen were all at their wits' ends just trying to keep the girls from shooting off in all directions to explore whatever new sight caught their fancy.

"I hope to God that we retrieved everyone and everything from the train," Stephen told Max with a wry grin as the train rolled out of the station and on with its journey.

"Have you ever left anyone behind on a jaunt like this before?" Max asked as they crossed the tracks and made their way through the station and out to the street.

Stephen's answer was an ominous look that had Max laughing in spite of the dire implication.

"We got her back eventually," Stephen defended himself, then started laughing himself.

It felt good to stand shoulder to shoulder with Stephen as they appreciated the humor of the situation. Max's life had been far too serious and much too filled with decorum until that point. There was something freeing in being in the midst of youthful chaos and high spirits. It connected him to all the things he'd never been allowed to enjoy when he was young like these girls. It connected him with Stephen on a level that felt like a precursor to something else.

"Those must be your father's," Stephen said, nodding to a line of black, lacquered carriages with the Eastleigh crest.

Max had been too busy studying the curve of Stephen's lips and the way his spectacles were just slightly askew from carrying and shepherding girls to notice. Dammit, how Stephen did things to him. Things that were entirely inappropriate to show with two dozen girls and Annie watching them. But if he ever had the chance to get Stephen alone....

"We should be able to fit six girls per carriage," Stephen said, turning from the row of carriages to the two lines of girls waiting behind him. "With one extra in one of the carriages. That means each of us can accompany a carriage with the oldest girls taking one for themselves. Beatrice, do you think you can supervise a carriage of older girls on your own?" he called to one of the girls who looked almost as old as Annie.

"Yes, sir," she answered, standing taller and sending sideways looks to her friends, as though she had been chosen for a special duty. Indeed, she had.

"Right. Let's soldier on, then," Stephen said.

Max regretted the fact that he wouldn't be able to ride with Stephen to his father's estate, but he understood the necessity of supervising all of the girls. He understood that even more when Jane insisted on riding with him and sitting on his lap, which was just a ploy for her to attempt to win her scissors back by picking his pocket. She failed, which resulted in a tantrum, which agitated all of the girls riding with him.

By the time the carriages rolled up the long, winding drive to his father's estate, Max had refereed a shouting match, stopped two girls from fisticuffs, dried six sobbing sets of eyes, and listened to fifteen minutes of inane jokes about bodily functions that would have made his Eton chums proud.

The girls were definitely ready to break free and scatter as they flew out of the carriages in the small courtyard in front of Eastleigh Manor's grand entrance. Stephen and Annie looked as though their journeys from the train station had been just as eventful as Max's. Donavan, his father's butler, broke his usually stoic composure to gape at the sea of girls as they dashed about the courtyard, like ants exiting a disturbed anthill.

"Donavan," Max called to him, striding forward to greet the butler. "Thank you for sending the carriages. This is Mr. Stephen Siddel of the Briar Street Orphanage and his associate, Miss Annie Ross."

Annie gazed up at Donavan and the façade of the house as though she'd reached the Pearly Gates and Donavan was St. Peter. Her mouth fell open, but she failed to produce a single sound.

Stephen broke away from where he was attempting to gather the girls into two lines again, as they had been at the station, to greet Donavan. "It's a pleasure to be here, sir," he said. Max's face heated with charm and embarrassment. Clearly, Stephen had no idea how to greet servants.

"Good day, sir." Donavan handled the faux pas with grace and understanding, nodding to Stephen in return. He shifted to Max. "Your father and mother are in the summer parlor, my lord."

Max's heart dropped to his gut. "I thought Father was in London and Mama was still attending Claudia."

"They returned yesterday, my lord," Donavan

explained. "When they received word that you intended to host your friends for a weekend." He peeked sideways at the shrieking, giggling girls dashing around the courtyard, investigating the architecture, smelling flowers, and, in Jane's case, picking up stones from the drive and hurling them into the fountain at the center of the courtyard.

"Oy! Stop that!" Beatrice shouted at her, as loud as a fishwife.

Max swallowed. "Father isn't going to send us all away, is he?" he asked Donavan with genuine concern.

"He is not," Max's father answered himself as he stepped out onto the front terrace, looking as dour as ever. "But he does wish you had consulted him before offering the use of his property as though it were a holiday resort."

"Father." Max's face heated even more as he scrambled up the stairs to greet his father, tripping on the way. He cursed himself and did his best to look presentable as he reached the terrace and stepped across to shake his father's hand, but he felt like a fly who had escaped a spider's web, only to be drawn back in again. "I didn't think you'd mind."

His father answered with a sharp hum, clasping his hands behind his back once Max was finished shaking. "I had the old barn on the Gifford's farm prepared to house these children," he said, studying the girls with a frown as Annie and Beatrice and a few of the older girls rushed to get them in lines. The girls seemed to sense they were in the presence of someone important as Max's father looked on and sobered surprisingly quickly. "And Mrs. Knight has given leave for Dora to set up a kitchen of sorts in the Gifford house to feed them."

"Thank you, Father. That's very generous of you," Max said, though he wondered if setting Stephen's girls up on the Gifford farm was a way to keep them out of sight and out of mind. The farm's fields had been absorbed into the estate's holdings a few years before, when old Mr. Gifford retired, and the barn and farmhouse had been empty since then. The girls would be comfortable, but distant.

"Your generosity is very much appreciated, your grace," Stephen said, approaching with the humble manner Max found both attractive and uncomfortable.

When Max's father stared down his nose at him, Max jumped back to Stephen's side to usher him forward. "Father, I'd like to introduce you to Mr. Stephen Siddel," he said with a smile, placing his hand on the small of Stephen's back as he swept him forward.

Max realized his mistake as soon as he'd made it. His father was utterly magnanimous as he greeted Stephen, even deigning to shake Stephen's hand, though their stations were miles apart. But Max could tell that he'd smiled too broadly, stood too close to Stephen, and glanced too openly at him by the way his father's jaw clenched and his frown grew disappointed.

"Charmed, I'm sure," his father said in muffled tones.

"Your kindness in hosting my girls truly astounds me, your grace." Stephen bowed deeply. When he straightened, he adjusted his spectacles. "Many of my girls have never seen the country before. This is the chance of a lifetime for them. I'm certain they will remember you forever."

Max's father hummed and nodded. "Donavan will see to any of your needs. The farm is only a short walk from here. And I understand that your charges sing?"

"They do, your grace." Stephen nodded deferentially. "And we would be happy to sing for you and your family this evening, if you would like."

"My wife would enjoy that very much," Max's father said. He turned to Max. "A word with you, son."

The look in his father's eyes was unmistakable. He was about to be told off. He was certain his expression communicated as much to Stephen when he turned to him. "It's probably a good idea to walk the girls down to the farm right away," he said in a low voice. "You can take that path, through the woods—don't worry, it's small and not particularly dark—and on over the hill."

"Understood," Stephen said, the slight flicker of his eyebrow indicating that everything was understood.

As Stephen turned to wrangle the girls and their baggage and speed them on their way, Max turned back to this father.

"You know how I feel about you conducting your abominations on any property belonging to me," his father said without preamble.

The comment stung Max on several levels, not the

least of which was because he was entertaining the idea of doing exactly that.

"Father, there is nothing between Mr. Siddel and I that you need to worry about." *At least, not yet.* "I am a patron of his orphanage, that is all." *For the time being.* "This truly is a golden opportunity for those poor girls. You cannot imagine how bleak their lives are in London. I believe some of them have never breathed fresh air or felt a gentle breeze on their faces in their lives."

His father narrowed his eyes slightly, clearly unconvinced.

Max gave up with a sigh. "I promised you I would never embarrass you or cause you public shame in any way, and I stand by that. But you can hardly think Mr. Siddel and I would even have the possibility of engaging in inappropriate behavior with twenty-five little girls in need of our constant attention this weekend."

Again, his father hummed, though this time his shoulders loosened and his expression softened as though he believed Max. "I never did understand your tastes," he said as though the topic were the last thing he wanted to talk about. "Your mother would like a concert, though. See to it that those waifs are ready to perform by five o'clock." He turned to head back into the house.

"And will I be invited for supper afterwards?" Max asked, a hint of resentment in is voice.

"Are you going to insist your Mr. Siddel dine with us?" his father asked, turning back to him, but not fully.

"Yes," Max answered without room for argument.

His father nodded. "Then no, you will not be invited."

Without another word or look, his father walked on into the house. Max let out a heavy breath, sagging. He shouldn't have expected anything different. Not only was he a superfluous, younger son without any chance of inheriting the ducal title, he was perverted in his father's eyes. He had been since adolescence. Anyone who wondered why he wanted out of his own family needed to look no further than that.

Max turned and headed down the path, hoping to catch up to Stephen. He supposed that most sons were caught in embarrassing situations by their fathers during adolescence, but he doubted many had their father walk in on them while they were fellating a school chum. He'd never been more than a liability in his father's eyes since that day.

"He knows, doesn't he?" Stephen asked as soon as Max caught up.

"Yes," Max said, falling into step with him.

Stephen settled into a grave frown, pushing his spectacles up his nose. "Is he the sort to cause trouble about it?"

"No, he's the sort to cover his eyes and plug his ears and pretend nothing is amiss, as long as I do absolutely nothing to draw attention to myself," Max answered.

A relieved smile spread across Stephen's face. "All is well, then." When Max sent him a wary look, Stephen shrugged and said, "We never did have anything to worry about from those who fear their own reputations through association with us."

Max tilted his head to the side. "You raise a good point."

"Sir, what is that?" One of the girls broke away from her friends to rush to Stephen's side. She took his hand as though it were a perfectly natural thing to do and pointed out over the pasture they walked beside.

"That's a sheep," Stephen laughed.

"I thought sheep were white," the girl said. "That one is brown."

"Sheep come in all colors, Katie," Stephen explained. Several of the other girls fell into step with them, looking impressed by the knowledge. "So do cows and chickens," Stephen went on. "You are all going to learn such a lot this weekend."

They reached the abandoned farm after a refreshing walk. True to what his father said, several members of the estate's staff had tidied up the barn and laid out several pallets for the girls to sleep on. The farmhouse chimneys were smoking, and the scent of bread and stew wafted out from the kitchens. There were plenty of activities on hand for the girls to partake in as well, from hoops and balls that had been brought down from the nursery Max had shared with his siblings growing up to a copious amount of old drawing paper that was going yellow around the edges and a variety of pencils. In no time, Stephen had the girls sketching flowers and trees or throwing the balls to each other and through hoops.

"If that isn't a scene of idyllic bliss, I don't know what is," Stephen said with a happy sigh once all the girls were deeply occupied.

"They all look so happy," Max agreed, standing shoulder to shoulder with him, a smile on his face as he watched the scene. It filled him with a kind of warmth that was different from anything he'd felt before. It was a pure sort of satisfaction, an enjoyment of innocence and a deeply humbling awareness of the part he'd played in helping such innocent souls to thrive. "No wonder you enjoy your position as their guardian so much."

"It has its moments," Stephen admitted with a sideways grin. Clearly it was more than just moments to him, it was his life. "Though you haven't yet witnessed an outbreak of vomiting or head colds." He paused, chuckled, face turning pink, then went on with, "Or the overwhelming awkwardness of a girl blossoming into womanhood, but thinking she's dying because of the blood."

Max winced, then burst into laughter. "God. Of all the people ill-equipped to tackle a situation like that...."

Stephen shrugged. "Mrs. Ross handles it for the most part. I've long since had the mystery of female functioning spoiled for me. It's no more embarrassing than being a boy of that same age in an 'interesting state' after a wrestling match with a schoolmate."

Max snorted with laughter, finding himself more than a little aroused at the thought of adolescent Stephen getting worked up by what had likely been an innocuous sporting activity. "Those were the days," he sighed, shaking his head.

Stephen turned his head away from the girls, looking at Max with a degree of longing in his blue eyes that had Max's cock aching. Stephen's gaze dropped to Max's lips for a moment before he glanced over his shoulder to the barn. "We should make certain everything is in order for tonight," he said, his face coloring.

"Oh?" Max turned to follow him to the barn. He would have followed him into the fires of hell, if that was where he'd been headed.

"I'm curious about the sleeping arrangements and the way these pallets have been set up," Stephen said in a perfectly natural voice, though Max was certain there was more to the invitation to investigate the barn with him. Stephen's body moved with ease as they crossed through the open barn doors and into the relative dimness of the barn interior, but the brief look he sent over his shoulder was anything but relaxed.

"I'm not sure if Donavan and the others expect us to sleep in the barn or if we're to have beds in the house," Max said, playing along and pretending the arrangements were what Stephen wanted to see to.

As soon as they turned the corner and dipped out of sight of the others, Max acted on the signals he was certain Stephen had sent. He grabbed Stephen's waist and pivoted with him until Stephen's back hit the dusty wall of the barn, and leaned into him, slanting his mouth over his. The surprise burst of command had Stephen gasping. Stephen tensed for a moment as though he might reject Max's boldness, but that hesitation vanished with a sigh. Stephen gripped the front of Max's jacket, taking command of the intimacy. Feeling the force of Stephen's sudden passion and the ferocity of his kiss made Max smolder as though he were burning from the inside out.

He groaned deep in his throat and intensified their kiss, tossing his arms around Stephen and tugging him even closer. Their bodies pressed together. The hardness of Stephen's growing erection against his hip was so tempting Max couldn't breathe. He gripped fistfuls of Stephen's clothes as their mouths melded, tongues teasing and tasting each other, wishing he could rip those clothes right off to explore Stephen's naked body. He'd never wanted anyone more in his life, as evidenced by the dangerously primed feeling in his groin. He was in serious danger of losing control right then and there, but none of that mattered as long as he had Stephen's tongue in his mouth and his body flush against his.

The bounce of a ball rolling past gave them just enough warning to jerk apart before Jane dashed into the barn. Max breathed heavily, straightening his jacket as best he could as Jane retrieved the ball. When she picked it up and turned to discover Max and Stephen standing there, panting and probably red-faced and disheveled, she only registered mild surprise.

"What are you doing?" she asked, tilting her head to the side.

"We...um...that is...." Stephen shifted anxiously, tugging at the hem of his jacket.

"We were just moving some of these old bales of hay to make more room for you lot," Max jumped in, kicking the bale that, blessedly, sat next to them. "It's strenuous work."

Jane barely even shrugged. "Can I have my scissors back?" she asked.

"Certainly not," Max said with feigned indignation. "Take your ball and go play outside."

"Okay." Jane dashed back out into the sunshine.

Max turned to Stephen, letting out a breath of relief that turned into a nervous laugh. "We need to be more careful," he managed to squeeze out.

"I'll say," Stephen said, his eyes wide with warning.

Max surged closer to him, sliding a hand around his back and bringing his lips to within an inch of Stephen's. "I want you so badly that I don't know what to do with myself."

Stephen let out a shaky breath laced with longing before stealing another, deep kiss that spun Max's head.

"No," Stephen said, pulling back and shaking himself before sucking in a deep breath. "We definitely cannot do this here or now." The way he looked at Max said that he desperately wanted to do everything and more. "It's too dangerous. We need to focus on the girls."

"As long as you know I want you," Max said, dropping all pretense and fixing Stephen with the sultriest look he could manage. "And that it *is* going to happen."

Stephen's answering look was the sort of thing that would fuel Max's hottest dreams for a long time to come. As hesitant as he could see Stephen was, they both knew where they were headed, and if he were honest, Max was certain the journey they took to get there would be as delicious as the destination.

CHAPTER 6

Stephen couldn't believe his audacity. Or his foolishness. Especially given the circumstances. Once they left the barn to supervise the girls as they played, he and Max were excruciatingly careful to keep their distance. The way he felt, the way his blood pounded through him and his heart refused to settle, anyone who so much as glanced at the two of them together would sense in an instant the carnal spark that snapped between them. And there was simply too much at stake for the whole world to become wise to the attachment they were forming. There was too much at stake for him to form it. But how was he supposed to pull back now?

That held especially true that evening, when they scrubbed the girls as clean as they could with the farmhouse's limited resources and marched them back up the hill and through the tiny stretch of woods to the estate house to perform for Max's family.

"I didn't realize my brother George would be here," Max said in a grim voice, swaying far too close to Stephen for either of their good, as they waited in the hallway just outside of a large parlor, where Max's family waited.

Stephen glanced carefully at Max, still feeling the charge of their kiss in spite of attempting to force his focus onto the girls and the performance for the better part of the afternoon. "Is there anything I should know about your brother?" he asked.

Max snorted. "Only that George is a shameless reprobate and a bully," Max growled. When Stephen raised his eyebrows at him in question, Max went on with, "He's only in the country to escape his gambling debts for the summer. Father will pay them off before the next session of Parliament, of course, but that's only a temporary measure. In all likelihood, George is here to dry out and to avoid God only knows how many ladies he's sullied as well."

"He sounds like a delightful man," Stephen drawled.

The two of them exchanged a wry look of camaraderie. The sight of Max's hazel eyes flashing and his shapely mouth—a mouth that he could remember the taste of vividly—threatened to create an embarrassing bulge in Stephen's trousers. He cleared his throat and looked away, staring straight forward into the section of the parlor that he could see. The girls. He had to focus on the girls. The consequences of letting that focus slip were too great.

"I wonder what's taking them so long," Max said, speaking Stephen's own thought aloud.

"Sir, I'm tired," little Ivy said, breaking out of line to stand by Stephen's side. She took his hand and leaned heavily against his leg.

"It won't be long, sweetheart," Stephen told her, resting a hand on her head.

"I want to go back and play with the sheep," Katie said from the restless rows of girls behind him.

A few of the others voiced their agreement.

"Can we sleep in the grass tonight?" Ginny asked, yawning.

"Yes, I want the stars watching me as I sleep," Ursula agreed. "God can see me better that way."

More chattering and agreement rose up from the girls. Stephen glanced over his shoulder at them, meeting Annie's eyes where she stood at the back of the pack and warning her they were about to have a mutiny on their hands. Annie nodded and began shushing the girls nearest her.

Stephen turned to Max. "You don't suppose there's any way we can speed this process along, do you?"

His question was followed by a thump and a crack as Ivy's sister, Lori, accidentally knocked a porcelain figure of a shepherdess off a gilded table in the hall where they waited. The shepherdess broke into several pieces, and

Lori looked as though the police would come to cart her away at any moment.

Max's lips twitched as though he didn't know whether to laugh or groan. "I'll go see what's holding them up," he said, striding forward into the parlor.

Stephen crossed to Lori, bending to pick up the pieces of the shepherdess and then to hug the girl. "Quick. Get back into line and they'll never know it was you," he whispered.

Lori did as she was told. Stephen walked the line of girls, urging them to silence as if they were all a part of the conspiracy. They responded as well as could be expected, falling back into line somewhat.

A few minutes later, Max stepped back out into the hall. "They're ready now," he said, then moved closer to Stephen and murmured, "I recommend keeping the girls, especially the older ones, away from George."

That comment sobered Stephen in a hurry. Just because he spent all of his time around innocent, young girls didn't mean he was as innocent and unaware of the dangers that could befall them as they were. "I'll take my lead from you. Arrange the girls as you see fit."

Max nodded, then led the way into the parlor. Stephen felt rather like he was leading a small parade. That feeling shifted to the sense he was leading his precious charges to their doom as they entered the parlor. The room was exquisitely decorated. The furniture had been cleared from one side of the room to make way for the girls and to form an audience. Max's father and mother sat front and center on a small sofa. His father looked impatient, but his mother seemed delighted by the prospect of entertainment. Max favored her in many ways, including the kindness in her eyes. That much put Stephen's mind to rest.

The other members of their aristocratic audience shattered his calm. Max's brother, George, was easy to pick out. He was older than Max by several years, but they bore a resemblance. Except that George was red-faced and puffy from drink and could barely sit up straight. A sour-faced woman sat near him, sending him disgusted looks. She must have been George's wife. What shocked Stephen was that a dozen other guests in fine clothes and in various stages of inebriation sat in the audience. They cooed and gawked as the girls filed in and took up their places at the front of the room.

"Aren't they just the most darling things you've ever seen," a middle-aged woman with a powdered face said in a voice that was far too loud for evening. "Like charming little street urchins."

Stephen's back was up in an instant. He fought to smile at the audience. "Ladies and gentlemen, may I introduce the choir of the Briar Street Orphanage."

He stepped to the side, beaming with pride, and gesturing toward his girls, all of whom beamed at him. Annie had taken a seat at the piano in one corner of the room and began to play.

"Who told that filthy slut she could touch our

piano?" George bellowed as Annie played the opening notes of the first song.

Annie fumbled, filling the air with jangling, discordant notes. She jerked toward Stephen with large, frightened eyes that filled with tears.

The audience was taken aback, but none of them did more than gape at George. Max's mother lowered her head to stare at her hands in her lap, but she remained silent. Max's father merely glared at George.

"She's not bad looking at that," George slurred on. "I've got some ivories she can tickle if she'd like." He guffawed and reached for his trousers.

"George!" Max hissed, stepping away from the side of the room, where he'd taken up a post to watch, and marching to his brother. He leaned close to hiss something at George that Stephen couldn't hear.

Stephen took the opportunity to stride across the room in front of the girls, heading toward the piano to rest a steadying hand on Annie's shoulder. "Ignore him," he whispered, trying his best to smile. "He's a drunken lout. Max warned me of as much. Just play."

Annie nodded and faced forward, though her hands shook as she touched the piano keys. She began to play the opening notes of their first song again.

"...and we all know that you wouldn't know a tasty piece of arse if it came up and flashed its tits at you." George raised his voice in whatever argument he was having with Max just as the girls started in on the first verse of their hymn.

More of the noble audience gasped or muttered in shock than before, but still no one lifted a finger to settle George down. Max did his best to counter George's bellowing, but it was clear George thought about as much of him as he did of a beggar in the streets.

"Get away from me and go play with the rest of the girls," George shouted, shoving Max away, though in his blurry state, he had little strength. "That's what you've always wanted, isn't it?"

The girls faltered and fumbled their way through the song. Only Beatrice, a few of the other girls, and, surprisingly, Jane were able to keep singing with clear and steady voices. Jane glared at George in a way that made Stephen glad Max hadn't given her scissors back. The rest of the girls were quickly descending into silence at best, weeping and sobs at worst.

Stephen did the only thing he could think to settle them. He stepped away from Annie and into the middle of the group, joining the song in his high tenor. The girls looked to him with fear and anxiety in their eyes, but as he sang, more and more of them found their voices. They inched closer to him, clustering around, the two on either side of him grabbing his hands.

Somehow, they made it to the end of the song. Max gave up trying to argue with his brother and stepped to the side, arms crossed in fury. Stephen hesitated, meeting Annie's eyes as she glanced to him in horror, silently asking whether she should go on or whether it was over yet.

Stephen peeked at Max's mother. The duchess was as anxious as Annie. She shifted this way and that, apparently attempting to judge the mood of her guests and her son.

"Oh, just get on with it, we haven't got all night," Max's father growled at last, sending several of the girls back into fits of sobbing. "George, if you cannot behave yourself, then kindly leave."

"I know when I'm not wanted," George said, rising shakily to his feet. He leered at Max, then snorted. "Unlike some of us."

Stephen's gut clenched with pure hatred as George stumbled out of the room, glaring at Max as though Max were a worm. Rarely did Stephen allow himself to feel that level of disgust in anyone, but George would forever be an exception to his rule of approaching everyone with compassion. Especially since it was clear George had hit his mark in hinting that Max wasn't wanted. The way Max's posture crumbled and his face fell filled Stephen with the urge to rush to him and take him in his arms the way he would any of his girls when their hearts had been crushed.

No, he wanted to do far more than simply kiss it and make it better with Max. Far more.

He forced himself to put those desires aside for the moment and nodded to Annie to go on. The room settled after George's departure, and the girls were able to get through their entire repertoire without any more incidents. That wasn't to say that their audience embraced them with open arms and wild applause when they finished, though.

After a smattering of applause, the loud woman from before they'd begun said, "Well, that was decidedly anti-climactic."

Most of the others glanced back and forth to each other in embarrassed agreement.

"I thought it was lovely," Max's mother said, rising and stepping forward to smile at the girls. "You should all be so proud of yourselves. It must be very hard to learn those songs and to sing so...memorably after being born in the gutter and raised on the streets."

Stephen's heart fell so hard and so fast that he was tempted to indulge in tears like his girls. "Thank you very much, Lady Eastleigh," he said with as bright a smile as he could manage. "You are too kind."

Max's mother gave him one of the most condescending smiles he'd ever received. "I trust that you and your darling charges will enjoy your accommodations for the night."

She couldn't have dismissed him more clearly if she'd pointed a finger at the door and ordered them to leave. Stephen nodded, not having the heart to protest or say more, and shuffled his girls out of the room. Annie slunk away from the piano, leading the way, as the two lines of bowed heads and stooped shoulders hurried out of the parlor and down the hall to flee the house.

"I am so, so sorry," Max said, jogging to catch up with Stephen as they headed out into the cool, April evening.

"I've never been so embarrassed by my family in all my life, and that's saying something."

"It's not your fault," Stephen said, sending him a weak smile as Max fell into step with him.

"If I had known my father and George would behave like that, I never would have suggested you sing for them," Max went on. "Even my mother's behavior was unforgiveable."

"I should have been ready for it," Stephen sighed, pushing a hand through his hair and adjusting his spectacles. "I should have known that the country sort would look down on my girls." It was the kindest way he could think to say that aristocrats like Max's family, possibly like Max himself, saw themselves as infinitely superior to those who had been born into challenging circumstances.

Max must have sensed the meaning behind Stephen's statement. He grabbed Stephen's arm and pulled him to a stop. "I'm not like them," he said in a firm voice, meeting and holding Stephen's eyes with sharp seriousness. "You know I'm not like that."

The girls continued on, following Annie down the path that would take them back to the barn. Stephen watched them, waiting until they were well out of earshot before turning back to Max.

"I know," he said, letting tenderness into his voice. He wavered, wanting to lean into Max, but knowing the risk he ran by letting his guard down, especially after the miserable concert.

"You saw the way they treated me too." Max moved

in where Stephen hadn't dared to, raising a hand to touch one of the buttons on Stephen's jacket. "In fact, I have half a mind to think that the bad behavior tonight was a punishment to me for coming here in the first place, for reminding them I exist."

"It's unconscionable," Stephen hissed. "Who do they think they are to cast someone as wonderful as you aside and to treat innocent girls like that, when they have no more control over their fate than the lilies of the field?"

"They think they're the bloody Duke of Eastleigh and his heir," Max answered, a world of hurt and heartache in his voice.

Stephen swayed toward him, but checked his impulse to take Max in his arms and kiss him until all was right with the world. They stood in plain sight of anyone who might come out of the house, or even look out the windows. It was dark, but not so dark they wouldn't be seen.

"We should walk on," he said, clearing his throat to hide the gruffness of desire in his voice. He already felt anxious about letting the girls out of his sight for so long.

Max nodded, and they continued down the path, but not so fast that they would catch up to the girls. Stephen was so tempted to reach for Max's hand, if only to feel the comfort of their fingers entwined, that it drove him to distraction. The battle within him was quickly growing to a full war. He couldn't forget Alice and the consequences of indulging himself before, no matter how much more Max meant to him than that clerk years ago.

After several long minutes of silence, he said, "I'm pulling the girls out of Lady Bardess's concert next week."

"What? You can't do that," Max said, more alarmed than Stephen expected him to be.

Stephen shook his head. "What's to say that they won't receive the same, miserable reception there as they received tonight?"

"Lady Bardess's concert is specifically for groups like your girls," Max said. "The audience knows what to expect."

"I won't put them through that again," Stephen said. Just like he was loath to put them through the consequences of following his cock again.

"But you need the money the concert will bring in," Max argued.

"I have you. As a patron." Stephen couldn't help but smile a little, the warmth in his heart reaching out through the cold that surrounded him after what they'd just been through.

"As more than that," Max said in a voice deep with emotion.

Stephen trusted him. It came as a shock that reached to the innermost parts of his heart. Perhaps giving in to what was growing in him where Max was concerned wouldn't spell disaster this time. He threw caution to the wind and took Max's hand.

For a moment, the look of devoted affection that came into Max's eyes, illuminated by moonlight, shone through poignantly. All too soon, Max's expression went grave.

"I have some of my money held independently of my family," he said, "but I rely on them for a greater share of it. I would gladly turn my back on them and make what I can of myself with what I have, but if I did, that would put you and your girls in a precarious position."

Stephen's heart squeezed with alarm, making it difficult for him to breathe. Yes, he found himself outrageously attracted to Max, physically and emotionally, but they'd only just met in the grander scheme of things. And here Max was talking about throwing his entire life and his family aside? For what?

The possible answer to that question made Stephen dizzy with possibility and with fear. Things never ended well when one person gave up everything for another without truly knowing them.

"Of course, there may be other answers," Max went on before Stephen could voice his concerns. "There's always The Brotherhood."

Stephen frowned, slowing his steps. "What do you mean?"

"They directed me to you," Max said with a shrug. "Others may be eager to donate as well. In fact, there's an event in a few days, a ball, of sorts."

"A Brotherhood ball?" Stephen's brow shot up. "With dancing?"

Max's whole countenance changed as he smiled

bashfully. "Yes, if you can believe it. I would relish the opportunity to dance with you."

Stephen continued to gape at him, even as Max's smile widened. "You want to dance with me at a ball hosted by The Brotherhood." Stating it bluntly did nothing to make the possibility seem less surreal in his mind.

"Wouldn't it be grand?" Max asked, tightening his hold on Stephen's hand. "Say you'll come with me. We could talk to some of the wealthier members of The Brotherhood about donating to the orphanage. If there's enough interest, you might be able to skip Lady Bardess's concert. Though I still think you should explore every avenue for funding."

Stephen gaped and sputtered for a moment, trying to come up with a solid reason why he couldn't possibly accompany Max to a ball consisting entirely of men like them. "I have nothing even remotely suitable to wear to a ball," he argued.

"I'll buy you a suit," Max insisted.

Stephen widened his eyes at Max in partial offense and let go of his hand. "Is that how you want things to be between us?" His voice pitched high with indignation.

"I want us to enjoy each other's company," Max argued, a distinct pleading note to his voice. "And if that means me footing the bill for a silly old suit, then so be it."

Stephen shook his head. "I've been around The Brotherhood enough to know that even though they admit men from all strata of society, it's mostly well-born gentlemen. I would feel out of place."

"You wouldn't, I swear," Max told him.

Stephen was running out of excuses. He had to admit, in his heart of hearts, the idea of attending such a unique ball with Max intrigued him.

"When did you say this ball was?" he asked with a defeated sigh.

"On Wednesday," Max answered, beaming from ear to ear. "I'll send a carriage around to pick you up at eight o'clock."

"You don't want to arrive with me?" Stephen's heart did flips of joy and uncertainty in his chest.

"I'd rather surprise you once you get there," Max answered with a wink.

One wink, and Stephen was sunk. "All right, then," he said, feeling himself heat like a furnace. "I'll go."

"Excellent." They had made it through the woods and were nearing the farmhouse. The girls had grown louder the farther away from the house they got. But Max still took the risk of leaning in and kissing Stephen's cheek. "You won't regret this, I promise you."

CHAPTER 7

"You look lovely."

Stephen was unnerved to find Annie standing at the end of the hall, gazing at him as though he were Michelangelo's David come to life, as he stepped out of his room, dressed to the nines. His bedroom was the only one on thé ground floor, tucked at the back of the building next to the kitchen. In spite of that, the area saw little traffic, so it was startling to find Annie waiting for him with wide eyes and pink cheeks.

"Thank you," he said, adjusting his spectacles, then tugging at the hem of the expensive suit jacket that had arrived by special courier for him that morning. "I feel rather like a dressed-up dancing bear."

"Oh no." Annie rushed to his side as he made his way up the side hall to the main hall. "You look as though you were born to wear clothes like that." Her cheeks grew even pinker as she took in the details of his broad shoulders, trim waist, and everything else that the decidedly showy cut of his new suit had on display. Not to mention the cobalt blue cravat that he knew full well set off the blue in his eyes. The cut of the suit alone was enough to make him suspicious about what Max was up to.

No, it wasn't, he told himself with a barely-concealed smirk. He knew exactly what Max was up to. What he wondered was whether he would abandon years' worth of convictions about where his responsibilities lay for the chance to feel Max's mouth on his again.

"One could argue that I was born to dress like this," Stephen said in a wry voice as they turned the corner and headed for the front door. Several of the older girls who had not yet been sent to bed peeked out of the great hall and gaped at him as he passed. "My family is gentry, after all."

"You've never told me that," Annie said, looking at him with even more awe.

"I never tell anyone," Stephen said with a sideways grin. "My father is a knight, much good though it ever did him. The family does well enough with our property in Wiltshire, but they disapprove of my choices in life." Which was putting it lightly. All except the uncle who had left the orphanage to him upon his death. But then, Stephen had always expected he and his Uncle Dennis had more in common than the family let on.

The carriage that Max had sent to fetch him was already waiting outside. Being sent for, like a mistress in the night, embarrassed Stephen to no end, but taking the offered carriage was a damned sight more convenient than walking halfway across London in the dark or paying for a hired hack.

"Make sure the girls all get to bed on time," he told Annie. "And for God's sake, keep sharp objects away from Jane. She's grown far too macabre for a ten-year-old these last few weeks."

"Yes, sir," Annie answered, still staring at him breathlessly.

"Well, aren't you just the bee's knees," Mrs. Ross said, rushing out from the great hall, as if she didn't want to miss getting a look at him before he left. Her expression twitched with mirth. "That's quite the ensemble." She raked him up and down with an overtly impressed look.

"I feel horrendously overdressed," Stephen said, inching toward the door and taking his coat and hat from the pegs beside it.

"Lord Hillsboro has fine taste," Mrs. Ross went on. Her smirk grew and she crossed her arms.

Stephen let out a breath, grabbing his coat. She knew. Of course she knew. Given her background, how could she not know? "It's a frivolous expense," he said, meeting her eyes firmly and hoping she caught his insistence on subtlety for the sake of Annie's innocence. "I don't know how I'll repay him."

"I do," Mrs. Ross murmured, sending him a saucy look.

Stephen cleared his throat and turned away to hide the way he was certain his face had gone beet red. "I'm not certain how late I'll be," he said awkwardly. "I have the key to the kitchen door, though, so you can lock up as usual."

"I'll keep a lamp lit in the kitchen for you," Mrs. Ross said, her voice laced with humor.

Stephen fled her teasing gaze and Annie's starry-eyed admiration as fast as possible. The driver of the carriage seemed impatient to be on his way, so Stephen hopped into the carriage without pausing to make conversation.

The ride to The Chameleon Club seemed both to last a lifetime and to be over before he was ready. By the time he stepped down in front of the utterly nondescript building facing Hyde Park and hurried up the steps and inside, his heart was beating like a drum calling an army to war. The Chameleon Club was far grander than his usual surroundings and intimidated him anyhow, but the moment he stepped inside the marble lobby, he knew he was in for far more than an evening spent with people he was certain would be his betters.

Rather than being quiet and sober as it usually was, the club was lit up with elaborate candelabras and rang with the sounds of music and conversation from somewhere deeper in its depths. The walls leading from the lobby to the great hall at the heart of the club were festooned with swaths of colorful silk and veritable fountains of flowers. There were even two rows of luminarias lining the upper hall to direct guests into the heart of the ball. The whole club was alive with brightness, color, and excitement.

Best of all, as Stephen approached the entrance to the great hall, he spotted Max standing there, waiting for him.

His heart all but stopped in his chest before racing as it never had before, and he stopped where he was, jaw dropping. Max was dressed in a finely-tailored, forest green suit. It accentuated his narrow waist and broad chest. His hair seemed curlier than usual in a way that instantly made Stephen want to run his fingers through it. His eyes were outlined with kohl, and if Stephen wasn't mistaken, he wore just a touch of rouge on his cheeks and his lips. Stephen had never cared much for men wearing cosmetics, but the effect on Max was dazzling.

That effect was magnified by a thousand as Max spotted him, their eyes met, and he smiled. If Stephen hadn't already been smitten, he would have lost himself completely in that moment.

"I've been waiting for you," Max said, striding forward and eagerly taking Stephen's arm. "So?" he asked, drawing Stephen into the great hall and the swirl of sound, color, and magnificence it contained. "What do you think?"

Stephen thought he'd been horribly overdressed, but at one glimpse of the great hall transformed into a ballroom, he felt as drab and pedestrian as he knew he was. Beauty spun all around him. The hall was decorated with the same silk and flowers as the lobby, only more so. There were so many candles illuminating the room that

Stephen worried the whole thing would turn into a conflagration, but it was gorgeous all the same, bold, yet artistic. More than half of the men in attendance were dressed in colors and ornaments that made Max look as underdressed as Stephen felt. A few were even dressed in elaborate evening gowns.

Perhaps the most elaborately dressed of any of the guests Stephen could see was a man with dark hair, piercing blue eyes, and a suit jacket that glittered with purple and green iridescence as he moved through what appeared to be a throng of admirers, heading toward the dais where a small orchestra played. Not only were his eyes heavily outlined with kohl, his lips were bright red. He wore an abundance of diamond jewelry on his ears, wrists, fingers, and around his neck. The overall effect was to make him shine like more than just a star, like the entire night sky.

"Good Lord, is that Everett Jewel, the actor?" Stephen asked, leaning closer to Max to be certain he was heard over the noise.

"It is," Max laughed, taking his arm, as bold as he pleased. "I saw him in Julius Caesar last year. He certainly knows how to draw a crowd."

That was putting it mildly. At least a dozen men crowded around the base of the dais as Jewel mounted it. They watched, enraptured, as he turned to the orchestra, which stopped playing, issued an order for songs, then faced forward again to sing as the musicians launched into a popular melody.

"What in heaven's name is his jacket made out of?" Stephen asked as he and Max made their way around the room to find a place to stand and watch the carnival of activity. "I've never seen anything like it."

"Beetle wings, if I'm not mistaken," Max answered. "They're imported from India and have that fascinating, iridescent quality."

"It must cost a fortune."

Max laughed. "Jewel has a fortune and more to spare. You should ask him to donate to your girls. I'm sure he'd be happy to."

Stephen dragged his eyes away from Jewel's sultry performance of a song that was growing lewder by the verse to gape at Max. "I could never, in a million years, approach a man like that and ask him for money."

"He's a man, the same as anyone else," a slightly familiar voice said by Stephen's side.

Stephen jumped and turned to find the most strikingly beautiful man he'd ever laid eyes on just inches away from him. He was thin with pale skin, blue eyes, perfectly coifed hair, and a sensuous mouth. He was dressed in a lavender suit with grey edging that made him look delicate and ethereal, but power radiated from him. The juxtaposition of softness and ferocity instantly put Stephen off-guard. Stephen had met the man before, but couldn't place where.

Max glanced past Stephen to see who was interrupting and his face lit up. "Lionel. It's good to see you." He reached to shake the captivating man's hand, staying unusually close to Stephen as he did. "May I introduce you to my friend, Stephen Siddel. Stephen, this is Lionel Mercer."

"The orphanage owner," Lionel said, sending Max a teasing grin. He offered Stephen his hand. "It's a pleasure to meet you again."

Stephen's mouth dropped open before he could think. The memory of meeting Lionel Mercer the one time he'd enlisted the help of Dandie & Wirth rushed back to him. "I'm surprised you remember me."

Max laughed. "Lionel remembers everyone he's ever so much as heard of. He was the one who suggested I invest in your orphanage."

"And it seems my instincts were correct," Lionel added, fixing Stephen with a saucy stare.

Stephen didn't know whether to laugh or be terrified by the elegant man in front of him. "Thank you," he said with a deep nod, falling back on manners. "I am in your debt."

Lionel hummed enticingly. "I love it when handsome men are in my debt."

The look he raked Stephen with from top to bottom was overtly sexual. It sent an odd chill down Stephen's spine. Aside from Max, and a few other men from his past, no one had ever attempted to devour him with a look.

Strangely, Max didn't seem to mind the look. "I brought Stephen here tonight because he's on the fence about letting his girls perform at Lady Bardess's concert next week."

Lionel made a sour face. "I don't blame him one bit. Lillian Bardess is a bitch."

Stephen's brow shot up. He'd come to the same conclusion, but to hear the sentiment expressed aloud and so bluntly was a shock.

"I told Stephen that he should search out alternative patrons at the ball tonight," Max went on.

"A wise decision," Lionel said, glancing across the room. "Lord Metcalf just came into some money, although he has his sister's family to support. Mr. Greenhill has had a profitable year, but I'm not sure I would wish that association on someone as kindhearted as you." He glanced to Stephen, who wasn't sure whether to be offended or grateful. "There's always Lord Chatsworth, but you'd never get rid of him and his tedious stories once you let him through the door."

"Isn't that the truth," Max said with a shake of his head.

Stephen had the sudden, uncomfortable feeling that Max was part of a whole, wide world that he had nothing to do with. And if they truly didn't have as much in common as he wanted to think they did, how long would it be before Max grew tired of him?

"No," Lionel said with a showy sigh. "Even I have to admit that your most likely choice for a new patron for the orphanage is Everett Jewel."

Stephen flinched in surprise. "Him?" He glanced

across to the dais, where Jewel continued to perform in a manner that seemed better suited for a dance hall than an assembly of gentlemen.

"He has a particular interest in orphans," Lionel said in a flat voice, crossing his arms and narrowing his eyes at Jewel. "Considering that he was one."

"You don't like the man?" Stephen asked.

"Everyone likes Everett Jewel," Lionel answered in a bitter voice.

"He's just jealous." A tall man with dark hair and patrician features sauntered up to Lionel's side and threw an arm around his shoulders. "Aren't you, Lionel?" He grinned at Lionel as if they shared an inside joke. Stephen recognized him as David Wirth.

"Absolutely not." Lionel shrugged David's arm off his shoulders and tilted his chin up in what must have been intended as a frosty gesture. Stephen wasn't fooled, though. The two men had to have been more than business partners.

"David." Max nodded to the man. "Good to see you. Allow me to introduce you to my friend, Stephen Siddel. Stephen, this is David Wirth of Dandie & Wirth, solicitors."

"We've met, remember?" Stephen shook the man's hand, beginning to feel overwhelmed by the sheer number of people at the ball and the fact that Max seemed to know them all. "Though it was years ago."

A round of applause broke out before Stephen could figure out how to make conversation with David and

Lionel. On the dais, Everett Jewel took a bow, the movement causing his beetle-wing jacket to glitter as though he were some sort of mythological creature.

"And now, let's dance!" Jewel declared in a loud voice.

The orchestra struck up a decidedly wild waltz, and before Stephen knew it, the center of the great hall transformed into a swirling crush of dancing couples, all of them male. Stephen was suddenly struck with the fear that Max would ask him to dance. Yes, he wanted to be in Max's arms, but who would take the lead? He barely knew how to dance as it was.

Max turned to him, his eyes sparkling with exactly the invitation Stephen both longed for and dreaded, but before he could do more than open his mouth, Lionel grabbed Max's forearm.

"I'm not missing out on the fun," Lionel declared, as mischievous as an imp. "Come on, Hillsboro."

Stephen's mouth continued to hang open as Lionel yanked Max away, causing him to lose his balance. Max sent an apologetic look to Stephen over his shoulder as Lionel whisked him into the crowd, then deftly assumed the woman's stance for the waltz. Underneath Stephen's shock at the pure surreal feeling of the situation, jealousy as green as Max's suit rose up.

He was startled when David slapped a hand on his shoulder and said, "Don't worry about Lionel," with a laugh. "He suffers from an overabundance of pride, and that pride tends to be wounded whenever Everett Jewel is in the same room with him."

"Oh," Stephen said clumsily, glancing from David to Jewel, who was making a show of choosing a dance partner from half a dozen men vying for the honor, to Max and Lionel turning circles among the others on the dance floor.

David let go of Stephen's shoulder and clasped his hands behind his back, staring out at the revelry on the dance floor. "Events like this are rare for The Brotherhood. Usually we like to keep things staid and professional." When Stephen couldn't think of a reply to the statement, David glanced to him and said, "To avoid accusations of lewdness and debauchery, of course. There are plenty of other establishments for our sort to frequent if that's what they're looking for. But it is nice for everyone to get a chance to let their hair down now and then."

It took several awkward beats of silence and an increasing sense that he didn't belong for Stephen to realize David's words were testing him. As soon as it dawned on him, he blinked and faced the man. "Max dragged me here tonight to see if I could recruit donors for the orphanage I run, since I'm having second thoughts about another source of revenue."

David's mouth pulled into a lopsided grin. "I wasn't accusing you of anything. Anyone with eyes can see you and Max are smitten with each other."

It might have been better if the man had accused him

of trolling the ball for a partner for the night. Stephen's whole body heated with self-consciousness. "My girls are my first priority," he said defensively. Even though he could sense that David Wirth wouldn't think less of him for being enamored of Max. No one in the vast room would. In fact, he was standing in the only place in the world where he could be surrounded by people who would not only not hold his feelings for Max against him, they would encourage them.

"I worry about Max sometimes," David went on, watching as Max and Lionel whirled around the dance floor, laughing. "His family situation is not ideal."

Stephen hummed, forcing his shoulders to loosen and standing in imitation of David. It dawned on him that David, too, was wearing a relatively plain suit and hadn't painted his face or added extra adornment to his attire either. "I've met his parents and his brother, George."

David grimaced. "George Eastleigh is an abomination."

Stephen laughed suddenly. When David raised a questioning eyebrow at him, he said, "That's a word that is usually reserved for our sort. But you're right, it fits men like George Eastleigh far better than us."

A suddenly serious look came over David's face. "How have you met the Eastleigh family? I was given to understand that they had all but banished poor Max from the family."

"We visited Eastleigh Manor over the weekend," Stephen confessed. The memory of the kisses he'd shared with Max rushed to his head. The visceral memories of the way Max had tasted and the way his body had felt so tantalizingly close to his made it difficult for him to concentrate for a moment. He cleared his throat and went on with, “My girls sang for Lord Eastleigh and his family.”

David seemed far more interested than Stephen would have thought. “And how did you find our friend George?” he asked intently. “How did he behave around your girls?”

“Abominably,” Stephen answered. A chill passed down his spine, but he wasn’t certain what it signaled.

David nodded as though the single word were enough of an answer to whatever deeper question he had. He frowned, seemingly lost in thought.

“Is something wrong?” Stephen asked, unable to bear the tension.

David remained in this thoughts for a moment before glancing up at Stephen. “I’m not certain.” He shifted his weight. “I’ve been part of a new investigation into several young people who have gone missing.”

The very idea of children disappearing had Stephen on edge and wishing he could run home to make sure every one of the tender souls in his care was tucked safely in bed. He knew entertaining his feelings for Max was a bad idea. But as fast as that thought hit him, he shoved it aside. The girls were safe. His heart was safe.

“It’s a new investigation,” David continued. For a moment, he looked as though he would say more. Instead, he shook his head and drew in a breath. "I shouldn't bother you with the details. I abhor premature anxiety." He paused, then added, "Though if you hear of anything that might aid in the investigation, any more tales of children going missing, please let me know." He reached into the inner pocket of his jacket and pulled out a card, handing it to Stephen.

Stephen took the card, reading it quickly. All it said was "Dandie & Wirth, solicitors" with an address in The City. The previous meeting Stephen had had with David and Lionel had been there, at the club. He nodded in thanks and tucked the card into his jacket pocket.

David took a breath and rolled his shoulders, glancing out into the dancing crowd once more. His wry grin returned. "I haven't seen Lionel in this good a mood in months."

"Are you—" Stephen started, stopping when he realized his question might be rude.

David laughed and shook his head. "Lionel is my business partner, nothing more." His expression clouded slightly as he resumed watching Max and Lionel. "In spite of the rumors you might have heard." It was enough to make Stephen wonder if he was telling the truth, or rather, if David wished he were lying.

The conversation lagged. Stephen couldn't think of anything else to say, and David seemed more interested in watching the throng of dancing couples. As soon as the waltz ended, the orchestra struck up another song. There was a burst of activity as partners were traded and new ones were sought out. Stephen grinned like an idiot when Max let go of Lionel and headed straight toward him.

"Our time has come," he said, mischief in his eyes, reaching for Stephen.

"I don't know how to dance," Stephen protested as Max grabbed his hand and drew him out toward the dance floor. "That is, I don't know how to dance this way."

"Then I'll teach you," Max said with a flicker of his dark brows. He shifted in such a way that Stephen was naturally whisked into his arms, then grabbed Stephen's right hand and positioned his left on his shoulder. "Like this. One, two, three, one, two, three."

Shivers of excitement bounced through Stephen, even though he was doing something simple. Max held him closer as he caught the rhythm of the steps, which sent his pulse soaring. Strangest of all was the complete acceptance of the way they moved together, enjoying the dance and the chance to be so close. It was a degree of acceptance that Stephen had never felt before, one that spun his head more than the circles he and Max turned. He never would have imagined that he could find acceptance quite like that.

"Perhaps it is a good idea to let the girls perform at the concert after all," he said as the waltz ended, another began, and Max showed no signs of letting Stephen go.

Max laughed. "We're dancing away the night, enjoying each other's company, and you're thinking about the Bardess concert?"

Stephen shrugged, slipping his arm farther around Max's shoulders. "I'm suddenly filled with confidence. I feel as though I could do anything."

"Anything?" Max arched one eyebrow, his eyes sparkling.

"I feel as though I could lead the girls on a charge to storm the ramparts of Bardess Mansion, much less let them sing for their supper there," he said with a smile. "In fact, I might even be brave enough to ask Everett Jewel for his support as well."

"You're too late there," Max said with a grin. "He left with a few friends two songs ago."

Stephen stood straighter, glancing around in surprise. How long had he been dancing with Max anyhow? It didn't feel as though it mattered that he might have lost his chance to enlist the patronage of the scintillating Everett Jewel as long as he could keep Max in his arms.

"What a pity," he said with a lopsided grin. "I suppose we'll just have to keep dancing."

"How fortunate," Max said, his expression heating. "Because I don't have any intention of letting go."

CHAPTER 8

In the end, there was only one choice. Stephen would have been a fool if he didn't take advantage of every opportunity to raise funds for the orphanage. But he wasn't entirely pleased with his decision.

"We will all be on our best behavior, won't we?" he asked his girls as they lined up in two rows in the front hallway of the orphanage.

Various responses of "Yes, Sir!" "We will!" and "Only if Jane stops pulling my hair," resounded in the wake of his question.

Stephen smiled in spite of his misgivings. It wasn't his girls who gave him pause. They were absolutely lovely, every one of them. His heart swelled with pride as he walked down the hall, checking each cherubic face for smudges and making sure hair ribbons and ruffles were all in place and buttons were done up correctly. He loved every one of the mischievous little imps as though they were his own, which was quite a family. And until a few, short weeks ago, he would have insisted that he had been blessed with more than enough love in his life.

The truth about love, how much he had, how much he needed, and from whom, wrapped itself around him in the unlikeliest of forms when he reached Jane at the end of the row. She glanced hopefully up at him and asked, "Will Max be at the concert?"

Stephen's smile widened in spite of himself, and his heart danced a jig in his chest. "He most certainly will," he told Jane, unable to hide his excitement, resting a hand on her shoulder. "But you should call him Lord Hillsboro."

Jane snorted. "He told me I could call him Max. He's my friend."

"He's my friend too," Stephen confided in her with a wink. Though he would be lying if he said he wasn't hoping for much more. He was hoping that Max was as devoted to the girls as he was, which would mean he could let his heart go without losing sight of his responsibilities.

It was probably foolish to display his emotions so openly with all his girls, Mrs. Ross, and Annie clustered around him, but none of them were paying much attention to him, as the carriages Max had hired on their behalf to take them to the Bardess mansion had just arrived. And little Jane was far too young to have the first clue what the flush that came to his face when he thought about Max or the way he had a hard time containing his smile or catching his breath when he remembered the way they'd danced together, or the passionate kiss they'd shared in the barn, meant. Once again, innocence and ignorance were the most effective means of protection he could possibly hope for.

"I don't know why Lord Hillsboro insisted on spending unnecessary money to hire these hacks," Mrs. Ross complained to Stephen as he headed back to the front of the lines. "It's an unnecessary expense. The Bardess mansion is only a mile away. We could walk."

Stephen answered her with a stern look. "Lord Hillsboro likely understands that it would be cruel to make twenty-five young girls walk a mile to perform a concert, then to walk home. This is a delightfully generous gesture on his part."

"I'll just bet it is," Mrs. Ross said with a smirk, crossing her arms, her mouth twitching into a teasing grin.

Self-consciousness flooded Stephen. Mrs. Ross was anything but innocent or ignorant. "Lord Hillsboro is the patron of this orphanage now. He takes his responsibilities toward us seriously."

"I'll just bet he does." Mrs. Ross's grin widened.

Stephen's face heated even more. "We should be thankful to have such an open-hearted and dedicated patron."

"You'll be thanking him on your knees, then?" Mrs. Ross's eyes flashed with wickedness.

"Oh, yes, what a splendid idea," Annie said, bouncing up to join the conversation. "We should all pray for Lord Hillsboro."

Stephen nearly choked, his whole body going hot. "Um...er...yes." He coughed. "We should all pray for him."

Mrs. Ross looked as though she were having a hard time not bursting with laughter.

"I know I am certainly grateful for this fine suit he bought you," Annie went on, her eyes shining. She stepped close to Stephen and brushed his shoulders as if clearing away dust, then ran her hands down the lapels of his jacket with a look of longing.

Stephen writhed with discomfort at the bold and possessive gesture, but he couldn't even begin to imagine how to tell Annie her affection was misplaced. As unnerving as she could be, he did care for her. Like a sister.

"Well," he said, awkwardly taking her hands and removing them from his person. "We'd better be on our way if we are to make it to the concert in time."

Annie didn't seem fussed by being put off. She grinned as though Stephen had made a thousand promises to her and proceeded to organize the girls and shoo them out to the carriages eagerly. Stephen and Mrs. Ross lingered behind, making sure all of the girls stayed in line and made it out to the carriages without dawdling or being left behind.

"You can't avoid breaking her heart, so don't even

try," Mrs. Ross told him in a wistful voice as they closed up the orphanage.

Stephen let out a heavy sigh. "I have an obligation of care for her as much as I do to the girls," he said, leaning close enough so that no one would overhear.

"Yes, but you have an obligation to yourself as well," Mrs. Ross said. When Stephen merely raised his brow in surprise, she shifted her stance, leaned in closer, and said, "I've known you these ten years and more. I've never seen your head turned by anyone the way it's been turned by Lord Hillsboro. Yes, there was that dalliance with that fine piece of arse from the docks—"

"Which ended in disaster, if you remember correctly," Stephen hissed.

Mrs. Ross blinked at him. "Disaster? I thought you simply grew tired of him."

Stephen shook his head, having a hard time believing Mrs. Ross didn't remember. "Alice," he whispered.

Still, Mrs. Ross didn't seem to have a clue.

"She landed in the situation that killed her because I was too busy dallying with Davenport to keep an eye on her," Stephen went on.

Mrs. Ross's mouth dropped open. "Is that what you think? Why you ended things with that fool?" When Stephen merely looked guilty, she let out a wry laugh. "Alice would have gotten herself in trouble no matter what you did, even if you'd tied her to your wrist." She narrowed her eyes as she studied Stephen. "My boy, if you so much as think of letting that sorry incident keep you from what I'm seeing between you and Lord Hillsboro now—"

"And what are you seeing now?" he asked, afraid of the answer.

"Love," she answered with a shrug. "And enough heat to keep us all toasty-warm through the harshest winter."

Stephen was mortified. "I was hoping it wasn't that obvious."

Mrs. Ross barked a laugh. "Poppet, when the two of you are together, it makes everyone on the street randy. Have the two of you even...." She raised her eyebrows questioningly.

"No," Stephen whispered, restless and self-conscious.

"Well, why not?" she laughed.

Stephen sent her a pointed look.

"Good Lord, man. Let the past and sweet Alice rest in peace." Her look of censure turned into a saucy grin. "You and Max are both gagging for it. Let go of your fear. Trust me. You'll feel much better once the two of you have traded off taking it up the arse a few times." She slapped his shoulder and marched on to the nearly-loaded carriages.

Stephen was left standing where he was, shocked to stillness, gaping at her. But he supposed that was what he got for hiring a former prostitute to run his business with him. And she did raise a vital point. Was it time to leave the past in the past and to get on with it?

He shook his head as soon as the question popped

into his mind. Of all the times to contemplate the intimate joys of sodomy, right before a children's concert was not one of them. He cleared his throat and rushed to climb aboard one of the carriages. Soon, they were all speeding toward Bardess Mansion.

Within minutes of arriving at the stately, Georgian home, all of the misgivings Stephen had had about the concert and the house itself returned in full force.

"I'm still not certain about this," he sighed to himself as he, Mrs. Ross, and Annie shuffled the girls out of the carriages and into the cavernous front hall.

"About the concert?" Annie was by his side, as cheerful and moon-eyed as always.

Stephen met her enthusiasm with a compassionate smile. "About a great many things."

"I think it's a lovely idea," Annie said, hopping forward to clasp his arm. "Isn't it romantic? A fine, large house, everyone dressed in their best, lords and ladies coming from all over London to hear us sing." She added a sigh to the end of her list. "It's almost as though we were in a fairy tale."

Stephen was afraid his smile looked more like a wince. Ignorance was one thing, but naiveté was another entirely.

He started prying Annie away from him, but was interrupted by Max approaching from a side parlor and saying, "Isn't this the most beautiful sight I've seen all day."

Stephen's blood instantly pumped harder, and to all

the wrong places. Max stared firmly at him as he spoke, but shifted his smile of appreciation to the girls in just enough time not to raise suspicion.

"You all look like a treat," he told them.

The girls responded with wide grins, pink cheeks, and giggles. Stephen knew exactly how they felt.

"Sir told us you would be here," Jane said, breaking from her place in line to throw herself at Max for a hug. Something else Stephen wished he could do. Max embraced her warmly, causing a ridiculous twist of jealousy in Stephen's gut. "Sir tried to tell me I wasn't allowed to call you Max," Jane went on, sending Stephen an extraordinarily amusing dirty look.

"Nonsense," Max laughed. "As I've told you all, you may call me whatever you'd like." The girls giggled and beamed wider as Max stepped subtly to Stephen's side and whispered in his ear, "Except for you. I have a few other ideas for what you can call me."

A delicious and completely inconvenient shiver passed down Stephen's spine. "Not now," he hissed in return. "Remember where we are."

Max hummed gravely, as if genuinely chastised, and stepped away. Stephen was happy to leave it at that, until he spotted Annie watching the two of them with a confused frown.

"Right, young ladies," Stephen said, clearing his throat and jumping into action, deeply alarmed at the possibility of Annie working out the truth at an inconvenient time. "Let us all be on our best behavior and sing our hearts out."

"Yes, Sir," they answered, angelic and delightful, giving Stephen hope that things might just work out after all.

In the back of his mind, Max wondered if he should feel guilty for teasing Stephen in public. Probably, but the way Stephen's face went red, the way his blue eyes sparkled, and the way his breath caught was too much of a delight for him to resist. He half expected Stephen's spectacles to fog up with every flirty look or suggestive comment he made.

"We're supposed to wait in the parlor across the hall from the conservatory," Stephen told him as they walked, side by side, down the hall, following the footman who had been sent to fetch them.

"I hate waiting for things," he replied, knowing full well his spirits were too high for his own good. He brushed his hand against Stephen's making it look as casual as possible.

Stephen blushed harder. Max had a hard time resisting the urge to yank him into an unused room to snog him senseless.

"What do you mean, my presence is required in the conservatory?" The booming voice of Sister Constance dented Max's feisty mood. "I will supervise my children in the parlor."

Ahead of them, a pair of footmen were doing a poor job of attempting to subdue Sister Constance and the pair of nuns with her. Stephen lost his flushed, unsettled look, switched to a frown of command, and marched forward. Max followed him, glancing over his shoulder to Mrs. Ross and Annie to make sure they had a handle on the girls.

"Lady Bardess said she wishes the orphanage owners to attend to the guests in the conservatory," one of the footmen was trying to explain.

"That's fine," Stephen said, stepping into the confrontation. "We can line the children up in rows at the side of the room instead of putting them in the parlor."

Sister Constance was clearly in a towering rage. Max had a hard time not laughing as she turned that rage on Stephen, especially because he could see she liked his suggestion. "You stay on your side of the room and I'll stay on mine," she growled at Stephen. "I don't want your undisciplined ruffians stealing the donations that are meant for us."

"I can assure you, we have no intention of stealing anything," Stephen said.

His reassurance wasn't helped by a sudden crash that turned out to be one of his girls attempting to slip a tiny figurine into the pocket of her dress and knocking over a larger one on the table in the hall.

"None of that," Mrs. Ross said, stepping forward to smack the girl's hand and to put the figurine back.

Sister Constance humphed and crossed her arms as though her point had been proven.

The two footmen looked as though they were about to have hell's fury brought down on them. "Lady Bardess insists the children be kept out of sight in the parlor while the adults attend to her guests," one of them said.

"Lady Bardess can have all of us in the parlor or all of us attending to her guests," Stephen insisted with the streak of boldness that Max found irresistible. "Now if you will excuse us, I need to arrange my girls in the conservatory."

Stephen gestured to Mrs. Ross and Annie, sending Max a look, then marched boldly past the footmen and into the conservatory. Max followed, giving Sister Constance a deliberately cheeky look as he passed her.

"Oh, no you don't," Sister Constance said, snapping her fingers at the two nuns with her. They shuffled her pressed and starched orphans into lines, then followed Stephen and his girls into the larger room.

A large number of guests were already assembled in the Bardess's conservatory by the time the two choirs entered the room and lined up against opposing walls. Several conversations stopped and the high and mighty of London oohed and aahed over the sweet lines of orphans. Max knew a great many of the people there, if only by reputation. He spotted Alistair Bevan at the far end of the room, caught up in conversation with Lady Matilda Fairbanks. To his immense disgust, he also spotted his brother, George, leering into some young debutante's décolletage. But before he could catch his brother's eye to give him a piece of his mind, his attention was pulled elsewhere.

"Good heavens. What is the meaning of this?" Lady Bardess said, charging toward them with a scowl. "I thought I ordered these children out of sight until it is time for them to sing."

"Wouldn't it be a better idea for your guests to see the very children they are here to contribute to?" Stephen asked, somehow managing to look deferential, even though he was defying Lady Bardess. Perhaps it was the way he adjusted his glasses and met her ire with a smile so sweet it could attract honey bees.

Lady Bardess sniffed and tilted her nose up. "I am not accustomed to having my orders ignored, Mr. Siddel."

"I beg your pardon, my lady." Stephen bowed with a near reverent degree of apology...all of which Max could see was feigned.

Lady Bardess clearly didn't know how to respond to the mix of command and acquiescence. "Well, I suppose we could just start the concert," she huffed. She turned and glanced across the room to a man Max recognized as her butler. "Chambers." She snapped her fingers at the man. "Begin the concert."

The butler nodded to Lady Bardess, then proceeded to the dais at the front of the room. "My lords and ladies," he announced in a booming voice. "If you would kindly take your seats, the concert will begin."

Max watched as the buzzing room of aristocrats

broke off their conversations and rushed to get the best seats. He had an easy time predicting which of the society mavens would rush to sit at the front, which would hide at the back, making eyes at their illicit lovers, and who would nestle in the middle so that they could fall asleep without being noticed. What surprised him was the way George sauntered to an aisle seat near the very front. George noticed Max, but failed to acknowledge him in any way whatsoever.

Max stayed right where he was, a few feet from Stephen's side, watching the whole thing like an outsider. He should have been in the thick of the crowd with the guests by right of birth, but in his heart, he knew he didn't belong there. He was something other, something not quite suitable for fine society. He hadn't fit with their lot for years.

With a warm flash of shock, he realized that he did belong somewhere after all. He belonged right where he was, standing against the wall beside a ramshackle group of orphan girls. He belonged by Stephen's side, regardless of title or wealth or any of the external trappings of birth that had been thrust upon him. He was so certain of his place that he didn't even mind the curious looks darted his way by old school chums or friends of his siblings. The world of the people sitting in the chairs in front of him should have been his own, but it wasn't. He'd always been on the outside, but with Stephen by his side, the outside felt right.

"We have a new addition to our yearly concert this

year," Lady Bardess was in the middle of saying from the dais, where she'd quickly taken over from her butler. "Please give a warm welcome to the girls of the Briar Street Orphanage."

Lady Bardess held out a hand to Stephen's girls as her guests applauded. Stephen, Mrs. Ross, and Annie quickly shuffled the girls to the dais, where Annie took a seat at the piano, her eyes going wide at the magnificence of the instrument. Across the room, Sister Constance stared daggers at Stephen, likely for what she would consider stealing the prime spot in the concert's order.

The girls sang magnificently, much to Max's relief. Far better than they had at his father's house. Even George seemed more interested, though the way he studied the girls with a look of appraisal set Max's teeth on edge. Stephen beamed with pride at the girls through the entire concert. Max watched him rather than the girls, unabashedly nursing the affection he had for the man. He found himself in serious danger of unmanning himself at one point during a quaint, old love song when Stephen peeked in his direction and met his eyes. The electricity that passed between them was so potent that Max had to force himself not to look in Stephen's direction for the remainder of the concert in order to protect both of their reputations.

As soon as the girls were done singing, the two footmen from the hall ushered them off the stage and into the hall while Mr. Chambers, the butler, escorted Stephen and Mrs. Ross back to the side of the room where Max stood. For a moment, Stephen looked as though he would follow his girls, but the butler wouldn't allow it. He twisted and turned to watch them as they left while Sister Constance's choir was introduced and took to the stage. Max was certain that the only thing preventing Stephen from charging off after the girls was the fact that Annie slipped out to the parlor with them.

"Don't worry too much," Max whispered to Stephen once they were standing side-by-side again, as Sister Constance led her choir in a series of hymns. "Annie will keep them from stealing everything in the room and tearing down the wallpaper."

Stephen managed a weak smile for the quip, but Max could tell he was on edge.

That edginess stayed with him, like an aura Max could sense, as Sister Constance's children finished their performance and were whisked out of the room, the same as Stephen's girls had been. And similarly to Stephen, Mr. Chambers made certain that Sister Constance and her nuns stayed in the conservatory.

"Now," Lady Bardess said, taking the stage again and smiling at her guests. "I'm sure you would all like to approach the leaders of these lovely choirs with questions about their dear, dear orphanages and ways to donate money to them. Off you go."

The room erupted into chattering conversation as soon as Lady Bardess ended the official entertainment. Within seconds, Stephen and Mrs. Ross at one side of the room and Sister Constance and the nuns at the other side of the room were inundated with curious and questioning noblewomen. The men didn't seem particularly interested in charity of any kind. Max even spotted a few, like George, Lord Chisolm, and Lord Martindale, leaving the room entirely.

"I'll mingle and put in a good word for you," Max told Stephen before stepping away, intent on making his way through the crowd to drum up donations from some of his old school chums.

"I was hoping to catch you, Lord Hillsboro," Lady Bardess said, grabbing Max's arm and dragging him to the front of the room before he could get far.

"Lady Bardess," Max greeted her, trying not to wince. "Your concert has been a triumph."

"Yes, of course," she sighed. Her face pinched into a sour expression. "I detest having so many people crawling through my home, though. And do not get me started on my reservations about having children running through the halls." She spoke of the children as though speaking about an infestation of rats.

Max frowned, even though he was forced to do the gentlemanly thing and offer his arm to escort her on a turn around the room. "Why do you host the concert every year if you like neither children nor company?"

Lady Bardess made a noncommittal sound and shrugged. "My father, Lord Chisolm, enjoys them."

Suspicion crawled down Max's back. "I'd forgotten Lord Chisolm was your father." He paused, then went on with, "Strange that he rushed out of the concert so quickly, considering how much you say he enjoys them."

"I believe he and my brother, Lord Burbage, have some sort of business to attend to." She brushed off Max's implied question, stopping and turning to him with a fetching grin when they reached the corner of the room. "I'm more surprised to find you still keeping company with the orphans, Lord Hillsboro. Didn't I hear that your father was about to be invested with a new title for service to the queen in the orient?" Her eyes sparkled with avarice.

"You know more than I do, apparently," Max said. "I haven't spent significant time with my family for months now. My interests lie in a more charitable direction than my father tends to be capable of."

Lady Bardess laughed and slapped his arm as though he'd deliberately told a joke. "You are droll, Lord Hillsboro. I am eternally shocked that some fine lady hasn't snatched you up." Her eyes continued to glitter.

Max was so used to being hunted for sport by women seeking titles and connections that he shrugged her flirting off. "Few women are interested in a fourth son," he said, attempting to be charming. "You should see the way they throw themselves at my brother Charles, though, after poor Elizabeth passed away last year." In fact, he found the way the dozens of salivating noblewomen threw themselves at his still-grieving brother to be disgusting.

"Do not discount yourself as a prize, Lord Hillsboro,"

Lady Bardess continued to flirt. "You are a man with charms of his own." She traced her fingertips down the length of his sleeve, biting her lip as she did. Max couldn't work out whether the woman truly was ignorant of how little interest he had in her or whether she was teasing him in an attempt to get him to admit his secrets.

A commotion near the door that the children had been escorted out through drew Max's attention, saving him from having to come up with a way to flirt with Lady Bardess. One of the footmen who had taken them out pushed his way through the crowd in an attempt to get to Stephen. Max watched as the man leaned in to whisper something in Stephen's ear. A moment later, Stephen broke away from the women he was speaking to and hurried to follow the footman out of the room.

"Excuse me, Lady Bardess," Max said, breaking away from her and dodging his way through the crowd.

By the time he arrived in the parlor, all hell had broken loose.

"Stop that at once, you little tart," Sister Constance was yelling at Beatrice.

All Beatrice was doing was attempting to pry one of Stephen's younger girls off of one of Sister Constance's charges. The two girls were going at each other with fists and feet, kicking, punching, and even biting. They weren't the only ones. The entire room was a sea of screaming, tussling, fighting children. Max could barely tell where Stephen's girls ended and Sister Constance's orphans began.

"He bit me!" one of the girls yelled.

"She tried to take my rock," a boy from Sister Constance's orphanage screamed in return.

"Someone pinched me," another girl wailed.

Within seconds, half of the children were screaming and crying while the other half did their best to give each other black eyes and bloody noses.

Max charged across the room to Stephen, pulling fighting children apart as he did. "Looks like we should probably get them all out of here and into the carriages as fast as possible," he said, not sure whether to laugh or turn into the disciplinarian he knew he wasn't.

"Agreed," Stephen said with the most ominous look Max had ever seen from him. "Make sure the carriages are by the front door and I'll wrestle this lot into them."

Max nodded, stepping away. He cast a look over the writhing sea of hot, angry, belligerent children, marveling at how a pack of little girls could go from sweetness and light to little hellions so quickly. He supposed that was just what children did sometimes. It was madness, but as he jerked and dodged his way through the melee to the door, racing down the hall to make sure the carriages were ready, his heart felt light. He would take a tiny battle of naughty children over the stiff and stolid arrogance of the upper classes any day.

CHAPTER 9

Max never would have imagined it would take so much time and effort to convince a wild pack of little girls to settle down long enough to pile into carriages and head home.

"Six to a carriage," Stephen called over the screaming, struggling mass of girls as they ran this way and that in front of Bardess Mansion. "Hurry along, now. The quicker we settle down, the faster we'll get home." He shoved a hand through his hair and adjusted his spectacles, obviously at his wit's end. "Max, fetch Ursula from the flower garden over there and get her into a carriage."

Max nodded and leapt into action. He didn't mind Stephen ordering him about, even though he was a viscount and Stephen was a humble orphanage headmaster. In fact, he rather liked it in ways that were best not to think about with two dozen young girls running amok all around him.

It didn't help that Sister Constance ushered her own rabble out to the street before all of Stephen's girls were secure in the carriages. Whatever argument had caused them to fight in the first place renewed, only outside, the children were armed with rocks and handfuls of dirt to throw at each other.

"Ivy, Lori!" Stephen shouted, managing to still appear kind and fatherly, even though he was clearly irritated. "Get away from that shrub! All of you, into the carriages."

"I should expect nothing less from a pack of undisciplined scallywags," Sister Constance growled as she pushed, shoved, and swatted her own orphans into another set of carriages.

"I would be happy to debate methods of childrearing with you later, Sister Constance, but not now," Stephen told her.

Mrs. Ross wasn't as polite. "Shut your gob, Connie. You always were an old windbag."

"Why, I never!" Sister Constance clapped a hand to her chest, but Max was certain she was about to retaliate with equally strong words, or even a tight slap.

He didn't get a chance to see it, though. He was too busy collecting Ursula from the flower beds by scooping her up around the waist and hoisting her under one arm like a rugby ball. He plucked Ginny from the other side of the flowers and carried her under his other arm to the lead carriage, handing them to Beatrice inside.

"Has anyone seen Jane?" he asked, striding toward

Stephen, but taking a detour to catch one of Sister Constance's boys and carry him to his own carriage.

"She's in here," one of the girls yelled from the middle of the line of carriages.

"As long as she hasn't found a pair of scissors," Max muttered.

"Quickly," Stephen said once Max returned from delivering the boy to Sister Constance. "I think they're all tucked inside. We should escape while we can." The flash of mischief Max loved so much had returned to his eyes.

Max nodded to him and raced for one of the carriages, hopping inside. The ride back to Briar Street felt rather like being trapped in a sardine can filled with live sardines. The girls were restless and overexcited from the afternoon. Max was elbowed, kneed, poked, and groped so many times that he swore he would be covered in bruises. And he had never been happier.

There was another bout of frantic activity when the carriages dropped the girls off at the orphanage. The orphanage of the Sisters of Perpetual Sorrow was just up the street, and several of Stephen's girls attempted to renew their battle by racing toward Sister Constance's carriages as her young ones climbed down. Stephen and Max had their hands full catching them and wrestling them back into the orphanage.

"Who needs a gymnasium when they have a pack of wild little girls?" Max panted as he and Stephen managed to get the last of the girls inside and into the great hall.

"Now you know how I stay so fit," Stephen laughed in return.

Max met the comment by raking him up and down with an appreciative gaze. "Thank God for wild orphans."

Stephen blushed pink, his eyes dancing with desire for a moment.

"You need to feed this lot before there's another mutiny," Mrs. Ross said as she passed the two of them, escorting Fanny into the great hall. "Save your flirting for later."

The woman's frank statement was enough to sober Max. He made a horrified face at Stephen. Stephen answered with an expression that made him look like a naughty schoolboy who had just been chastised—a look that stirred Max's blood and stiffened his cock.

"You can help me serve the stew," Annie said, marching past them and out to the hall. Surprisingly, she glanced to Max, not Stephen. "It's been simmering all afternoon. And I baked rolls early this morning, so those will be ready to serve too."

Stephen nodded to Max to go with Annie. As the two of them headed down the hall to the kitchen, Max cleared his throat and shook his shoulders out, and did everything he could think of to tamp down his hunger for Stephen.

"Are you going to marry Lady Bardess?" Annie asked

the second they reached the kitchen. She didn't stop moving, heading for the large, fragrant cauldron sitting on the most massive stove Max had ever seen, but she glanced over her shoulder to him with a suspicious look.

The question caught Max off-guard. "Er...um...no, I'm not," he answered, perplexed at how self-conscious Annie's stare made him feel.

"It's just that I heard someone at the concert saying that you would most definitely marry Lady Bardess, and that it would be a perfect match of wealth, position, and convenience."

Uneasiness prickled down Max's spine. Wealth and position were harmless words, but convenience implied far too many other things. "I'm not inclined to marry," he said, gathering up a tray full of wooden soup bowls as Annie pointed across the room to it.

"I'm going to marry Mr. Siddel," she said without looking at him.

Awkward prickles inched down Max's spine. "Are you?" he asked, uncertain whether he should encourage her fantasy or dissuade her from it. The possibility that Stephen had arranged something between the two of them for convenience's sake also crossed his mind, bunching his shoulders and filling his gut with acid.

"Yes." She was smiling when he brought the tray full of bowls over to her. "We've been intended for each other these many years now. I'm more than ready to say yes to his proposal, whenever he chooses to make it." She sighed, lowering her shoulders. "I do wish he'd hurry."

It was all Max could do not to visibly sigh with relief. Stephen hadn't promised the poor girl anything. "Stephen might not be the marrying kind either," he said carefully, loath to hurt Annie's feelings. She was sweet, after all, and he liked her.

"Oh, he is," Annie reassured him, her smile growing wider. "Mr. Siddel is the kindest, most generous man I've ever met. But I can see in his eyes that he longs for a wife."

"Can you?" Max's insides heated and quivered at the thought, not of a wife, but of a lifelong partner.

Annie nodded bashfully. "He is so strong on his own, but sometimes you can just tell that a man needs a mate to be perfectly happy. Mr. Siddel gives so much love to others, but I can tell that what he truly wants is for all that love to be returned to him."

"Yes, I can see that," Max said, losing himself in an indulgent smile. Mad as it was, considering the mountain of circumstances surrounding them, he wanted to fill that role in every way possible.

"That's why I don't think it will be long before he proposes," Annie went on, ladling stew into the bowls as Max laid them out on the tray. "There's been something different about him these last few weeks. I can't quite put a finger on it, but he seems...." She glanced up at the stove's chimney for a moment. "Primed," she finished at last. "He seems ready at last."

Max couldn't help but interpret her words carnally. He, too, had a strong feeling Stephen was primed and ready, like a man deep in the throes of passion, just on the verge of orgasm. The comparison and the imagination of Stephen's impassioned expression when he came had Max hard as a rock in no time. It took everything in him to concentrate and shove aside his desire to focus on serving supper.

Luckily for him, it was easy to cool down while carrying a tray of stew and rolls up through the great hall while ravenously hungry little girls all but attacked him in their hurry to eat. Max didn't have a chance to think of anything but avoiding being bitten and stopping skirmishes from breaking out between the girls. He'd never seen them in such a mood before. Not that he'd been with them long. It was a miracle that he, Stephen, Mrs. Ross, and Annie were able to eat their own suppers before the new trial of getting everyone up to bed, washed, and tucked in for the night began.

It was well past dark by the time the last girl had her hair braided, her nightgown tied, and her pillow fluffed for her. Max had never nestled a child into bed for the night before, but he found the whole thing charming. Mrs. Ross and Annie were so exhausted by the end of it all that they dragged themselves straight to bed in the upstairs room they shared. That left Stephen and Max to walk back downstairs together, shaking their heads and laughing tiredly at the chaos of the day.

"They're not usually like that," Stephen laughed, rubbing his eyes under his spectacles.

"Even if they were, that's still the most enjoyable

evening I've had in a long time," Max said as they reached the downstairs hall. He glanced toward the door, but found himself dreading the thought of leaving.

Stephen smirked at him. "You wouldn't have rather spent your evening at some fancy ball, pretending to court high society ladies?"

Max laughed. "God, no! That's the last thing I would ever want to do."

"I'm glad to hear it." Stephen's eyes sparkled with raw emotion. His lips twitched into an inviting grin. For a long moment, he looked as though some sort of inner debate was raging behind his ardent stare. Max held his breath, heart pounding until Stephen asked, "Do you want to spend the night?"

Joy and relief shot through Max. "Do you have a spare bed?" he asked, knowing the answer.

"No," Stephen answered, staring straight at him, unflinching and hot.

A giddy sort of relief shot through Max. Finally. He launched himself at Stephen, wrapping his arms around Stephen's torso and bringing his mouth crashing down over his. It was like the floodgates had been opened at last, for both of them.

Stephen made the most delicious sound of carnal acceptance deep in his throat as Max thrust his tongue against his. Stephen clung to him, digging his fingertips into Max's sides as they tumbled toward the closest wall, pressing up against it for support as their mouths ravaged each other. Max had never wanted to be a part of someone else the way he wanted to meld with Stephen. He tugged at Stephen's clothes, moaning in triumph as their lips pressed together, teasing and exploring each other.

"I want you," he panted, freeing Stephen's shirt from the waist of his trousers and stroking his hands along Stephen's bare flesh. "I've wanted you from the moment I first saw you."

"And I've wanted you too," Stephen echoed restlessly.

He followed his words by reaching for the front of Max's trousers and stroking his growing erection through the fabric. The jolt of pleasure that hit Max had him groaning loud enough to wake anyone upstairs.

"Ssh." Stephen silenced him playfully with a kiss powerful enough to take Max's breath away. But he also increased the pressure of his stroking, driving Max mad with desire. So much for being a mild-mannered, sweet, father-figure. Stephen was a fiend when it came to temptation.

"We'd better move," Stephen said at last in a shaky voice, prying himself away from Max. He grabbed Max's hand and led him quickly down the hall, past the kitchen, and on to a quiet bedroom at the back of the house.

Max knew in an instant it was Stephen's room. Everything about it, from the furnishing to the decorations, were pure Stephen. The single bed was neatly made with simple but well-made linens. The plain curtains were drawn over two, small windows on one side of the room while a wardrobe and washstand stood against the opposite wall. None of the furnishings or the carpet matched, and they were all clearly second-hand, but they'd been well taken care of. One entire wall held small photographs of girls, presumably ones who had grown up under Stephen's care, then gone off into the world. The display was tender and adorable, and it made Max want Stephen even more, in spite of its sweetness.

"Will anyone hear us in here?" Max asked the vital question as he advanced on Stephen, his hands going straight to the buttons of Stephen's disheveled jacket.

"The room above this one is for storage," Stephen panted, shaking his head and fumbling with Max's buttons. "Though I don't recommend screaming."

The very idea of screaming as the two of them made love made Max dizzy. "I don't know if I'll be able to stop myself," he said, throwing himself into Stephen's arms once he'd unbuttoned his jacket and waistcoat.

Momentum sent them reeling backward. The back of Stephen's legs knocked against the side of his bed and he lost his balance. They both spilled across the bed, still trying to grope and undress and kiss each other clumsily. It was madness, and it was magnificent. Max couldn't contain his laughter as he pulled at whatever piece of Stephen's clothing he could get his hands on, fighting to expose flesh and peel away layers. Stephen did the same with him, and Max wriggled and writhed to shed his jacket and everything else. Their struggles only served to grind their bodies against each other, heightening the pleasure.

"God, I've wanted to touch you like this for so long," Stephen panted, sliding his hands up Max's sides under his shirt. It was all Max could do to wriggle out of his shirt as quickly as possible. Stephen's touch burned like magical fire across his skin.

He felt exactly the same, but was too far beyond words to express it. Instead, he yanked Stephen's shirt up over his head, knocking his spectacles askew as he did. Stephen tried to straighten his spectacles as Max threw his shirt aside, but Max stopped him. His hands shook with need as he gently removed Stephen's spectacles and reached to set them on the bedside table.

"How well can you see?" he asked, balancing himself over Stephen, who looked beyond perfect on his back, chest bared.

"Well enough," Stephen answered, surging up to grab Max's face and to draw him down for a kiss.

Max groaned as their mouths melded, tongues exploring each other. Kissing only satisfied him for a moment, though, as amazing as it was. He told himself that he would spend hours upon hours just kissing Stephen in the future, but in that moment, he wanted more.

He broke away from Stephen's lips, kissing a trail down his neck to his chest. Stephen sucked in a breath, arching into him. There was so much about the man to love—his unfettered reactions, the delicious scent of his skin, the pleasured sounds he made as Max kissed his way lower, stopping to flicker his tongue across one of Stephen's nipples as he did. Max wanted to slow time down so that he could relish every last detail of their first time together, but the urgency pounding through his own body wouldn't let him.

He shifted lower, climbing off the bed for a moment. Stephen looked worried, until Max picked at the laces on his shoes and pulled them off his feet. He paused to remove his own shoes, then shamelessly shucked his trousers and dropped them as he straightened.

Stephen let out a sound of pure joy. "I knew you'd be beautiful," he said breathlessly.

Max grinned, taking his time approaching the bed to give Stephen a look. His cock stood up eagerly, and since Stephen was drinking in the sight, Max stroked himself slowly to give him something more to feast his eyes on. Stephen made a wild sound of need in response, fumbling with the fastenings of his own trousers.

Max leaned toward the bed, pushing Stephen's hands aside so that he could do the honors himself. Once the fastenings were undone, he grabbed hold of the useless trousers and tugged them down. Stephen's impressive cock sprung up, sending a shudder of need down Max's spine. He tore off Stephen's trousers entirely, then stroked his hands up Stephen's thighs, nudging them apart as he did, to reach his goal.

He'd waited for what felt like so long to touch Stephen, to feel his heat and hardness in his hands.

Stephen was impressively large, thick and straight. Max's arse tightened in anticipation of how Stephen would feel inside of him.

"Do you have anything we can use as lubrication?" he asked breathlessly, lowering his head toward Stephen.

Stephen made a strangled sound. "No. I haven't needed it for years."

"Me either," Max said, answering the unasked question of how long it had been since he'd had a lover himself. "Never mind," he went on, bending close enough for Stephen to feel the heat of his breath against the head of his penis. "I don't want to risk us hurting each other, but there are worlds of other things we can do."

He followed his statement by kissing the head of Stephen's cock before drawing it slowly into his mouth as though it were candy. Stephen made the most delicious sound Max had ever heard as he gripped the bedcovers on either side. His hips jerked up, driving him deeper into Max's mouth. He found the involuntary gesture hopelessly erotic and carried it farther by seeing how deep he could take Stephen.

It truly had been years, but Max remembered exactly what he needed to do to make the experience as pleasurable and comfortable for both of them as possible. It helped that Stephen's taste drove him wild, as did the desperate look of pleasure that pinched Stephen's face as Max sucked him. Taken as a whole, every bit of evidence of Stephen's pleasure only fired Max's own, making him reach for his own cock even as he gripped the base of Stephen's.

"I can't hold out," Stephen panted, suddenly reaching for Max's shoulders. "I don't want...."

Stephen couldn't finish his sentence, but Max understood that he wasn't ready for the whole thing to end yet. He let Stephen's cock go, sliding up so that their bodies touched in as many places as possible. He kissed and nibbled at Stephen's chest and shoulder on his way up to his lips. Their mouths met with such passion that Max felt himself as dangerously close to the edge as he felt Stephen was.

"God, I love you," Stephen gasped, grabbing a handful of Max's backside with one hand and digging his fingertips into Max's back with the other.

The declaration hit Max like a tidal wave, filling his heart with the same pre-orgasmic fire that had his groin poised, throbbing on the edge of release. He couldn't remember a time when anyone had said they loved him, anyone at all.

"I love you too," he panted, jerking his hips against Stephen's in a deliberate effort to speed things to a blissful completion.

Stephen gripped Max's thigh hard, spreading his legs enough to slip his fingers against the pucker of his arse. It didn't take much more than that, laughable as it seemed on one level. With their bodies entwined, rutting against each other, their mouths and tongues tangled, and their hands reaching and groping, it was only a matter of moments before Max careened over the edge, spilling himself across Stephen's belly. Stephen gasped as he did, and moments later cried out in release as he came as well.

It was clumsy, messy, and almost amateur in its artlessness. In Max's mind, they'd hardly done anything to achieve such a spectacular result. But they'd both been so hungry for each other and, he suspected, hadn't experienced any pleasure at all for so long, that it seemed like the blink of an eye before they were lying in a tangled, sweaty pile, desperately clinging to each other as they fought to catch their breaths.

"That was surprisingly good," Max panted as they shifted to lie in each other's arms, limbs entwined, stealing kisses between breaths.

"It was," Stephen said with a smile that was both satisfied and mischievous. "And once we've recovered, we can try again and do even better."

Max had never heard anything so wonderful in his life. He hummed deeply in agreement before surging against Stephen for another passionate kiss. He had the feeling that it wouldn't take long for either of them to be ready to go again, and he wouldn't have had it any other way.

CHAPTER 10

Stephen couldn't remember the last time he'd slept so hard. In more ways than one. He couldn't remember the last time he'd been so exhausted either. The girls had run him ragged during the day, and Max had pushed him to his limits through the night. It was pure bliss to wake up, still feeling groggy but utterly content, with Max stretched beside him, one arm thrown over his chest, the deep, slow rhythm of his breath against Stephen's shoulder.

Somewhere deep in the recesses of Stephen's mind, the thought that he should feel guilty for waking up naked in a bed with another naked man tickled him. He instantly pushed it aside in favor of a lazy smile. In spite of the wild way they'd made love the night before, there was nothing salacious or wicked about being with Max. In the throes of passion, they'd confessed their love for each other. It had come as a surprise to Stephen, but he stood by everything he'd said, every kiss, every touch, every soul-deep orgasm they'd shared. Max was his heart, and nothing could possibly be righter than the two of them being together. Better still, Max loved the girls as much as he did. That alone was so unlike the tragic affair of his past that he wondered why he and Max hadn't ended up in bed sooner.

He wasn't sure how long he lay there, grinning over his brilliant good luck, before Max stirred awake. Max stretched and sucked in a breath before lifting his head and glancing around with a confused frown. He looked utterly charming with his dark hair a mass of messy curls and one side of his face pink from pressing against the pillow, his lips still swollen and shapely from a thousand passionate kisses. Stephen's heart leapt in his chest as Max rubbed his eyes with one hand and propped himself on his other arm.

"Where am—" he started, then glanced down at Stephen. A lazy, almost silly smile spread across his bleary face. "Oh."

He bent to kiss Stephen, in spite of the fact that they could both use a good scrub and their teeth cleaned. Stephen didn't mind the lack of cleanliness at all. There was something intimate about it. He slid his arms around Max's back as Max shifted to cover him, sneaking one hand down to caress Max's backside.

"This is a lovely way to wake up," he said when Max broke their kiss and settled his head on the pillow beside Stephen's, evidently still not fully awake.

"Are we awake?" Max asked. "Because this feels more like the most beautiful dream I've ever had."

Stephen chuckled, holding him closer. The vibrations of his laughter sent eddies of pleasure through him. Judging by the way Max caught his breath and by the stiffness of his cock as it pressed against Stephen's belly, the feeling was mutual. His own arousal was rushing to the point where he would have to do something about it... a sensation that filled him with excited anticipation.

"I want to wake up like this with you every day," Max said, inching closer and nibbling on Stephen's earlobe.

The gesture was so erotic that it blasted the last haze of sleep right out of Stephen. He muscled to his side, flipping Max to his back and covering him. "Who's to say we can't be like this every day?" he asked, grabbing Max's thigh and hiking it over his hip. The movement brought them into such intimate contact that Stephen couldn't help but jerk against him, reveling in the sensation of their pricks pressed tight between them.

"That would be heaven," Max sighed, reaching up to thread his fingers through Stephen's hair.

Something bitter squeezed its way into the pleasure and joy of the moment. The implication of a thousand difficulties in the two of them just being together and greeting every day the way they were, was too great to ignore. Innocence and ignorance could only protect them if they protected themselves by keeping their distance. At that moment, distance was the very last thing Stephen wanted.

"If I could change the world so that the two of us could be together freely," he said, reaching between them to stroke Max's penis, "I would in a heartbeat. You know that."

"I do," Max said with a groan, sliding his hand down to hold Stephen's erection.

"You're all I've ever wanted," Stephen went on, finding it hard to speak as Max teased him to greater and greater degrees of pleasure.

Max answered without words, sighing loudly and stretching up to capture Stephen's mouth in a fiery kiss.

There was no telling how long they had. The pleasure they sought to give each other was as rudimentary as it got, but they kept at it, stroking and caressing each other while trying to kiss between increasingly desperate panting. Stephen longed for more, for the most intimate joining they could manage, but that took planning, and at the moment—

The door to his room banged open, causing him to tense so abruptly that he was surprised he didn't pull several muscles. Max jerked beneath him, hissing a curse. A tell-tale burst of liquid warmth spread between them. It would have made Stephen laugh if Mrs. Ross hadn't charged deeper into the room with a look of uncharacteristic fear in her eyes.

"The two of you need to finish up and get your sore arses out to the great hall," she said, utterly nonplussed by the sight in front of her.

Stephen twisted to the side, his cock still throbbing

with imminent release that had been stopped cold, pulling the bedcovers up to his shoulders like a priggish young miss. "Jesus, Mrs. Ross," he gasped, glaring at the fuzzy shape of her that was all he could see without his spectacles.

"I...I can explain," Max stammered, out of breath and red-faced.

Mrs. Ross clucked and shook her head. "I didn't fall off the turnip cart yesterday, Lord Hillsboro. I dare say I know more about what the two of you have been up to than you do. That's not the point." She shifted to frown at Stephen as he reached over Max to grab his spectacles from the bedside table. "Jane is missing," she said.

Stephen's alarm shot to dizzying heights when he put on his spectacles and saw just how anxious Mrs. Ross looked. "She's what?"

"Missing." Mrs. Ross raised her voice. "Possibly since last night, since the concert."

"But she was in one of the carriages that took us home, wasn't she?" Stephen sat, exposing more of himself and Max than he would have liked to as he did. He was still erect and growing more uncomfortable in body and spirit by the moment. Guilt flayed him. He'd known something like this would happen if he let himself go.

"I asked about Jane," Max said, sitting as well and glancing awkwardly around, as though he wanted to get out of bed but didn't dare to with Mrs. Ross right there and the evidence of his orgasm a little too apparent. "I was told she was in that middle carriage."

"Whether she was or not, she isn't here now," Mrs. Ross said. "So get up and come out to the great hall right away." She turned to go, but paused in the doorway, pivoting back to face them. "But finish up first," she said with grim practicality. "You'll be in no shape to tackle a crisis with blue balls."

She sailed out of the room, shutting the door loudly behind her.

Stephen let out a breath, sinking back against the headboard and rubbing a hand over his face. It was all his fault. He knew better, but he'd put himself first yet again, and disaster had befallen. It made his soul feel like shattered glass as he surged forward in an attempt to climb over Max and out of bed.

"Where are you going?" Max stopped him with a hand to his chest.

Stephen blinked at him incredulously. "To find Jane," he answered. Flickers of resentment licked at his insides like flames as he stared at Max, but he forced himself to let go of it all. It was his fault, not Max's, that they'd ended up as they were.

"First things first," Max said with a serious look, peeling back the bedcovers to expose Stephen's cock, still standing straight up against his belly. Max reached for it, curling a hand around him and stroking.

"What are you doing?" Stephen gasped, caught between his instinct to pull away and the pleasure that thundered through him, just as he battled between his instinct to tell Max to leave him to his responsibilities and his desperate need to hold him close.

"Mrs. Ross is right," Max said. "You won't be able to properly concentrate with a cockstand, so...." He jerked harder.

It was one of the oddest moments of Stephen's life. His body responded eagerly to his lover's touch while his mind raced off to the crisis at hand. And yet, in a completely unconventional way, the intimacy of the utilitarian act was even more powerful than the most romantic of private moments. It was as if it were a sign that Max might make it easier for him to fulfill his responsibilities instead of holding him back. But the guilt of the past refused to leave him entirely. He was grateful to be close enough to coming already that it didn't take long for him to find relief.

"Do you have a clean shirt I could borrow?" Max asked when they finally made it out of bed and washed up as best they could without a full bath.

"I should."

The fact that they wore the same size shirts settled into the back of Stephen's mind as they rushed to dress. He would contemplate how sweet it was that they were of a size where they could share clothes later. In that moment, all that mattered was Jane.

"Who was the last person to see her?" he asked several minutes later, as he and Max marched into the great hall.

The girls were all seated at the two long tables,

finishing up their simple breakfast. Most of them appeared anxious, but their faces lit with hope when he and Max arrived.

"She stood next to me at the concert," Ginny offered, her eyes wide as Stephen and Max walked past her, heading to the front of the room.

Annie blinked in surprise at the sight of Max. "Lord Hillsboro," she said, stepping away from the table where she'd been collecting breakfast dishes from the girls who had finished. "When did you arrive?"

An inconvenient knot formed in Stephen's gut. Of all the times for Annie to begin to notice things, she had to pick now. "Does anyone remember seeing Jane here during supper last night?" Stephen asked, hoping to side-step any uncomfortable questions.

"I don't think she was here," Beatrice answered with a miserable expression. "I'm so sorry, Sir. I should have kept a better eye on her."

"It's not your fault, sweetheart," Stephen said, knowing exactly how Beatrice felt. He changed direction so that he could give Beatrice the fatherly hug he knew she needed. "Jane is difficult to keep track of in the best of times."

"I was certain I locked up before going to bed last night," Annie said, following Max with a frown as he strode to the head table for a cup of tea. "And I was the one who opened them this morning. Why didn't I see you come in?"

Stephen stepped away from Beatrice, letting out a

frustrated breath. He would have to deal with that situation now instead of later. "Lord Hillsboro spent the night," he said, marching toward the table as though his intention was also to fix a cup of tea.

"He did?" Annie blinked in surprise, then her eyes narrowed as she glanced between Stephen and Max.

Max couldn't have looked guiltier if he'd tried. His face was bright red and his movements were tense as he poured a cup of tea for himself and one for Stephen. Stephen was certain he looked just as awkward as Max, but there was nothing he could do about it.

"Who was it that told Lord Hillsboro Jane was in the carriage with them?" he asked, turning toward the girls and speaking loud enough to be heard.

"It...it was me, Sir," Lori said, raising her hand with a miserable expression. "But I was wrong. I thought it was Jane, but it was Millie instead."

Several of the older girls murmured anxiously, as if they knew what the admission meant.

"She didn't come home with us after the concert, then," Stephen said, adjusting his spectacles and taking a long gulp of tea before heading back down the row of tables to where Mrs. Ross stood by the door. Max followed him, and Annie kept close on his tail.

"If you stayed the night, then where did you sleep?" Annie asked. "We don't have any guest rooms, and all of the beds are taken at the moment."

Max sent Stephen a sidelong look, asking what he should say to Annie's questions. Stephen clenched his jaw and frowned, wondering himself. The whole issue was nothing more than an irritation compared to the real problem at hand, but he didn't think Annie would drop the matter anytime soon.

As he reached Mrs. Ross at the back of the room, he decided the time had come to throw caution to the wind. "He shared a bed with me," he told Annie bluntly, then turned to Mrs. Ross. "Is it possible that Jane climbed into one of Sister Constance's carriages by mistake?"

"Lord Hillsboro shared a bed with you?" Annie's brow was deeply knit in confusion. Her gaze turned unfocused, as though she were trying to figure things out but couldn't.

Mrs. Ross sent Annie a frustrated look. "It's none of your concern, girl. All you should be thinking about right now is Jane." She turned to Stephen. "It might be possible. Jane wouldn't have gotten into the wrong carriage by accident, though."

"She would go home with Sister Constance's children if she wanted to cause mischief," Max suggested.

"And Jane always wants to cause mischief," Stephen agreed, feeling more confident. "Let's go bring her back."

He started into the hall, Max right behind him. Annie started to go with them, but Mrs. Ross grabbed her wrist and held her back.

"Not you, my dear," she said. "You need a lesson in keeping your nose in your own business. Besides, the girls need you right now, and they're what's important."

Annie didn't look happy to be left behind, but she

stayed as Stephen and Max fetched their coats and hats and started up the street to the Sisters of Perpetual Sorrow.

"She'll be there," Max assured him as they strode swiftly up the street. "Sneaking off to the wrong orphanage is just the sort of thing Jane would do."

Stephen sent Max a grateful smile, wishing he could reach for his hand, if only for the comfort it would bring him.

His heart sank straight into his feet when they reached the Sisters' orphanage, only to find it in just as much of a tizzy as Stephen's. The second they stepped through the front door, it was obvious something was wrong. An air of panic met them, and the nuns were rushing about in such a state that they didn't stop to greet Stephen and Max.

Stephen had to catch one of the young nuns by the arm as she scurried past. "What's going on here?" he asked.

"Oh, Mr. Siddel." The young woman clutched his hand with worry in her eyes. "It's Jerry, sir. And Robbie. They've gone missing, and we can't find them anywhere."

Stephen's gut clenched in dread. He glanced to Max only to find the same, anxious emotion radiating from him. "Where is Sister Constance?" Stephen asked, taking charge as much as he could.

"In the classroom, sir." The young nun launched forward, gesturing for Stephen and Max to go with her.

The classroom was a scene of chaos. Sister Constance

stood in the middle of a sea of upended desks and opened cupboards. Several of her older children appeared to be searching every nook and cranny while Sister Constance watched. The moment the older nun spotted Stephen and Max, her expression of heartfelt anxiety flashed to anger, and she marched toward them.

"Where are they?" she demanded, instantly in a towering fury. "What have you done with those boys?"

"Nothing," Stephen answered, firm enough, he hoped, to calm the woman down.

"Nonsense," Sister Constance went on, reaching Stephen and standing toe to toe with him, her eyes blazing and her nostrils flared. "We all know that Jerry loves to run down to your disorganized swamp of an orphanage whenever the notion takes him. I should have known that's where he and Robbie have gone."

"They aren't with my girls," Stephen said, glaring at the woman.

"Jane is missing as well," Max added. "The last time anyone saw her was at the Bardess concert. We thought she might have gone home in the wrong carriage and is hiding here."

"I would never allow such indiscipline within my walls," Sister Constance boomed, but there was far more fear than arrogance in her expression for a change.

"Have Jerry and Robbie been seen since the concert yesterday?" Stephen asked, ignoring Sister Constance's show of bravado.

"No," the woman admitted, lowering her voice.

"Were they at supper last night?" Max asked.

"No." Sister Constance's shoulders sagged anxiously, and she seemed to shrink under her wimple. "After their horrible behavior at the concert, the entire lot were sent to bed without supper." She chewed her lip in worry and regret, looking more like Mrs. Ross than ever. "I should have counted them. I should have inspected them all myself to be certain they were there. But I was so out of sorts myself...." She shook her head, her face pinching with regret.

Stephen's heart went out to her, and he rested a hand on her arm for a moment. However much of a dragon Sister Constance might have seemed most of the time, he knew she cared about the children in her charge. It was just a shame they had to go through what they were now faced with before she showed that side of herself.

"We'll help you search the orphanage one last time," Stephen said. "There is a chance that all three of the little ones are hiding around here somewhere. Your building is far larger and more elaborate than ours, what with the chapel attached to it and all. The three of them, Jane, Jerry, and Robbie, could all be hiding and playing a prank on us."

"If they are, then I'll wring their precious little necks," Sister Constance said with a sniff, standing straighter.

"I'll be right there with you," Max said, sending Sister Constance a friendly smile.

Sister Constance glanced to Max as though seeing

him there for the first time. She frowned at him, as though attempting to figure out exactly why he was there so early in the morning, but gave it up and turned to Stephen.

"I'll accept your help this once," she said. "The children have to be around here somewhere." She turned and marched off toward the hall, gesturing for Stephen and Max to follow her. As she did, she muttered, "And if they're not here, I don't know what I'll do with myself."

CHAPTER 11

Max kept his mouth shut as he, Stephen, and Sister Constance searched through the stodgy orphanage and its adjacent chapel. Sister Constance and Stephen wouldn't have liked what he had to say, and he suspected they already knew the truth themselves. Jane, Jerry, and Robbie were not hiding. They were not playing a game or being mischievous. They were missing.

"I won't hold back on using the strap once we find them," Sister Constance said with false anger as they searched the rows of pews in the chapel, her wimple flapping each time she leaned over to check under the seats. "Discipline must be maintained, after all. Spare the rod, spoil the child."

Max glanced across the room at her from where he'd gone to check behind the organ. If he had a foundling child that needed to be deposited in an orphanage, he would have chosen Stephen's over the Sisters of Perpetual Sorrow any day. Stephen raised his girls with tenderness and love, whereas Sister Constance ruled her roost with discipline and reverence. But half an hour in the woman's company, seeing the concern for her children that she couldn't hide, and Max was convinced that there was a heart beating under the dark grey of the woman's habit.

"I don't think a lack of discipline has anything to do with this," Stephen said, striding up the aisle from the chancel, adjusting his spectacles and rubbing his face. He had grown more agitated by the second and was now pale and wan. "They're not here."

Max left the organ and marched quickly to Stephen's side. Sister Constance continued to check the pews, her expression pinching with more and more worry as she looked. It was clear she didn't want to give up the search and that she didn't want to face the truth.

"We need to call the police," Max said what it was clear Stephen was thinking as well. He reached for Stephen's hand, but Stephen yanked away, not meeting his eyes. Foreboding dropped into Max's gut like a rock.

Sister Constance snapped straight, looking as though she might weep. "But calling the police is such a drastic measure. It means—" She clapped a hand to her mouth to hold in what Max was certain was a sob.

Stephen let out a breath and crossed to the back of

the chapel so that he could put an arm around the older woman's shoulders. "I'm afraid we've reached the point where denying the truth isn't going to help us or the children, Sister," he said in a rich, kind voice that plucked at Max's heartstrings. Mostly because Max could see Stephen was deeply disturbed himself. "We have to face the truth that they are genuinely missing."

"But what has happened to them?" Sister Constance asked in a tremulous voice.

"We'll find out," Stephen reassured her with a soft smile. "And we'll bring them home, where they belong. But first, I need you to fetch the police."

Sister Constance nodded, leaning slightly into Stephen for a moment before seeming to remember her dignity. She cleared her throat and stood straighter, back to being the sergeant-major she usually was. "I'll send for them at once."

She squared her shoulders and left the room, back to appearing to be in command of the situation.

Max watched her go, walking slowly to Stephen's side at the back of the chapel. The drafty old space felt somehow colder than it should for a late-spring morning. The patches of sunlight streaming in through dirty stained-glass windows were more ominous than comforting. The overall sense of gloom and helplessness grew deeper as Stephen drooped, losing the comforting aura of command that he'd worn just moments before. He let out a sigh and rubbed his eyes under his spectacles.

"I don't know what to do," he said quietly.

Max closed the gap between them in a heartbeat, attempting to fold Stephen into his arms for a tender hug.

Stephen wrenched away from him. "Not now," he hissed.

Max clenched his jaw, rippling with misery at the rejection. "Now is exactly the right time for comfort and support," he said, fighting not to sound angry.

Stephen sent him a mournful look that swept all of Max, as though he wanted nothing more than to find comfort in his arms but couldn't bear to. "It's my fault that the children are missing."

"Your fault?" Max flinched in disbelief.

Stephen turned away, a guilty flush reddening his face. "I shouldn't have given in to temptation. My duty is to protect my girls at all times, and every time I put my own desires first...." He let out a breath, rubbing a hand over his face.

Max frowned, crossing his arms and resting his weight on one leg. "Every time?" he asked, knowing the comment wasn't random and feeling a burst of jealousy because of it.

Stephen's whole face pinched. He turned slowly back to Max. "Several years ago, I lost one of my girls, Alice. She died in childbirth at the age of fourteen."

"Stephen, I'm sorry." Max let his arms drop and took a step toward him.

Stephen held up a hand to ward him off. "It was my

fault that she ended up with child in the first place. I had a lover at the time, and I gave too much of my attention to him and not enough to my duties. A local lad seduced Alice, but I was too preoccupied to notice or do anything about the affair."

Anger flooded Max, but not directed at Stephen. At least, not over what had happened all those years ago, or even because Stephen had had another lover. Max was indignant that a mistake from the past was causing Stephen to push him away now.

"Stephen," he said frankly, moving even closer to him. "Even I can see that whatever happened was not your fault, and I barely know any of the details. Regardless, the situation we're in now is entirely different. Don't take it out on me."

Stephen jerked to stare at him with wide eyes. "I'm not taking it out—" He stopped abruptly, pressing his lips into a tight line. "I just want to find Jane and the boys," he went on in a distracted voice, shaking his head as he marched past Max to the chapel door.

Max was ready to tear his hair out from frustration. He would be damned if he'd let Stephen's guilt shut him out, but he didn't know where to begin to wheedle his way back into the man's heart. "You were right to send for the police," he said as he followed Stephen to the hall. "They'll know how to widen the search."

"I just can't believe no one noticed Jane and the others were missing yesterday." Stephen marched ahead, tense as a tiger. "I can't believe I didn't notice."

"You can't blame yourself for this," Max said, catching up to him. He caught Stephen's arm, holding him still. "You are an excellent father to your girls, but it is a massive job. You're doing everything right."

"Am I?" Stephen broke away from him, taking a long step back. He studied Max as though he were a perplexing problem. "Am I the man you seem to think I am?"

"Of course, you are."

"Or am I a selfish cad who puts his own desires above those of the children in his care?"

Max took a half step toward him, resting a hand on the side of Stephen's face. "You are not to blame for any of this," he said, meeting and holding Stephen's eyes with stalwart strength.

Stephen shook his head, but placed his hand over Max's, holding it to his cheek. "I've been good for years, but one night of abandon, and this is the punishment I get."

Max's heart rejected the notion so vehemently that he nearly laughed. "No one is punishing you for enjoying yourself." When Stephen's expression turned doubtful, he went on with, "What we did, what we feel for each other, it isn't wrong, Stephen. You have every right to a life of your own, every right to give your heart and body away."

Stephen's wary look deepened. He pulled Max's hand from his face, though their fingers remained entwined, and glanced back toward the chapel. "I can think of quite a few authorities who would disagree with that sentiment," he said in a wry voice.

"Fuck them," Max said, a giddy thrill passing through him at the idea of using coarse language in a church. "Most of the people who made those rules are stodgy pricks who wouldn't know love or pleasure if it shouted in their face. And your heart is so big that there is more than enough to lavish on your girls and to give it to a lover, whether that's me or not." It hurt to add the last bit, but it was something Stephen needed to hear.

Stephen's lips twitched, but a smile didn't fully form on his worried face. "I will never be as sure of myself as you are." He paused, then added, "And I have no wish to give my heart to any other lover but you."

Max swayed closer to him, squeezing his hand. "Thank God for that." He was desperate to kiss Stephen, but wasn't sure he dared to. "And I have to be sure of myself. I've tried the alternative, and that way lies misery. The world isn't going to accept me, so I have to accept myself. And I accept you, Stephen. I accept you just as you are."

At last, a smile blossomed on Stephen's gorgeous face. His blue eyes turned suddenly glassy behind his spectacles, as though he'd never heard such tender words before, as if he'd never expected to hear them. Max changed his mind about daring. In spite of standing in a church hall with the possibility of being interrupted at any moment, he slipped an arm around Stephen's waist and pulled him close, slanting his lips over Stephen's.

It was a sweet kiss and a brief one. Just as it reached into Max's soul, making him want more, they heard the clatter of footsteps on the flagstones around the corner from where they stood. The warning gave them enough time to jump apart and head toward the corner before a young nun with a tear-stained face met them.

"The police are here," she said in a wispy voice. "Sister Constance sent me to fetch you."

"Lead the way," Stephen said, back to sounding as though he were in command, though his cheeks were flushed and his eyes glowed.

By the time they reached the entryway of the orphanage, Sister Constance had revived her towering temper as she addressed a single police officer in a disheveled uniform.

"There are children missing, sir," she shouted. "Young children. None of them older than ten. You must do something about it."

The officer raised his hands as though to ward Sister Constance off. Max was alarmed at the banality of his expression. "Now, now, Sister. I'm sure it's nothing to get upset about," he said in a cockney accent.

"Missing children are most certainly something to get upset about," Stephen said, raising his voice as he marched to join the conversation. "Three children, a girl named Jane, a boy named Jerry, and another boy named Robbie, have been missing since yesterday afternoon," he went on. "They were last seen at a concert hosted by Lady Bardess at her home in Mayfair."

The officer looked at him as though he had snatched a mug of beer out of his hands for no reason. "And what do you expect me to do about it here, in Limehouse, if the kids went missing from Mayfair?" he demanded, his tone as slovenly as his appearance.

"I expect you to do your job and open an investigation into the children's whereabouts," Max said, adding his weight to the confrontation.

The officer jerked back, staring incredulously at him. "Who are you when you're at home?" he asked with far more sass than Max was accustomed to.

"I am Lord Hillsboro," Max said with as much imperiousness as he could manage. "My father is Lord Eastleigh."

The officer seemed to shrink a bit as he realized he was speaking to a nobleman. All the same, it was clear that he either didn't entirely know his place or he didn't care about hierarchy. "Look, m'lord," he began, ignoring Sister Constance and Stephen entirely. "So you've got three kids missing. Kids go missing from places like this all the time."

"Then they should be found," Max insisted.

The officer's face pinched. "Maybe where you come from, m'lord. But around here?" He shrugged as though none of it mattered.

"These three children are precious to us," Stephen insisted, glaring at the officer.

Again, the officer shrugged. "I'm guessing the kiddos are orphans?"

"What does that have to do with anything?" Max demanded.

"No one much cares about orphans, do they?" the officer said. "That's why they're orphans to begin with. Folks dump 'em off on you lot because they're not wanted. So why should I waste my time turning over stones to find a few whelps that no one wants anyhow?"

Max was so appalled by the man's attitude that it turned his stomach. "These orphans are very much wanted," he insisted.

"They are loved," Stephen agreed.

"You will do your duty and find them," Sister Constance added.

The officer sighed and rubbed a hand across his stubbly chin impatiently. "Look. You can lodge a complaint with the district office if you'd like. I doubt anyone will care much, though. We've got thieves and murderers to catch. These streets are rotten, all of them. No one cares about kids when businesses are being robbed blind and blokes are being stabbed in the alleys."

"But you can't just—" Sister Constance started.

Stephen silenced her with a raised hand. "We understand," he said in a seething voice. "You're not going to help us."

"No, sir, I'm not." The officer nodded.

"Then get out," Max growled.

Between him and Stephen, and even Sister Constance, they must have presented an intimidating enough front to unnerve the man. He touched the brim of his hat and scurried back out to the street without another word, looking glad to be rid of them and the problems.

"I've never seen anything so irresponsible and callous in my life," Sister Constance huffed once the man was gone.

Max exchanged a glance with Stephen that said they'd both seen more than their share of unfair treatment for unfair reasons.

"What do we do next?" Max asked. "Since the police aren't going to be of any help."

"Maybe not these police," Stephen said, rubbing a hand over his stubbly chin. "There has to be someone who will help, though."

Something tickled in the back of Max's mind. He could have sworn he knew of someone who had mentioned something about searching for missing children recently, though he couldn't place his finger on it.

"We should return to Bardess Mansion," Stephen said after a few intense moments of silence. "Someone there might have seen the children."

"Do you think they could still be there?" Sister Constance asked. "Could they be hiding belowstairs?"

"Possibly," Stephen said, though from his expression, Max could tell he didn't think so.

"There's only one way to find out," Max said.

They jumped into action. Max went out to find a cab —not an easy task so deep into the bad end of the city—

while Sister Constance informed her nuns of what they were planning to do and Stephen dashed back to tell Mrs. Ross and Annie their plan. It took the better part of an hour, but at last they were on their way to Mayfair.

Unfortunately, they were met by the same level of indifference there that the officer had shown them.

"Missing children?" Lady Bardess tilted up her chin and sneered at Stephen when he asked about Jane, Jerry, and Robbie. "Good Lord, what would I know about that?"

"The last time any of them were seen was here, at the concert," Stephen told her, clearly trying to hold his temper in check. His jaw was tight and his back as rigid as a statue.

"That doesn't mean I know anything about them." Lady Bardess looked aghast at having to speak to Stephen at all, let alone answer his questions. The way she curled her lip at him, at his unshaven appearance and threadbare suit, filled Max with disgust. And he was supposed to be allied with her and people of her class instead of Stephen?

"Perhaps we could speak with your staff," Max said, throwing caution to the wind and stepping toward Lady Bardess on the off chance she would be more amenable to speaking with him. "Servants always see things that we don't." He was disgusted with himself for grinning and flirting with the woman, but if it would help them find the children, he was willing to do almost anything.

Irritatingly, Lady Bardess responded to his forwardness, though not in any sort of helpful way.

"Why, Lord Hillsboro, your concern for these waifs is charming." She batted her eyelashes at him and shifted her shoulders in a way that accentuated her bust. "Your father must be so proud."

Max's mouth twitched into a humorless smile. His father hadn't been proud of him in a decade, if not longer. "As I have told you many times before, Lady Bardess, the Briar Street Orphanage is my particular cause. When one of its charges goes missing, it is of great concern to me."

Lady Bardess laughed as though he'd told a clever joke. She sauntered forward to take his arm, pulling him away from Stephen and Sister Constance to take a nonsensical turn about the room. "I think you are charming to support such a pedestrian cause as a London orphanage when most of our friends are patrons of much more exciting foreign establishments. There's something so exotic about patronizing institutions in the orient to Christianize those poor, lost souls."

"My interests are closer to home," Max said through a clenched jaw.

"Which I find so sweet." Lady Bardess glanced at his mouth, which Max supposed was intended to be an invitation of some sort.

"Truly, my lady, any information you might have about these dear children would be greatly appreciated." He found himself contemplating the horrific notion of letting the odious woman drag him aside for a snog if it would pry just the slightest hint of the children's whereabouts from her.

"You know, I've never cared about children," Lady Bardess said, turning to face him as they reached a window near the far end of the room. She traced her fingertips along the lapels of his jacket. "My interests are far more...adult." She lifted her gaze to meet his eyes.

The situation was laughable, but Max wasn't amused. "My lady, I'm afraid you misunderstand my intention in coming here today."

"What do your original reasons matter?" she flirted. "Send your friends away and you and I can discuss far more important matters than those wretched orphans. I've heard that your mother is intent on marrying you off at last." Her eyes flashed with avarice.

"Perhaps some other day, my lady." Max walked a fine line between putting her off completely and trying to pry information out of her. "The sooner we locate these children, the sooner I will be free to pay social calls."

He was certain his ploy worked when a splash of color came to Lady Bardess's face and her smile warmed. "In that case—" She leaned closer to him. "I wish you all the luck in the world in searching for those little dears."

Max held his breath, waiting for more information. When none came, he prompted her with, "Do you know anything at all that might help?"

"I truly wish I did." She sighed, laying a hand on his lapel and stroking his chest. "I was far too busy admiring the patron to pay much attention to the orphans yesterday. My father cares more about those sorts of causes than I do anyhow."

Disappointment crashed through Max. He let out a breath, stepping away from her. "Thank you for your help, my lady," he said. As an afterthought, on the off chance that they would need her help again in the future, Max took her hand, bent over it, and placed a gallant kiss on her knuckles. His gesture was rewarded with a look of carnal enjoyment that turned his blood cold. He would need a night and a day locked alone with Stephen where no one would disturb them to shake the way Lady Bardess's glance made him feel.

With that in mind, he turned away from her, catching Stephen's eye from across the room and sending him a look like he'd barely escaped the gallows. He hurried to Stephen's side as fast as he could.

"She doesn't know anything," he murmured bitterly.

"Dammit," Sister Constance hissed.

Max's mouth twitched into a grin, but he sobered his expression as the three of them took their leave from Lady Bardess and marched back through the hall, led by the butler, Mr. Chambers.

Max was already plotting their next move and hoping Stephen had a few ideas too as they reached the front door and Mr. Chambers turned to him with a frown.

"My lord, you are the brother of Lord Westerbrook, are you not?" Mr. Chambers asked.

Max blinked at the use of George's formal title. "I am," he answered cautiously.

Mr. Chambers's look soured. "Would you kindly pass along the message to him that the vase he shattered in his haste to retreat after the concert yesterday was over one hundred pounds and that the antique sewing scissors that were also found broken cost at least twenty pounds?"

Max frowned, though he wanted to roll his eyes at his brother. "I'll tell him," he answered the butler with a grin nod. Though, if it were up to him, it would be a long, long time before he would see the bastard.

"I guess that's that, then," Stephen said with a sigh when they stepped out to the street and started up the road to where it would be easier to hire a carriage.

Max stopped suddenly and glanced back at the house. "You don't think the fact that my brother destroyed a pair of scissors is a sign, do you?" he asked.

Stephen paused to turn back with him. "Jane is rather fond of scissors," he said, his expression growing more troubled.

"Is Jane clever enough to leave behind a deliberate sign?" Max went on.

"Or was she playing with those scissors and just happened to drop them as she was taken?" Stephen seemed to finish his thought.

They exchanged a look that communicated far more than words could. Max couldn't shake the feeling that the ruined scissors were proof that Jane had been taken from the house itself, and therefore Lady Bardess had to be involved.

"We left as empty-handed as we arrived," Sister

Constance moaned, several yards ahead of them, oblivious to their conversation.

"We need to find a police officer who doesn't think orphans from Limehouse are lower than the scum of the earth," Stephen said as he and Max strode to catch up to her.

"There have to be some out there somewhere," Max agreed. He blinked as inspiration hit him. "Someone in The Brotherhood might be able to help."

"The Brotherhood?" Sister Constance asked, then frowned. "That's not one of those non-conformist religious orders, is it?"

Stephen and Max exchanged a wary look. Max cursed himself for speaking out of turn. He cleared his throat. "In fact, it is, Sister. But I've found their contacts to be quite useful in the past."

As he spoke, Stephen's eyes lit with inspiration. "I know who could help," he said, his energy visibly renewing. He sent Max a significant look. "Someone I spoke to at a recent social outing. A chap from a solicitor's office."

David Wirth. It came back to Max in an instant. He remembered Stephen and David talking while Lionel whirled him around the dance floor at the ball. Stephen had mentioned the investigation into missing children in passing as they'd made their way home late that night. In fact, Lionel himself might be able to help with their particular situation. Max was fired up to go with Stephen before remembering his other duties.

"I have to go home," he said, his disappointment obvious. "I need to tell Father about George's indiscretions. But I'll check back in with you as soon as possible."

Stephen nodded as they reached a busier street and raised a hand to hail a cab. "We'll get to the bottom of this," he said. "One way or another. We'll find those children."

CHAPTER 12

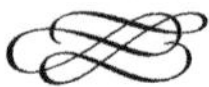

Max's thoughts were scattered and his mind was firmly still in Limehouse when he charged up the steps of his family's townhouse in Mayfair. He barely acknowledged his father's butler when the man opened the door for him, heading straight for the stairs that would take him up to his bedroom. He needed to bathe, change clothes, and think. Jane and the two boys couldn't have just disappeared into thin air after the concert. Lady Bardess might not have been directly involved, but he had a hard time believing she was completely innocent. If he was clever enough, if he combined forces with Stephen and, with any luck, David Wirth and Lionel Mercer, there had to be a way they could discover—

"So the prodigal son has returned home at last."

Max was jolted out of his thoughts before he'd made it halfway up the stairs as his father stepped out of the afternoon parlor. Irritation warred with a reluctant sense of guilt as Max stopped short and twisted to face him.

"I wasn't aware you'd returned from the country," he said, his heart thundering against his ribs from more than just his dash through the front hall.

His father's face remained as dark as a storm as he strode to the foot of the stairs. The way he glared up at Max made it feel as though his father were the one on a higher level while Max was forced to cower beneath him.

"I had business that brought me back to town," his father said, his expression darkening. "Imagine my surprise when I learned from Mr. Holmes—" he nodded to the butler, "—that you have not been home for days."

It was an exaggeration, but Max couldn't deny he hadn't been home the night before. His father wasn't a stupid man. Max knew exactly what the intent behind his comment was. He descended the stairs slowly, but stayed one step above his father, if only for the illusion of added height that the single stair would give him in the unpleasant conversation he was about to have.

"I'm nearly thirty, Father," he said. "Where I spend my time should not be any of your concern."

"It is my concern when you continue to live under my roof, surviving off of my money."

Max clenched his jaw. "I have money of my own."

His father snorted. "Barely enough to support you in the sort of decadent life you choose to live."

Max frowned, wondering what sort of life his father thought he lived. "I have no need to continue to live here," he said with what he hoped came off as a casual and confident shrug. "I'll move out immediately, if that's what you want."

"Why? So that you can go live with your pauper lover?" His father's expression turned dangerous.

As much as he hated it, fear coiled around Max's heart. He wasn't fool enough to think any sort of paternal love would keep his father from exposing who he was, or from turning him over to the authorities.

"I would think you'd be glad to be rid of me," he said instead, his voice hoarse with old and fading resentment over his father's rejection.

"Getting rid of you isn't the issue," his father said, as cold as winter. "The embarrassment of the whole thing is."

"Ah, yes. I would hate for you to be embarrassed by me," Max seethed. He blinked, tilted his head to the side, then went on with, "Oh, wait. You've been embarrassed by me for a decade now."

"Because you are a filthy perversion," his father said without pause. "You bring disgrace on us all with your sordid affairs and public carrying on."

Again, Max wondered if his father had the first clue what his life was truly like. It had been years since he'd had a lover. He wasn't the type to seek out empty pleasure or to flaunt his choices. Half of the reason he loved Stephen so much was because Stephen was the same. And not a single person of their acquaintance would ever look down far enough to see Stephen or the orphanage, or to take notice of Max's interests there.

Unless they had been to the concert.

"Did someone say something to you?" he asked, inching closer to his father in the hope that he would be able to pry whatever information he needed out of the man by standing up to him. "Did something happen at Lady Bardess's concert that you found embarrassing?"

He expected his father to flounder and struggle to answer, but the man snapped, "Lillian Bardess is exactly the bride you need. She is wealthy, respected in the only social circles that matter, and well-connected."

Max's brow shot up. "You want me to marry Lady Bardess?" The notion was so preposterous that he laughed.

"Want? No, son, I demand that you do," his father said with a grim laugh. "Before the veil drops from her eyes and she understands what sort of an abomination you are."

"No," Max said in no uncertain terms. "I cannot stand the woman."

"Your opinion of her is irrelevant. You will marry her."

Max gaped at his father. "Again, might I remind you that I am not some green youth. I am a grown man, and you have no right to make my decisions for me."

"He does when you're behaving like a blasted idiot." The confrontation was interrupted as George swayed into the front hall, a bottle of whiskey in one hand and a bleary look on his face.

Max sighed in exasperation. "If you want to talk about abominations, ask George to recount the tale of his behavior at the concert yesterday."

George snorted in indignation; a gesture that tipped him off-balance. "I behaved like a perfect gentleman," he argued, swaying to regain his balance.

"By staring into the décolletage of whichever lady you happened to be standing next to? By arriving drunk and rushing out of the room when the concert was barely finished even drunker? And where did you go when you fled? To vomit into some ornamental vase in an adjacent parlor?"

A sudden thought stuck Max through his anger. George had left the room before the concert ended. Lady Bardess's butler had said he'd broken a vase. He might have been in the hall, or even the parlor with the children, when Jane and the others vanished. George might know something.

"What happened to them?" he asked, stepping down from the stairs and crossing to stand toe to toe with his inebriated brother. "Did you see anything? Were you in the hallway when those children went missing?"

"I've no idea what you're talking about," George said, then hiccupped. The alcohol fumes radiating from him turned Max's stomach.

"The only children you need to concern yourself with are the ones you will get on Lady Bardess once you are married to solidify the alliance between our families," his father said, pulling himself to his full height and crossing to trap Max between himself and George.

"I will not marry Lady Bardess," Max insisted. "Nor any other woman," he added. In for a penny, in for a pound.

"You will do as you're told," his father seethed. "Lillian Bardess is the daughter of my friend, and she is in need of particular protection right now."

"I don't care if she's a member of the royal family," Max argued, daring to raise his voice. "I'm not marrying her. Now, if you will excuse me, I have a desperately important matter to attend to."

He turned to go, but his father grabbed his wrist so hard it hurt.

"Running off to bugger your pitiful lover, are you?" his father growled, leaning close enough to murmur threateningly into Max's ear. "Or perhaps some of those children of his?"

"Mr. Siddel's orphanage is for girls only."

"Men like you shouldn't be allowed anywhere near children," his father went on, ignoring the comment.

"Should they be allowed around men like George?" Max challenged him. "Or half of the arrogant, leering guests at Lady Bardess's concert?" He hadn't liked the looks that any of the members of his own social class had directed at the children. No wonder Stephen had felt so uneasy about the concert from the beginning.

"If you care about that man or those children at all,

you will cut off all contact with them at once," his father said, bending even closer to Max's ear, his expression threatening to the point of chilling Max. "It would be tragic if some sort of accident were to befall them, say, a fire. Or if your beloved Mr. Siddel were to be arrested on charges of sodomy and abuse of children."

Max swallowed hard, meeting his father's stare with pure hatred. He wanted to tell the bastard off and denounce everything he was saying. The trouble was, men like his father absolutely had it within their capability to destroy men like Stephen. The truth wouldn't matter when title and money spoke out against poverty and what the world saw as perversion.

Max shook his father off. "I will never, in all my life, understand why men like you and like George—drunken, cruel, faithless louts who destroy lives and innocence for pleasure—are praised and awarded the highest place in society while men like Stephen—good, kind, and brave—are deemed filth and threatened with imprisonment and worse. If that is the world you live in, then I want no part of it."

He jerked away, marching toward the stairs without a backward look, seething with hatred.

"You will not be permitted to leave the house unless I say so," his father called after him. "Holmes has been given orders to make certain you stay put until our meeting with Lady Bardess tomorrow."

Max nearly missed a step, but soldiered on. He wasn't

about to let his father see him sweat. He wasn't about to be locked in his room like a disobedient child either. The fact that his father had arranged some sort of meeting with Lady Bardess was a minor annoyance that he would easily get around. Once he was able to shift a few things into place, all the locks in the world couldn't keep him chained to a life he hated. And nothing or no one could stop him from helping Stephen to find Jane and the others.

Stephen glanced at the card David Wirth had given him during the dance at The Chameleon Club, then up at the nondescript building in front of him. He had the address right, he'd just expected to find more than an ordinary building, just like every other on the busy street. A small plaque beside the door listed the businesses housed inside, and the offices of Dandie & Wirth were among them.

It wasn't until Stephen walked through the door into the ground floor office that he knew he'd come to the right place. The building outside might have been plain and uninteresting, but the office itself was elegant and refined. Two leather-upholstered sofas sat facing each other near the center of the room. Bookshelves lined with everything from books to exotic art pieces stood around the perimeter of the room. A stove with a steaming kettle sat in a corner. The wallpaper and curtains were perfectly matched with the carpet. But the most striking feature of the room was the large desk that faced the door and the man who sat behind it.

Even though he'd only met the man twice, Stephen would have known Lionel Mercer if they'd encountered each other in a dark alley. Lionel was dressed in calming shades of blue that set off the color of his eyes. Not a hair on his head was out of place. The man exhibited the same otherworldly power that he had at The Chameleon Club. And as soon as Stephen stepped through the door, he stood to greet him like an old friend.

"Good morning, Mr. Siddel," Lionel said with a smile that was almost teasing in its welcome. "It's nice to see you again. How can I help you?"

Stephen cleared his throat and stepped deeper into the office. It was ridiculous that he should be intimidated by a man as elfin as Lionel Mercer, but he was. He removed his hat and said, "I was told that Dandie & Wirth might be able to assist with a serious problem I have." He cleared his throat and muttered, "Well, at least, David Wirth implied that he might be the sort who could help with this particular problem."

"We are experts in helping people with serious problems," Lionel said, coming around his desk with a look of extreme interest. He leaned against the front of the desk and crossed his arms. "What is the nature of your problem?"

"As you know, I run an orphanage in Limehouse," Stephen began, turning his hat in his hands nervously. It was ridiculous for him to be anxious around Lionel when he had been able to face down Lady Bardess as though he were her equal. Then again, Stephen wasn't certain anyone was Lionel Mercer's equal. "And yesterday, one of our children went missing. As well as two little boys from the home run by the Sisters of Our Lady of Perpetual Sorrow."

"Missing children?" The question was asked by David Wirth himself as he came out of the office at the back of the main room.

Stephen was relieved at the sight of the man. Whereas Lionel filled him with an odd sort of intimidation, David made him feel as though help had arrived. It was an uncanny juxtaposition of personalities.

"Yes," Stephen said. "A little girl from my orphanage and two boys from the Sisters'. I was given the impression in our last conversation that you might know what to do about children that have gone missing."

"Unfortunately, we do," Lionel said, pushing away from his desk and crossing the room to the stove, where he set to work making tea. Stephen watched him for a moment, his brow inching up over the ease with which such a powerful man rushed to make tea for a visitor.

"When did these children go missing?" David asked, gesturing for Stephen to have a seat on one of the sofas.

"Yesterday," Stephen said, feeling confused, but taking the offered seat all the same, "my children and the Sisters' performed at a benefit concert that was held at the Bardess mansion. Afterwards, we realized that three of the children were nowhere to be found."

David's expression filled with alarm, but with a certain measure of triumph as well. "You've come to the right place, Mr. Siddel," he said as Lionel returned to the sofa to hand Stephen a cup of tea. "We're already investigating this kidnapping ring, and we won't stop until we bring it down."

Stephen nearly dropped the teacup and its contents on the floor. "A kidnapping ring?" His gut filled with dread and guilt. Not even a sip of the excellent tea could tamp it down. "I can't—" he stammered, finding it suddenly hard to catch his breath. Shock turned to fear within him as all the possibilities of what might have happened to Jane and the boys closed in on him. "We have to do something," he said, his hands starting to shake so badly that tea splashed over the edges of his cup.

Lionel cleared his throat and quickly took the cup and saucer from Stephen's hands. "You're in luck. We've been doing something for weeks now."

"My dear Jane," Stephen went on in a strangled voice, barely hearing him. "And Jerry and Robbie. I'm not ignorant enough not to know what happens to children who have been taken like that." His pulse shot up so fast and hard that it made him dizzy and he thought he might be sick. His heart felt as though it were being turned inside out.

David shifted to sit beside him, taking his hand. "It's all right, Stephen," he said as though they'd been friends for decades. "We are aware of the situation, and believe me, we are doing everything humanly possible to resolve it."

"You will be pleased to know that there was a vital break in the case just yesterday," Lionel added, sitting on Stephen's other side. His manner suddenly shifted from intimidating to comforting as though he were an actor who had switched masks and committed to a whole new role.

"A break in the case?" Stephen forced himself to take a deep breath and pull himself together. He wasn't going to find Jane if he fell apart.

David's expression grew serious. "The police prevented a ship full of children from leaving Batcliff Cross Dock last night."

A surge of hope filled Stephen so suddenly that it made him dizzy all over again.

"Dozens of children were rescued, and some of the men responsible were captured by police," Lionel added.

"Jane," Stephen said, twisting to grasp David's hand with both of his. "Did you find a girl named Jane Pratt?"

David glanced past him to Lionel. Lionel's face pinched into a frown. "We did not," he said. "The children all gave their names, but there wasn't a Jane among them."

"What about Jerry? Or Robbie?" Stephen's emotions ran riot, ricocheting between hope and despair.

"There was a Bob," David said with a sympathetic wince. "He was a lad of about thirteen?"

Stephen slumped where he sat. "No. Robbie is barely seven, as I understand it."

"So your children weren't among those who were rescued," David said, drawing the same, horrible conclusion Stephen had.

"That means there's another cell of this group out there, as we feared," Lionel said, speaking to David as though Stephen weren't there. "And I would be willing to bet that Chisolm is involved."

"Chisolm?" Stephen's back snapped straight. "As in Lord Chisolm?"

"The very one," David said gravely. "His son, Lord Burbage, was one of the men arrested last night."

"Although, as I understand it, he'll be released before teatime today," Lionel added bitterly. "Ah, the benefits of a noble title."

"Lord Chisolm is Lady Bardess's father," Stephen said as though he'd been punched in the stomach. He cringed, wanting to break down into tears, but knowing he couldn't. Not without embarrassing himself far more than he wanted to. "I knew I never should have let my girls perform at that house."

David let out a tight breath, releasing Stephen's hand long enough to rub a hand over his face. "It stands to reason that if Chisolm and Burbage are in the thick of this, Lady Bardess could be as well."

Stephen fought to think of the situation rationally, in spite of the fact that his heart was ready to break into a thousand pieces. He knew he'd been wrong to take his focus off the girls, no matter how much Max had argued otherwise. He should have known better. Still, he tried to reason. "I'm not sure Lady Bardess is a willing participant. She seems far too flighty for that."

"You'd be surprised," Lionel said with a drawl. "Women can get away with murder by pretending to have fluff for brains. Trust me."

Stephen did. He trusted Lionel and David implicitly, though he wasn't certain why, other than that they were like him. They had the capacity to understand.

"What do I do?" he asked, glancing from one man to the other. "How do I protect the rest of my girls, and Sister Constance's children as well? How can I help to find Jane and the others?"

David and Lionel exchanged a look that conveyed a deep level of communication before David said, "I'm sending Patrick to interview you." He paused, then went on with, "Officer Patrick Wrexham of the Metropolitan Police has been assigned, at my request, to work on this case. He has been coordinating the efforts to thwart this ring."

"Darling," Lionel interrupted David with a wry grin. "*We* have been coordinating the efforts."

David sent him a warning look that held just enough heat to raise questions about their relationship in Stephen's mind. "Patrick is officially coordinating the efforts. I'll send him to your orphanage as soon as I'm able."

"Thank you," Stephen said, letting out a breath, even though he was far from feeling relieved.

"In the meantime," David went on, "you should do everything possible to keep your girls safe and out of sight. Although I honestly don't believe these kidnappers are the sort to charge into orphanages and snatch children out of their beds. I wouldn't let your girls play unchaperoned in the streets, though."

"Never," Stephen said, balking at the idea. "Not even in the best of times."

David smiled, patting Stephen's knee. The gesture would have been condescending coming from any other man, but from David it was comforting. "Good," David said, standing. "I promise you, Stephen, we are doing everything we can to catch these villains and to bring them to justice. And we will find your Jane, and the others."

"Thank you again." Stephen stood, shaking David's hand. "Anything at all that I can do to help—truly, anything—I will do it."

"I'm sure you will." David walked him to the door. "We'll be in touch as soon as we know anything," he said.

Stephen said another round of thank yous, shaking Lionel's hand as well. For a slight, pale man, Lionel had a powerful handshake. Stephen felt better, but not good enough. As soon as he reached the sidewalk in front of the building, he paused. He should return home and see to his girls. Sister Constance deserved to know that there were people fighting in their corner and that there was hope.

But all he could think about was Max. He needed to tell Max what was going on. And he needed to tell Max he was sorry, but they would have to keep their distance for the time being. At least until he was certain the girls were safe. Even if it killed the both of them to be apart.

CHAPTER 13

Figuring out exactly where Max lived took longer than Stephen anticipated. Few people in Mayfair were willing to answer questions about the home of an aristocratic family when they were asked by a distressed and disheveled man in a threadbare suit and spectacles. It wasn't until Stephen practically got down on his knees and begged a passing maid for whatever information she could give that he was directed to the home of the Duke of Eastleigh, Max's father.

But learning the location of Max's home was only part of the battle.

"Excuse me," Stephen asked when a pinched-face butler answered the door at the imposing, Georgian townhouse. "Might Lord Hillsboro be at home?" He held his hat in his hand and tried his best to look as innocuous as possible as he addressed the man.

The butler stiffened, glancing down his long nose at

Stephen. "Wait here," he said in an ominous voice, then shut the door in Stephen's face.

Stephen took a step back, his stomach sinking. It wasn't a good sign. He hadn't even been asked to wait in the house, in spite of the fact that night was falling. The shadows that stretched through the square where Max's house stood were long and dark. Stephen couldn't help but think it was some sort of horrible omen, that he should have simply sent a note. Or better still, cut off contact with Max without a word. But no, he rejected that thought outright...which only caused him to doubt his intention to put Max aside at all. He would have given anything to be able to think straight.

He was forced to wait, hat in hand, far longer than he should have. Anger began to bubble up within him, but he tamped it down. He was there to reach Max, not to cause trouble with Max's family by creating a scene. But the more time that passed, the more he convinced himself that he at least owed it to Max to tell him everything David and Lionel had revealed. Otherwise, he would have stormed off, making a rude gesture at the house as he went.

Finally, just when Stephen's nerves were at their breaking point, the door opened once more. This time, the glaring figure of Lord Eastleigh himself stepped out into the chilly night air.

Stephen opened his mouth to speak, but the duke cut him off with, "He will not see you. Ever again. If you are sighted anywhere near this house again, I will have you arrested for trespassing, attempted thievery, and sodomy."

Stephen was so taken aback that he could only stand there and gape for a moment. It didn't matter that he'd convinced himself he was coming to Max's house with the intention of doing more or less what Lord Eastleigh had just ordered him to do. As soon as Lord Eastleigh issued his demand, the last thing Stephen wanted to do was obey it.

He recovered from his shock quickly, shutting his mouth, shaking his head, and saying, "I do not believe you have the authority to keep me away from my friend."

The duke reacted as though Stephen had used a term far more intimate than "friend". His eyes widened and his nostrils flared. "You dare to defy me? You? A pathetic aberration with delusions of grandeur?"

Stephen shifted his weight, crushing the brim of his hat as his hands formed into fists. "I came to inform Lord Hillsboro of advancements in an investigation into missing children," he growled.

The duke sucked in a breath, his body going rigid. "Advancements?" he hissed, but rushed quickly on to, "Filth like you should be kept as far away from children as possible."

Old, deep anger washed through Stephen. He'd lost count of the number of times the same, sordid assumptions about what his character must have been were tossed in his face. "I love every one of my girls as a father, and I care for them better than anyone else could."

The duke snorted a humorless laugh. "If you care for them as you say you do, you will leave this place and never show your face again. You will forget about my son, wipe him from your memory. If you do not, I will see to it that your precious little charges are handed over to the care of exactly the sort of men you claim not to be one of."

A chill raced down Stephen's back. The duke wasn't bluffing. The fact that he seemed so confident in his ability to find such "caretakers" for his girls was alarming.

He glanced past the Lord Eastleigh and into the house. The only hope he had was that Max was somewhere nearby, close enough to overhear the conversation.

"I'll go," he said, louder than he should have, taking a step back. "But this is far from over."

"There you are wrong," Lord Eastleigh said. He, too, took a step back, nodding to his butler, who slammed the door in Stephen's face.

Stephen let out a frustrated breath and turned to descend the stairs to the street. Jaw clenched, he clapped his hat on his head and thrust his hands into his coat pockets. He never would have imagined he'd feel worse for attempting to reach Max than if he'd gone straight home after his meeting with David and Lionel. Exasperation like he'd never known hung on him as he marched away from the Eastleigh house and on to a major road, where he could hail a cab.

His mood didn't improve at all when he returned to the orphanage.

"And just where have you been all day?" Mrs. Ross accosted him as soon as he hung his hat and coat on the pegs in the front hall. "We've all been in a right state here without you." Her expression was equal parts anger and anxiety.

"I've been everywhere." He let out a weary sigh. "At the Sisters' orphanage, Lady Bardess's house, a solicitor's office, Mayfair." He rubbed a hand over his face, knocking his spectacles askew, then straightening them. "Is there anything to eat? I haven't had a bite all day."

Mrs. Ross's expression softened for a moment before turning grouchy all over again. "The girls are just finishing their supper. If you're lucky, Annie has saved you a plate."

Of course, Annie had saved him a plate. The moment he stepped into the great hall, she rushed forward from where she was serving the girls, grabbing his arm and leading him up the aisle between the two tables to the head table.

"You look a fright," she said breathlessly, fussing over him as he took his seat. "I've been so worried about you all day, wondering where you've been and what might have happened to you."

She removed an upturned bowl from a plate sitting at his usual place, revealing a feast of cold roast, potatoes, and vegetables. Stephen was tempted to laugh at Annie's resemblance to a fine chef in a posh restaurant revealing the treats that lay under a silver serving dome. He was too tired to do much of anything but dig into his meal, though.

"Sir?" Katie asked, approaching the table once he'd consumed half of his supper.

"Yes, sweetheart?" he asked, following her with his eyes as she circled around the end of the table and came to stand right next to him.

Her eyes were round with fear and slightly red, as though she'd been crying. "Where's Jane?" she asked in a tiny voice.

"I'm looking for her, poppet," Stephen said, his heart melting.

Katie nodded and sniffed. "It's just...." She sniffed again, tears making her eyes glassy. "It's just that I miss her. And I think she ran away because...because I was mean to her."

Everything within Stephen wanted to weep right along with her. "It's not your fault, darling." Echoes of Max saying the same to him poked at the edges of Stephen's mind, but he ignored them to focus on Katie. He set aside his fork and knife, twisting in his chair so that he could draw Katie into his arms for a hug. "You've done nothing wrong."

"I know Jane was bad for dipping my hair in ink," Katie continued to sob, "but I shouldn't have put beetles in her bed the other night. And I shouldn't have cut her hair ribbon in half."

A bittersweet grin pulled at the corners of Stephen's mouth as Katie buried her face against his shoulder and wept. He'd always suspected there were far more things going on under his roof than he was aware of. Katie and Jane's antics seemed adorable compared to the truth.

"We'll find her, sweetheart," he said, stroking Katie's head. "Lord Hillsboro and I are working hard to bring her back. And we've enlisted the help of some important friends as well."

"Lord Hillsboro can find her," Katie said, standing straight and wiping her streaming face with the back of her hand. "Jane is in love with him."

Stephen smiled and kissed Katie's forehead. "She's not the only one."

A moment later, he blinked at his slip, his smile fading. Katie was far too young to grasp the implications of what he'd said. More than that, it was as if his heart had spoken all the things his mind had attempted to deny. Katie nodded, threw herself at Stephen for another hug, then shuffled back to her place at one of the long tables. Stephen smiled as best he could as she went, highly aware that nearly every pair of young eyes in the room was looking at him for reassurance and guidance.

"We will find Jane," he said to them all. "And Jerry and Robbie as well. Don't you worry about that. You're all too pretty to worry anyhow."

The silly words of comfort did their job. His statement was met by relieved smiles, and as the girls returned to their meal, their chatter grew louder and brighter. It was the best Stephen could hope for, particularly since his own worry was as deep and dark as ever.

"I'm glad Lord Hillsboro is helping," Annie said, her expression guarded as she took a seat at the table a few places down from Stephen. "He's a good man."

"Yes, he is." Warning bells sounded in Stephen's head at the way Annie didn't quite look at him. He schooled his expression to neutrality, picking up his fork and knife and returning to his meal. Annie had most certainly been standing close enough to him to hear his declaration of love for Max.

"He'll make quite a grand couple with Lady Bardess," Annie went on, uncharacteristic pointedness in her tone.

She'd definitely heard.

Stephen forced his hands to remain steady as he cut through his roast and chewed his bite. "I doubt the two of them will marry," he said as casually as he could.

"That's not the impression Sister Constance had after your trip to her home this morning," Annie went on, pretending just as much casualness.

Stephen swallowed awkwardly and reached for the glass of weak ale at his place. "Lady Bardess isn't the sort of woman Lord Hillsboro would be interested in," he said, slightly hoarse, after taking a drink.

"Sister Constance said the two of them seemed quite chummy." Annie glanced sideways at him. "She said that Lord Hillsboro was flirting up a storm."

If he was, Stephen reminded himself, it was to pry information out of her. And why was he so bothered by Annie's insinuations? She hadn't even been there. Plus,

Stephen damn well knew the truth of things. He still had sore muscles to prove it.

"Friendship is a lovely thing," Annie went on with just a hint of guile. "But marriage is the natural state that God intended us all to be in. We should be happy for Lord Hillsboro, and you should—" She snapped her mouth shut, her cheeks turning a bright shade of pink.

Stephen didn't need her to finish her sentence to know what she was thinking. He was all too aware of what she wanted from him, what she expected. It pained him that she would never get it, especially not now. But then again, he would never be able to marry Max, no matter how devoted they wanted to be to each other. And it wasn't entirely outside of the realm of possibility that Max would be forced into a marriage of convenience for the sake of his family. Some truths just couldn't be denied, no matter how distasteful they were. Just as he felt a deep conviction to put his girls above himself, would Max do the same and put his family before their love?

The dismal thought made the rest of his supper taste like ash in his mouth. He'd been a fool to think that love could be simple between him and Max. Nothing that far from what society accepted as normal could ever be simple. And yet, for a few, glorious days, he had hoped. Those hopes seemed to be fading fast now.

"I'll help you get the girls to bed," he told Mrs. Ross as he finished up his supper and stepped away from the table. "Perhaps they would like it if I read them a fairy tale tonight."

"Oh, yes, please!" A chorus of small voices rang from the tables as he moved to walk among his little darlings, ruffling their hair and bending down to give them kisses that he knew they all needed.

Focusing on his responsibilities and his heart's first joy helped to put Stephen at ease. At least, as much as he could be with Jane missing under the most frightening of circumstances. He tried to force himself to be cheerful for the other twenty four girls' sakes as he helped them scrub their faces and brush their teeth before bed, then as they all gathered in one of the dormitories, sitting on the floor so they could all be close, as he read from the orphanage's beloved copy of *A Treasury of Classic Fairy Tales*. It was exactly what they all needed to settle down enough for sleep.

Mrs. Ross and Annie were on their way to bed as well by the time Stephen finished with the story and headed downstairs. His heart was heavy with the weight of his frustrations, but light around the edges from the love and affection his girls had shown him as he wandered through the downstairs, locking doors, blowing out lanterns, making certain the fire in the kitchen stove was banked, and cleaning up the last remnants of supper. He wanted so desperately to believe that everything would work out for the best, that Jane would be found, that he could forget about his guilt and regret, that Max would be in his arms again soon, and that they would all have a happily ever after, just like the stories he'd read to his girls. His heart was filled with uncertainty, though.

That uncertainty stayed with him as he undressed, washed his face and brushed his teeth, just as the girls had, and began to crawl into bed. A tap at one of his bedroom windows stopped him short as he peeled back his bedcovers, though.

"Stephen," Max's muffled whisper sounded through the glass and the closed curtains. "Stephen, are you awake?"

Stephen rushed to the window and threw open the curtains. The alley behind the orphanage was almost pitch black, but there was just enough light from a few, stray lanterns in the windows of nearby buildings and from the moon for Stephen to make out Max's grim face. He scrambled to unlock the window and to shove the pane up.

"Max," he gasped, filled with relief and joy so suddenly that it made him dizzy. "What are you doing here?"

"I refuse to be a prisoner in my own home," Max answered, hoisting himself up through the small window. "Not that I truly consider that mausoleum to be my home."

Stephen stood back, his heart thumping hard against his ribs, as Max climbed through the window. He lost his balance at the last minute and tumbled to the floor with a thud. Stephen was so happy to have him there that he laughed in spite of himself, rushing to help Max to his feet.

As soon as he was on his feet, Max threw himself into Stephen's arms as enthusiastically as Katie had. Stephen wrapped his arms around Max with a moan of satisfaction, bringing his mouth crashing down over Max's. It was the most gratifying kiss he'd ever engaged in, primarily because he had been about to resign himself to not kissing Max again for a long, long time. Stephen threaded his fingers through Max's hair, pressing close to him and enjoying the nighttime coolness of Max's coat against the warmth of his thin pajamas. The world seemed right again with Max's scent in his nose and the taste of him as they devoured each other.

"Wait, wait," Max said, laughing for a moment before frowning, as if trying to force himself to sober up. "Before we lose our heads entirely...." He cleared his throat and unbuttoned his coat. "One of the footmen let me know that you came to my father's house earlier. He said you had something you needed to tell me about the investigation."

"Yes." Stephen stepped behind Max to take his coat and walked it to a chair in the corner of the room. "I went to see David Wirth and Lionel Mercer. It turns out they've known about missing children for quite some time now. There's a kidnapping ring at work in London."

Max lost all trace of good humor. "That does not sound good."

"It isn't." Stephen returned to him, starting in on the

buttons of Max's jacket. There was no point pretending they weren't going to end up naked and sweaty in each other's arms within a matter of minutes. That sort of intimacy was exactly what Stephen needed to turn the world back to right again, as paradoxical as it felt. One last indulgence was exactly what he needed. "But what is good is that there are people aware of what is going on. David said he would send an Officer Patrick Wrexham to help us as soon as possible."

"That's a blessing," Max agreed, letting out a breath and pulling his shirt out of his trousers as Stephen finished with his jacket buttons and started in on his waistcoat. Both of their efforts picked up speed and intensity as they went.

"We'll find them," Stephen said, filled with confidence for the first time all day. Blast his head, but his heart had known having Max with him, making him feel like a man, would renew his confidence. He wanted more of that feeling, all of it. "We'll find them and bring them home."

His patience wore thin, and he tugged Max into his arms, kissing him with command. Max sighed and sagged against him, signaling that he was Stephen's to do with as he pleased. The subtle surrender drove Stephen wild, increasing his ardor. He wondered what the high and mighty Duke of Eastleigh would think if he knew his son had handed over the reins of desire to a pathetic aberration with delusions of grandeur.

But only for a moment.

"I want you," he said breathlessly, reaching for the fastenings of Max's trousers. "Desperately."

"I'm yours," Max sighed in reply, fumbling with the buttons of Stephen's pajamas.

Stephen loosened Max's trousers and drawers, pushed them over his hips, and slipped his hands along Max's hardening cock. Max let out a sound of pleasure that had Stephen's prick jumping in response. He wanted to stroke every inch of Max's body, kiss and suck him, and satisfy him in every possible way. He could hardly draw breath with the urgency of his need and couldn't get Max out of his clothes fast enough.

Max wanted the same thing, as evidenced by the way he yanked his shirt off over his head and groaned in pleasure as Stephen shoved his trousers farther down his legs. They had to step apart for a practical moment to shed the rest of their clothes and Max's shoes, but in no time, they were back in each other's arms, skin to skin, mouths entangled. It felt so incredibly good to feel Max's iron-hard cock trapped against his hip that Stephen trembled.

"Wait," Max panted, breaking away from Stephen reluctantly. Mischief shone in his eyes as they met Stephen's. "I brought something."

He stepped around Stephen, marching to the chair where Stephen had discarded his coat. Stephen drank in the sight of Max's naked body—its firm lines and lean muscles, and especially his eager cock standing stiff and tall—as he riffled through one of his coat pockets. He came up with a small container, presenting it to Stephen.

The cool weight of the jar of lubricant in his hand sent Stephen's thoughts to the most carnal of places and had him aching to get Max on his back. He sent Max a look as if to warn him that he was about to be fucked into next Tuesday.

"I'm yours," Max said, breathless with ardor, sliding into Stephen's arms once more and drawing him toward the bed. His mouth pulled into a grin as they kissed. "And after you've had your wicked way with me, I fully intend to turn the tables on you."

Stephen laughed even as the intensity of his need catapulted dangerously toward the point of no return. And that was from merely the thought of what they were about to do alone. Max slipped eagerly into Stephen's bed, kicking the bedcovers into a ball at the foot of the bed and posing provocatively on his stomach, arse raised in invitation.

"Oh no," Stephen said, unscrewing the lid of the jar and joining Max in bed. "I want to see your face when we both come."

Max's eyes glittered with excitement as he twisted to his back, reaching for Stephen's pillow to prop under his backside. The whole thing was a blend of practicality and wickedness on a level that had Stephen certain he was part of some sort of erotic dream. He scooped enough of the lubricant from the jar to thoroughly coat his aching cock, making a show of stroking himself in an attempt to drive Max wild. Judging by the way Max bit his lip as he watched, his chest rising and falling in short pants as he spread his legs wide, it was working.

Stephen took another bit of lubricant before setting the jar and his spectacles on the bedside table, using it to tease the pucker of Max's arsehole. Max let out a ragged breath as Stephen tested him, first with one finger, then two, making absolutely certain he was ready. When he was confident, he stroked his way forward, fondling Max's balls for a moment before teasing him with long, firm strokes along his prick. He leaned forward as he did, balancing himself on one arm while raining soft kisses across Max's chest, flicking one of his nipples with his tongue, and nibbling his shoulder.

"Now," Stephen whispered into Max's ear, feeling erotic power surge through him, "I'm going to fuck you like you've never been fucked before." Max moaned in anticipation, the sound sending Stephen's senses soaring before he added, "Try not to scream so loud you wake the rest of the house."

Max started to laugh, but Stephen guided himself to exactly the right spot and pushed inside. Max's laughter turned into a sound that defied description, but carried every emotion that throbbed between the two of them. With surprising speed, their bodies accommodated to each other enough for Stephen to pick up the pace of his thrusts. What must have looked awkward and ridiculous to any outside observer felt like utter perfection to Stephen as he grasped one of Max's legs and deepened his angle of penetration.

Almost immediately, pleasure overtook any possibility of thought. Whatever worry Stephen might have had that he wasn't hitting exactly the right spot within Max was banished by the sounds Max made and the way his face contorted in pleasure, eyes rolled back as Stephen pounded into him. Watching Max's transformation from excited flirtation to pleasure to orgasmic ecstasy as his expression changed and his features pinched sent Stephen right to the edge. And when Max opened his eyes and stared straight up into Stephen's eyes, into his soul, with undiluted love and indescribable pleasure, Stephen exploded into an orgasm that shook him to his soul.

He cried out, defying his own order to stay quiet. The joy of it all, the intense intimacy of spending himself inside of Max, and the surprise delight of Max coming with a loud sound of release moments later, left Stephen pulsing with satisfaction. His movements slowed, and he untangled himself from Max only to collapse atop him, caught between trying to catch his breath and kissing Max until he was dizzy. They rolled to the side, embracing, touching, and kissing as though they were just getting started instead of floating down from the heights of ecstasy.

Soon, even that stroking and their efforts to meld together as intimately as possible slowed until they lay in each other's arms, trying to catch their breaths, overheated, sticky, and happier than Stephen could remember being.

"I won't ever let anything keep us apart," Max panted, threading his fingers through Stephen's hair and stealing another light kiss. "Not even you."

Stephen didn't know how to reply, didn't even know what he wanted anymore. Max felt too perfect in his arms to let reason keep them apart. Underneath his sated bliss, his heart beat with determination. "I will do whatever it takes to fight for the people who matter the most to me."

CHAPTER 14

Annie Ross was going to be a problem. Max knew it the second he and Stephen emerged from Stephen's room in the back of the house and attempted to pretend as though nothing were amiss with Max's presence at the orphanage so early in the morning again. Try as he did to behave as casually as possible, helping out in the kitchen by making coffee—his one culinary skill—while Stephen roused the girls from sleep and helped them dress and brush their hair for the day upstairs, Annie eyed him warily.

"But how did you get inside?" Annie asked with a frown as she cracked two dozen eggs into a bowl with the intent to scramble them for the girls. "I'm certain the doors were all locked."

"Stephen let me in," Max answered, keeping his face turned away from her. He was hot from the neck up, and not because of the steaming kettle he was minding. Annie might have been young and naïve, but naivety could only last so long.

"Why would he let you in so late at night?" Annie went on, sounding mostly as though she were talking to herself. "If the house is so crowded that you would be forced to share a bed with him again, why you would you bother to return at all?"

Max left the question unanswered. Mostly because Mrs. Ross strode into the kitchen with a sense of urgency.

"Stephen wants you in the great hall immediately," she told Max. "There's an Officer Wrexham here to speak to the two of you."

Max nodded and stepped away from the stove, abandoning the coffee preparations.

"Why doesn't he want me?" Annie asked, pausing her task with her whisk poised over the bowl of eggs.

Max exchanged a look with Mrs. Ross. Annie's question was far more loaded than she could possibly imagine.

"Scramble your eggs, girl," Mrs. Ross told her, then murmured as she and Max left the kitchen side by side, "Stephen's certainly never going to scramble them for you."

Max's mouth twitched into a grin, but he felt guilty for laughing at Annie's expense. "You're going to have to educate her about the whole thing eventually," he said quietly to Mrs. Ross. "Particularly since I fully intend to spend a great many more nights here."

Mrs. Ross humphed as they approached the doorway to the great hall. "She's most of the way to figuring it out already. And God help us all when she puts the last piece in the puzzle."

Max wished he could have laughed, but the knot that formed in his gut told him it was no laughing matter. Sweet as she was, Annie was a live shell waiting to explode.

"Ah, Max." Stephen stepped away from the table at the front of the room as Max and Mrs. Ross entered the great hall. An officer in a crisp Metropolitan Police uniform walked with him to meet Max in the center of the room. "This is Officer Wrexham."

"How do you do?" Max shook the officer's hand.

Wrexham was about their age and handsome, in a tough, stocky sort of way. His short-cropped hair was a playful shade of strawberry-blond that seemed at odds with his serious face and strong jaw. He had massive shoulders, and even with the uniform, Max could see the man had impressive muscles. And yet, there was a kindness in his eyes that put Max at ease. He was exactly the sort of man Max would have wanted spearheading the investigation into missing children.

"Mr. Wirth tells me you were with Mr. Siddel here at the Bardess Mansion concert where the children went missing." Wrexham got straight to business.

"I was," Max said with a nod, shifting to stand shoulder to shoulder with Stephen, his arms crossed. "I'm convinced there was some sort of foul play in the house during and after the children's performance."

Wrexham nodded. "There was an operation that

night, after the concert. Lord Burbage, along with several accomplices, were arrested at Batcliff Cross Dock and a ship containing several dozen kidnapped children was raided. The children were rescued, thank God."

Max felt as though all the breath had been squeezed out of them. "Did you find Jane and the others?" He glanced quickly to Stephen.

"They didn't," Stephen said, flushing. "I'm sorry, I meant to tell you the whole tale. That's why I went to your father's house. But then we were distracted." His face turned even redder and he adjusted his spectacles self-consciously.

"The girl who went missing from this orphanage and the two boys from the one up the street weren't among the children rescued," Wrexham went on without showing the least sign of discomfort at Stephen and Max's exchange. "We have ample reason to believe this kidnapping ring extends far wider than Burbage and the children who were rescued the other night."

"What sort of reason?" Max asked, clearing his throat to push aside the swirl of emotions that remembering his night with Stephen and the reasons they hadn't talked invoked in him.

"The level of sophistication involved in attempting to whisk a ship full of human cargo out of London indicates this is more than a one-off operation. The reports of missing children that I've been able to gather in the last few weeks extend back months, if not years." Wrexham paused, looking stricken for a moment. "Unfortunately, few people seem to care when the children of poverty go missing. They are seen as flotsam and jetsam anyhow, so no one bothers."

The way the man glanced meaningfully over the table of Stephen's girls sitting next to him instantly had Max wondering if Wrexham was an orphan himself and if he'd been one of those children no one cared about.

Wrexham sucked in a breath and shook his head, focusing on Stephen and Max once more. "We have other reasons to be suspicious as well. Lord Chisolm hasn't been seen since the day of the concert. Burbage was released from jail yesterday, and he, too, has now vanished."

The news hit Max like a fist in his gut. "They're both gone?"

"Yes," Stephen said in a grim voice. Evidently, Wrexham had informed him of the development earlier. "If that's not a signal of guilt, I don't know what is."

"The fact that noblemen of the highest order are involved in this ring doesn't bode well for our chances of thwarting it easily," Wrexham went on. "No offense, my lord, but nobs have every sort of convenience available to them when it comes to hiding, fleeing, and covering up the truth."

"I don't disagree with you, and I abhor it as much as you do," Max said, his jaw tensed.

"So how do we proceed?" Stephen went on. "How do we take action and find Jane and the others when everything is stacked against us?"

Wrexham sighed, rolling his massive shoulders. "One step at a time, I'm afraid."

"David Wirth seems to think that Lady Bardess must be involved in the ring as well as her father and brother," Stephen said, sending Max a wary, sideways glance that hinted there was more to the statement and his thoughts.

Max blinked, his breath catching in his chest. "She seemed so ignorant when we approached her yesterday." He wished he actually believed that she was ignorant.

"David seems to think that could be an act," Stephen went on, arching one eyebrow.

Max shook his head, not because he didn't believe it, but because he felt like he should have tried harder to wheedle the truth out of her during their turn around the room at Bardess Mansion the day before.

"I should speak to her again," he said, feeling more confident as a plan took shape in his mind. "For some Godforsaken reason, she seems to think I would make an ideal husband. If I can encourage that mindset, she may reveal something important without realizing it."

Stephen tensed by Max's side. It made perfect sense that he would hate the idea, but one quick glance at him was enough for Max to see Stephen would put up with whatever it took to get Jane and the others back. That sentiment warmed Max's heart and made him daring. He reached for Stephen's hand, squeezing it reassuringly, slow to let it go.

Wrexham noted the gesture, but his expression

barely changed. If anything, he relaxed. "You may be in a unique position in this investigation, my lord," he said.

"Call me Max, please."

Wrexham nodded. "Are you willing to return to Bardess Mansion to see what you can discover?"

"Absolutely," Max said. Knowing he could take action filled him with confidence and an eagerness to get started.

"In the meantime...." Wrexham turned to Stephen. "The section of Batcliff Cross Dock where Burbage's accomplices were found and arrested remains cordoned off by the police, but it won't be for long. Would you be interested in investigating the site with me in case the officers conducting the investigation—good officers, but men without the singular motivation that others might have—might have missed something?"

"Of course," Stephen replied, standing a bit taller as his confidence grew as well. "I'll go wherever you need me to as soon as we can."

"Good." Wrexham nodded. "Then we should leave right away."

Right away ended up being a good hour later, after Stephen oversaw the serving of breakfast and got his girls off to their lessons—a feat that was nearly Herculean, considering how distracted the girls were. Max had to wait to leave for Bardess Mansion until a reasonable hour for paying calls anyhow, so he helped with the girls as much as he could. It was uncanny to him how far shepherding a flock of energetic girls from room to room—not to mention handing out a few hugs and reassuring words to the ones who were traumatized by Jane's disappearance—went toward improving Max's mood and making him feel useful. Sometime, when the danger in front of them was over, he vowed to think seriously about upending his life entirely so that he could keep that feeling with him always. And so that he could keep Stephen with him always.

Those magnificent thoughts for the future stayed with him as he hired a carriage to take him to Bardess Mansion. He might actually be able to do it. Who would stop him from exchanging the cold and frustrating life of a minor noble, living at the whim of a society he hated, for the simple joys of a life working by Stephen's side? In a way, it was madness to contemplate. But there was no denying the rush of excitement the very idea of giving up his old life for a new one gave him.

He was still riding high on those thoughts when Lady Bardess's sour-faced butler led him into a bright morning parlor near the front of Bardess Mansion. But his cheery smile dropped with a thud the moment he was escorted into the room and found himself face to face with his father and George as well as Lady Bardess.

"What are you doing here?" he blurted before he could gather his wits about him.

"I could ask you the same thing," his father said with a growl, standing and moving closer to him. When he was close enough to hiss into Max's ear without Lady Bardess or George overhearing, he went on with, "I forbade you from leaving the house yesterday. Don't think I don't know where you've been."

"As I told you, where I've been is none of your concern," Max growled in return. He jerked away from his father, plastering on a smile and approaching Lady Bardess. "My lady, it is good to see you looking so well this morning."

In fact, the closer Max looked, the less well Lady Bardess looked. She was dressed impeccably in a morning gown of Belgian lace. Her hair was dressed in the latest style. She sat straight and wore a benevolent smile, but it didn't reach her eyes. Her eyes were those of a cornered animal ready to run at a moment's notice.

"I am so happy to see you again, Lord Hillsboro," she said with the perfect manners of a hostess. "Please do sit beside me." She patted the place next to her on the sofa with a flirtatious grin. That grin didn't meet her eyes either. "What brings you to my humble home this morning, my lord?" she asked, inching closer to Max once he'd had a seat.

"I, uh—" Max scrambled to come up with an excuse that wouldn't instantly make his father and his brother—who looked extremely out of sorts and wan, likely from drinking too much the night before—suspicious. "I heard a terrible rumor that your father and brother have abandoned you, and I wanted to make certain you are being looked after," he said. The best way to avoid disaster was to stick as close to the truth as possible.

"Oh, my father and brother haven't abandoned me at

all," Lady Bardess said, laughing so suddenly that it set Max's teeth on edge. "That is to say," she went on with a gulp, her entire demeanor changing in an instant, "they *have* abandoned me, but with good reason."

Max's pulse shot up. He fought to keep his easy smile in place as he studied Lady Bardess. Something was most definitely wrong. She picked at her lace gown as though she were about to be sent to the gallows. Her cheeks were a little too pink. Most telling of all, she shot a furtive look across the seating area to Max's father.

Max glanced across to his father as casually as he could. "Have you come to comfort Lady Bardess in her hour of need as well, Father?"

"You know that Lord Chisolm and I are friends," his father snapped.

A deeper chill passed down Max's spine. His father and Lord Chisolm were friends. The connection was unnerving, to say the least. It made Max feel sick to wonder if his father—and potentially George as well, for why else would he be there—might be involved in the kidnapping ring.

"As a friend, I would assume you know what has become of Lord Chisolm," Max said as casually as possible.

"He's been called abroad," his father said with an irritated shrug, as though Max were annoying for bothering to ask the question. "My understanding is that Burbage has gone with him."

"Yes," Lady Bardess rushed to say, her eyes glassy

with anxiety in spite of her smile. "Papa and Paul have sailed off to the Caribbean." Max caught the briefest hint of the glowering look his father sent Lady Bardess before she waved a shaky hand and went on with, "Or perhaps it was India. South America? I cannot remember. I never pay attention to those sorts of things. Not when there are far more interesting things to occupy my mind." She slid even closer to Max, taking his hand.

Max arched one eyebrow as he stared at Lady Bardess's hand on his. He wasn't certain what she was attempting to do until his father said, "Dear Lillian and I have just been discussing the many benefits of marriage."

"You're already married, Father," Max said in a tight voice, narrowing is eyes at his father, knowing full well where this was going.

"Not him, you dolt, you," George snorted, then winced, as though speaking aggravated a headache.

"Forgive me, but I have no intention of marrying," Max said, glaring at his father, then turning a kinder smile on Lady Bardess.

Lady Bardess gaped as though he'd signed her death warrant before smoothing her features. "But, of course, we will marry," she said with another high, piercing laugh. "You and I make ideal partners, for I am beautiful and wealthy and you are handsome and well-connected."

"I'm also—" Max stopped, losing his nerve to shout the truth. "—far too inconsequential for a woman of your standing, Lady Bardess," he recovered as best he could.

His father looked ready to murder him all the same.

"You do not give yourself enough credit, son," he said through a clenched jaw. The spite in his eyes said far more about what his father thought of Max's worth than his words. "Lady Bardess and I were just finalizing the arrangements."

"Padron me, the *arrangements*?" Max stared hard at him.

"It will be a June wedding," his father said.

"I'd like to see you pull together a wedding as grand as mine was in less than six weeks," George scoffed, as if he'd already won a prize. A prize Max had absolutely no interest in winning.

"I'm terribly sorry, Father, Lady Bardess, but marriage is out of the question," Max said.

"You will do as you are told or you will face the consequences," his father snapped, so loud that Lady Bardess yelped and burst into tears.

In an instant, Max's sense of the situation and his attempts to figure out what was truly going on shifted. Lady Bardess might not have been a direct accomplice in her father and brother's activity, but he would bet all the money he had and then some that his father was. The idea repulsed him. It also brought home the horrific realization that he would get further and uncover more information if he played along fully, taking things beyond the half-hearted flirtation he'd intended, rather than fighting at every turn. It also dawned on him that, as odious as she might have been, Lady Bardess might be in a dangerous position as well.

Max cleared his throat and rolled his shoulders. He met his father's eyes with as much gravity as he could muster. He already guessed what his father was thinking, but played along anyhow, pretending to come to a slower realization of the game his father was playing. It was clear he was threatening Stephen and the orphanage, as he had the day before. Carefully, Max let his expression morph into what he hoped his father would interpret as a sudden understanding of exactly who was in danger.

"I see," he said, lowering his eyes. "In that case...." He managed a weak smile for Lady Bardess, turning his hand so that he could thread his fingers through hers, since she hadn't moved her hand away from his yet. "A June wedding it is, then."

Lady Bardess let out a breath of relief, as though granted a reprieve from something.

Max's father smiled as though he'd won a major victory. "Good," he said. "I'll have your mother make the arrangements at once." He stood, gesturing for George to get up. "I believe our business is done here, for the time being."

Max let go of Lady Bardess's hand and stood. "Yes, I believe it is."

Max feigned defeat, but underneath the act, his heart burned with hatred and the desire to bring his father to justice. He would pretend to be the cowed and dutiful son now, but his father's days were numbered, as far as he was concerned.

"If you will excuse me as well, Lady Bardess," he said

as soon as his father and George were gone. "I have an urgent appointment I need to keep."

"Oh? Yes. Well." Lady Bardess was so distracted Max wasn't certain she'd heard him.

He left her to her own devices, hurrying out of the mansion and hailing the first cab he could. David Wirth needed to know about his father as quickly as possible.

CHAPTER 15

"The operation to stop those children being shipped overseas and the resulting arrests went fairly smoothly the other night," Wrexham explained to Stephen as the police carriage entered Batcliff Cross Docks. "We were successful in keeping our investigation a secret. None of the operatives of the ring knew we were coming for them until the very last minute."

"That's a blessing," Stephen said, though he was having a difficult time being completely optimistic about the whole thing. Not when Jane and the boys were still missing. Not when he still felt it was his fault.

"Another advantage we believe we have on our side is that the operators of this ring neither trust nor particularly like the very lowest classes," Wrexham went on as the carriage jerked to a stop beside a row of rundown warehouse buildings. "They have either overlooked those who they consider dirt or treated them badly, which means some of those people have been willing to talk to us."

"Have you learned anything interesting?" Stephen asked, his pulse beating with uneasy interest as the two of them climbed down to the bustling, crowded dock.

Stephen tried not to wince at the stench of rotting fish, brackish seawater, and the unwashed bodies of the dock workers and other unfortunate souls who packed the area. Despite his birth, he wasn't that far above any of the people around him, but even so, the differences in their circumstances of life were palpable. He wasn't about to turn into a snob, like too many of the aristocrats he knew, by treating those around him as refuse.

"We learned the exact location of the ship that was minutes away from sailing for the orient," Wrexham said, gesturing for Stephen to follow him down the line of dilapidated warehouses. "We also learned that the children were held here for days before being loaded onto the ship." He nodded to one warehouse building in particular.

Stephen's blood ran cold at the sight of it. He couldn't shake the image of Jane, cold, frightened, and miserable, being locked away in a place as frightening and hopeless as the dock.

His sense of foreboding only increased when Wrexham led him inside of the building—which was already being loaded anew with cargo from a newly arrived ship—and up a rickety flight of stairs to a storage room.

"Isn't it counterintuitive for this warehouse to be used for shipping when it's still the subject of an investigation?" Stephen asked as they climbed the stairs, glancing over his shoulder at the workers stacking crates.

Wrexham huffed an irritated breath. "The owner of this building was furious that we wanted to close it up at all. He complained about the money he would lose by letting it stay empty, and all because of a handful of brats no one cared about."

Stephen's gut clenched in anger. He could see Wrexham shared his outrage. It added to his estimation of the man's character.

"This might very well be the last time we get a look at the room where the children were held," Wrexham went on, opening a creaky door and letting Stephen into the storage room. "I've been told it'll be in use for cargo storage within a few hours." Wrexham paused, then added, "God damn the men who disregard the lives of vulnerable children in order to make a profit."

Stephen agreed with him wholeheartedly, but his thoughts were scattered by the stench that slapped him when Wrexham opened the door to the dark and dank storage room. The air was as rotten as could be and heavy with the smell of urine and worse. As Stephen's eyes adjusted to the darkness, he spotted lengths of chains and soiled shackles that had been abandoned against the walls. His eyes stung with furious tears and his heart bled at the thought that innocent children had been kept in such conditions.

"Can we open a window," he croaked, crossing to the tiny, dirty window at the other end of the room.

"They're nailed shut," Wrexham told him.

Stephen tried to open one anyhow, but gave up when he saw it was impossible. He turned to survey the room, his breath coming in short, shallow gasps. Whoever had held children in that room was evil incarnate. He didn't even want to think about where the children had been bound for or what sort of lives other children had been sold into. Everything within him burned with fury to think that men like him and Max were vilified and seen as abominations while the men responsible for everything around him likely walked free in society, lauded as upright members of the community.

"I will make whoever did this pay," he seethed. He'd never been so angry or so deeply hurt in his life.

"Not if I make them pay first," Wrexham growled.

Stephen glanced to the burly officer as he made his way around the room. Whatever the man's story, it was a sad one, he was certain. Wrexham glared at the space around him with fists clenched, looking as though he could be a champion boxer if he wanted to. He certainly had the rage in him. But there was also an unmistakable gentleness to the man. Gentleness and pain. He was the sort of man Stephen could be friends with.

Friendship could wait, though. Stephen turned his attention to the details of the room, painful as it was. He had the sense that the children had been moved in haste. Whoever had left bits and pieces of chains and shackles just lying around had been clumsy.

"Either the men who did this wanted to be caught or they had to act so fast that they couldn't clean up after themselves," Stephen spoke his thoughts aloud.

"My assessment exactly," Wrexham said. "And that of the detectives who looked the place over yesterday."

Stephen turned to him in surprise. "Did they find anything?"

Wrexham let out a wry laugh. "They spent fifteen minutes in here, if that. Even the Met doesn't think these children are important enough to warrant allocating valuable resources."

"But you're here," Stephen said.

"I'm not a valuable resource," Wrexham said in a hollow voice.

There was more to the man's statement than Stephen had time to process. He returned to studying the room, acutely aware there could be clues lying around that everyone else had missed.

He moved in closer to get a look at every corner of the room, studied the remaining chains and shackles, and tried not to lose the contents of his stomach at the alarming piles of refuse scattered around the room. Among the signs of misery and terror were a few incongruous pieces of paper and scraps of fabric or ribbons. He picked up one scrap of paper that seemed too large to be a torn-up receipt or bill of lading.

"Gretton Mill," he read aloud, brow furrowing. "Why would a paper with the address of a mill in Leicestershire be lying around here?"

Wrexham left what he was scrutinizing in the opposite corner of the room to stride over to Stephen's side. Instead of commenting, though, he handed Stephen another small slip of paper, his eyes wide with intensity.

Wrexham's paper was the stub of a train ticket. The letters "Leic" were printed in one corner where the ticket had been torn.

"Do you think it was purchased in Leicester?" he asked.

"It could have been," Wrexham said. "It very likely was."

"Is there anything else lying around from Leicester?"

Stephen's heart thumped against his ribs as he and Wrexham combed through the room, looking for any further clues. The trouble was, hardly anything was left. None of the other bits of paper or scraps of cloth bore any sort of clue. The address of the Gretton Mill and ticket stub were all they had to go on.

"You two, get out of here," a dock worker barked at them from the doorway, nearly shocking Stephen out of his skin. "Boss says to clean this mess up so the room can be used."

"This is a police investigation," Wrexham tried to argue with the man, crossing to glare at him.

The worker backed up a bit, but said, "I'm just doin' as I'm ordered, sir."

"We've found all we can find here," Stephen said with a sigh. It felt too much like admitting defeat. At least they had a weak lead they could pursue.

"There has to be something else to guide us," he said when he and Wrexham reached the street and the relatively fresh air of the dock. "Somebody has to know something."

"If they do, they're not telling," Wrexham growled.

"About them kids?" Their conversation was interrupted by a gnarled old man with one leg and no teeth.

Stephen and Wrexham turned to face him as though he were the King of Siam.

"Do you know something about the children who were held here?" Wrexham asked, approaching the man.

The old man snorted. "I know nothing," he said, a shifty look in his eyes.

"Please," Stephen pleaded with him. "Young lives are at stake. If you know anything at all, please share it."

"I said I know nothing." The man raised his voice, narrowing his eyes at Stephen. "Except that this ain't the only place I've heard the wail of young ones and their pitiful cries for their mothers." His face pinched with misery for a moment before returning to dismal anger.

"Where?" Wrexham asked. "Where else have you heard these sounds?"

"All over," the old man said. "Up and down the waterfront. Coming from ships." He snorted, then spit on the rotting planks of the dock. "This weren't the only place locking them up. There's more out there, and there will be more and more and more."

Uneasy prickles raced down Stephen's back. He wasn't sure the old man was entirely sane. But he believed him when he implied the ring was still as active as ever.

"We will stop them," he told the old man, no idea if he would want to be comforted or not.

The old man nodded sharply at him, then turned to hobble away on his crutches.

Stephen and Wrexham walked away as well, heading back to the police carriage. "I hope you're right," Wrexham growled. When Stephen glanced at him, he went on with, "That we'll stop them."

"We will," Stephen said without a shred of doubt. "I love Jane. She is my responsibility. And every other child. I won't rest until they're safe."

"Does that include investigating Gretton Mill in Leicestershire?" Wrexham asked. They'd reached the carriage and climbed inside. Once they were settled, Wrexham went on with, "I'm Metropolitan Police. They won't let me outside of London, not for this."

Stephen sighed at the injustice of it all and nodded. "I'll do what I have to do."

Wrexham dropped him back at the orphanage. They were silent through the whole trip, lost in their thoughts. Stephen felt as though he had the weight of the world pressing down on him. Jane was out there somewhere, but time was ticking down. He wasn't fool enough to think that whoever had taken her would keep her wherever she was indefinitely. But he refused to let himself believe it was too late.

His thoughts were a ragged turmoil as he alighted from Wrexham's carriage and crossed through the front door of the orphanage. He didn't pick up on how quiet the place was until he marched into the great hall, sniffing one of his sleeves and wondering if he would have to burn the entire suit of clothes if Annie couldn't get the stench of the docks out, and came face to face with Lord Eastleigh.

"Good God," Max's father choked, grimacing and pulling a handkerchief from his pocket to hold to his mouth and nose. "I knew you were detestable, but I had no idea to what extent."

Stephen ignored the slight, pulling himself to his full height as though he smelled of roses. "Your grace," he said in a tight voice, nodding with far less deference than the man likely thought was due him. "What brings you to our humble establishment today?"

Lord Eastleigh paid as little attention to Stephen's greeting as Stephen had paid to his cruel slight. "I've come to tell you that my son entered an engagement to Lady Bardess this morning," he said, a flash of victory in his eyes. "An arrangement he entered into willingly and eagerly, I might add."

Try as he did to dismiss the man's words, he felt as though he'd taken a knife to the heart. He couldn't bring himself to say anything in response.

"Furthermore," Lord Eastleigh went on, "if you seek to disrupt this arrangement or to even contact my son ever again, I will ensure that your orphanage loses all possibility of patronage."

"Yes," Stephen said in a hoarse voice. "So you told me before."

"And you didn't listen." Lord Eastleigh narrowed his eyes. He stepped in closer and whispered, "I know where my son was last night."

A paradoxical feeling of pride filled Stephen. Max had been with him, in spite of his father's efforts to control his life. Their love had proven itself to be more powerful than Lord Eastleigh's treachery.

Moments later, that feeling of pride collapsed. He and Max had won a minor battle, but Lord Eastleigh seemed poised to win the war. And the more attention Stephen gave to the fight, the less he would have for his girls, for Jane.

"My son will have nothing to do with you, do you understand?" Lord Eastleigh said, backing away and sneering at Stephen.

Stephen said nothing. He glanced past Max's father to where Mrs. Ross and Annie stood, watching the confrontation with wide, frightened eyes. In all the time he'd known her, nothing had ever put that look on Mrs. Ross's face. Stephen could only thank God that most of his girls were apparently tucked away in their classrooms, though Beatrice and some of the older girls watched the whole encounter from the far end of one of the tables, where they were studying. Stephen could only imagine the sort of education those girls were getting about the ways of the world at that moment.

"I cannot control your son," Stephen said at last, weighing his words carefully. "He is his own man. I will not stand in his way, no matter what he decides to do."

His words were vague enough that Lord Eastleigh narrowed his eyes, seeming not to be able to make out exactly what Stephen was saying. "I have warned you twice now," he said in a low voice. "I will not warn you again."

With that, the odious man marched straight past Stephen and into the hall, leaving the building without taking his leave or bothering to have someone show him out.

As soon as he was gone, Mrs. Ross and Annie let out the breaths they were holding. Annie burst into tears, burying her face in her hands. Mrs. Ross stepped forward, resting a hand on Stephen's arm.

"I hate to say it, lad, but that man is more powerful than all of us put together," she said. "I know it'll kill you, but you have to think of the girls before you think of yourself."

It was as if she'd spoken his thoughts aloud, though it stung him to his core to acknowledge it. Giving up Max would be like ripping his heart out and tossing it onto the trash heap, but it was becoming clearer and clearer that it was something he would have to do. Especially if Max had already seen the truth of things himself. Why else would he have consented to marry Lady Bardess?

"Officer Wrexham and I managed to find something that might be a clue as to the whereabouts of more children," he said in a rough voice, deliberately skating away from anything that had to do with Max or his crumbling heart.

"You know where Jane is?" Mrs. Ross asked, following him as he left the great hall and headed back to his own room to bathe and change.

"No," he admitted, heart heavy. "Not exactly. But I intend to investigate on the chance that she and the others were taken to Leicestershire."

"Leicestershire?" Mrs. Ross shook her head. "Why would they be there?"

"We found the address of a mill," Stephen said, sparing her the details that he would have done anything not to recall again for the rest of his life.

"What sort of mill?" Mrs. Ross asked.

Stephen shrugged as he opened the door to his room. "I don't know," he said. "But I'll be making a trip up north as soon as possible to find out."

"Do you need me to help make arrangements?" Mrs. Ross asked, helping him remove his coat and screwing up her face as she did.

"Possibly," Stephen said. "But there's one other person who might be able to help me as well. I need clean, presentable evening clothes," he went on. "I have to go to the club."

CHAPTER 16

The offices of Dandie & Wirth were closed when Max reached them after his harrowing morning with his father, George, and Lady Bardess. Finding the door locked and a small sign reading, "Back this afternoon" hanging on the doorknob nearly frayed the last of Max's overtaxed nerves. He stood in the hallway outside of the office for a few minutes, bristling with impatience and feeling like his life was on the verge of cracking apart.

He wouldn't ever marry Lady Bardess. That much was certain. Perhaps, if he hadn't met Stephen, he would have been able to go through with it, but now the whole idea was repulsive. The trouble was that if he defied his father outright, if he made any sort of public declaration or even committed himself to Stephen privately, there was no doubt that his father would use every spiteful bone in his body to ruin Stephen, his orphanage, and his girls.

He couldn't let that happen, even if it meant sacrificing himself by moving abroad. He could only hope it wouldn't come to that, though.

Nerves still twisting, he left Dandie & Wirth, headed to the only place he could think of where David Wirth or Lionel Mercer might be found or where he might be able to get the help he needed.

When he arrived, the Chameleon Club was busy with afternoon guests taking tea or simply spending time with friends. The aura of calm that pervaded the establishment was a far cry from Max's inner turmoil, but it was exactly the thing he needed. His shallow breathing steadied and deepened as he strode through the lobby and on to the main hall. A few men of his acquaintance were lounging around the massive space where the ball had been held what seemed like a lifetime ago, but most of the members who were present would be in the dining room farther down the hall.

Max nearly wept with relief when he spotted Lionel Mercer sitting alone at one of the dining room's tables near a window. The man was like a plant in his need to sit in some sort of light, which made his pale skin all the more noticeable. The room buzzed with the chatter of a dozen conversations as friends and acquaintances enjoyed tea or luncheon together. Max even spotted Everett Jewel seated at the table next to Lionel, in some sort of uncharacteristically serious conversation with a tall, thin man who had a notebook of some sort open on the table in front of him. Lionel sat alone with his back toward Jewel, but he seemed far too alert and irritated to be lost in his own thoughts, which made Max feel less guilty about intruding.

"May I have this seat?" he asked as he approached Lionel's table.

Lionel's dampened expression transformed into a broad smile of greeting. "Of course, Lord Hillsboro. Please join me."

As Max helped himself to a seat at Lionel's table, he caught Lionel glancing slightly over his shoulder, as if to judge whether Jewel and his friend were aware of Max's arrival. Indeed, Jewel looked up from his conversation, meeting Max's eye, and nodding with a grin that could only be described as amused.

Lionel turned fully around to glare at Jewel before facing Max, his mouth flattening into a tight line. "Show off," he muttered. "Don't pay him any mind. He feels the need to flirt with anything that moves."

Max couldn't help but smirk in spite of his frayed nerves. "Jealous?" he asked.

From the shock that spread across Lionel's face, Max would have thought he'd thrown a glass of red wine at the man. "Certainly not," Lionel hissed. "I could never be jealous of an overbearing, preening, arrogant, attention whore like that."

Jewel and the man with him laughed. Max doubted they'd heard Lionel's string of insults, but whatever had amused them, it caused splotches of red to break out on Lionel's porcelain cheeks.

"I dropped by your office just now," Max said, feeling it was wise to get straight to business before Lionel became too distracted by whatever feud he had with Jewel to be of any help. "It was closed. I'm glad I guessed correctly about where at least one of you might be."

"David will be along soon," Lionel said, rolling his shoulders slightly and sitting straighter, as though he knew exactly what sort of fool he was making of himself and was attempting to correct that. "He had to visit a client at home about a particularly delicate matter."

Max nodded, respecting whatever confidentiality the man had with his client. He hesitated for a moment, suddenly unsure of how much of Dandie & Wirth's business Lionel handled. There couldn't be much harm in confiding in the man until David showed up.

"I have a bit of gossip you might not have heard yet," Max began in a way he knew would pique Lionel's interest.

"Oh?" Lionel brightened, seeming to forget the inhabitants of the table behind him. Although Jewel glanced covertly in Max's direction. "I love gossip I haven't heard yet."

It gave Max no pleasure at all to say, "Lady Bardess is engaged."

"Do tell." Lionel perked up even more.

"To me," Max admitted with a growl. "Against my wishes, I might add."

Lionel's mouth hung open for a moment before his shoulders sagged and thunderclouds filled his expression. "I take it this is your father's doing?"

"It is," Max said, a fresh wave of fury tightening his chest.

Lionel uttered an exceptionally colorful curse under his breath. "I am so tired of our kind being pushed around and thrown into alliances we neither want nor can tolerate."

Jewel sat straighter at the table behind them, and his companion turned slightly, proving they were both listening.

Max met Jewel's eyes for half a second before focusing on Lionel. "I have no intention of going through with it, mind you," he said.

"Because you're in love with Siddel," Lionel said as if finishing his thought. His features softened momentarily before hardening all over again. "Has your father threatened him and his delightful little charges?"

"On more than one occasion now," Max sighed. "Which puts me in an impossible spot."

Lionel hummed in agreement, sitting back in his chair and stroking his chin. "There has to be a way out of it. There's always a way out, if you're willing to take it."

"I certainly hope so," Max said, leaning into the table and resting his hands on the tablecloth. "That's not why I was looking for David, though." When Lionel raised one eyebrow in question, Max went on with, "I have reason to believe my father, and possibly my drunken lout of a brother, are somehow involved in the kidnapping ring."

Lionel snapped straight so fast Max was afraid he'd fall out of his chair. But, of course, falling out of a chair was far too graceless for Lionel Mercer. What surprised Max was the way Jewel reacted. Every trace of snide humor dropped from the man's face, replaced by intense horror and interest. Lionel wasn't able to see Jewel's reaction, and Max wasn't eager to point it out for fear of distracting Lionel from the important matter at hand.

"What did he say?" Lionel asked. "Did he give specifics?"

Max shook his head, suddenly doubting his intuition. "It wasn't anything he said specifically. Only, he reminded me that he is close friends with Lord Chisolm and his son. He was at Bardess Mansion this morning before I arrived there, intent on speaking to Lady Bardess about the events of the concert where the children went missing, or so I gathered. My father seemed to know where Lord Chisolm and Lord Burbage are."

"Where are they?" Lionel asked, his eyes growing round.

"Abroad," Max growled. "The Caribbean, if Lady Bardess's slip of the tongue is to be believed. I'm not sure she is, though. She was highly agitated the whole time my father was there, which is another reason I believe the bastard is up to no good."

"My money is on Lillian Bardess being as guilty as anyone else in this whole affair," Lionel said, his brow furrowing. "I do agree that it's damning that your father knows Lord Chisolm's whereabouts when no one else does."

"There's more," Max went on. "Though I'm not sure how it's all connected. My father knows about me and Stephen. He threatened that if I continue my relationship with Stephen, he will make certain the Briar Street Orphanage suffers and implied that the girls would be sent to places that would give us all nightmares."

Jewel jerked as though he would rise out of his seat. "I've heard enough," he said in a loud enough voice that Lionel was forced to twist to face him, clenching his jaw as he did. "I won't let you keep me out of this investigation any longer, Lionel," Jewel went on. "You know I can help you in ways no one else can."

"Mind your own business, Jewel," Lionel hissed. "We all know that the only thing you care about is your own reputation and the spotlight that being part of this investigation will shine on you."

"This is not about my ego," Jewel insisted. "Though I'm beginning to think it's about yours."

Lionel's jaw dropped as he twisted to glare at Jewel. "I would never put my own interests ahead of those of innocent, defenseless children," he said, so angry his words came out as a whisper.

Max believed him. He also believed Jewel when he said, "You know that I have contacts in the underworld that you will never have access to. You need me in this."

He paused, then added in the gravest voice Max had ever heard, "And you know why."

The two men sat there, glaring at each other in silence. The intensity of their stares had the hair standing up on the back of Max's neck. He had the feeling that whatever Jewel was referring to, he didn't want to know about it.

His already heightened tension nearly snapped when Stephen's voice sounded directly behind him with, "I'm surprised to see you here."

Max jumped, whipping around to find Stephen staring at him with a cold and distant look. "Stephen." He leapt from his chair, but resisted the urge to embrace him. Something was wrong. The warmth had gone out of Stephen's eyes, and he held himself stiffly. "I came in search of David Wirth." Max glanced past Stephen to find David striding into the room.

Stephen sent David a look. "I met him as I came into the club."

"This looks like a meeting I won't want to miss," David said, reaching to shake Max's hand, nodding to Lionel, and sending a wary glance to Jewel and his companion. "Cristofori." He nodded to Jewel's friend, who nodded back. Max found David's presence settling, particularly since the man instantly gauged the situation in front of him and seemed to sense how volatile it was. "What's going on?"

"I want in on this investigation," Jewel said, rising

from his seat and stepping around Mr. Cristofori to stride to David's side.

"He wants another starring role," Lionel countered, leaning back in his chair and crossing his arms. "This one thinks his father is involved in the ring," he added, nodding to Max.

For a moment, Stephen's expression registered surprise. A moment later, it darkened into a scowl. "Your father paid me a visit this morning," he told Max. "He advised me of your upcoming wedding."

Max clenched his jaw tight, furious for a thousand different reasons. "We need to talk."

"Yes, we do." Stephen narrowed his eyes.

The intensity of his displeasure sent acid pouring through Max's stomach, not so much because he thought Stephen believed everything his father must have said, but because the same defensiveness that Max had worked so hard to break through weeks ago was back in place.

Before Max could think of anything to say to fight against that defensiveness, Stephen glanced from Lionel to David and went on with, "Officer Wrexham and I toured the warehouse where the children you rescued were stored before being taken to the ship this morning. We found evidence that could indicate the involvement of a place called Gretton Mill in Leicestershire."

The mood of the tumultuous conversation shifted, as though someone had shot a cannon into a building that was already on fire.

"I told you," Jewel seethed at Lionel, though Max couldn't figure out for the life of him what the reaction was all about. "I told you I should be involved."

"What would a man like you have to do with an investigation into missing children?" Stephen asked what Max was thinking.

Jewel turned to him, restless and short of breath. "What do you think happens to children who are taken?" He didn't give anyone a chance to answer before going on with, "Only a handful of things. Slave labor at mills and factories is one of the more fortunate outcomes." The intense flash of his eyes hinted to Max that he knew a little too well what he was talking about.

"I intend to travel to Leicestershire tomorrow to investigate this mill," Stephen said, glancing from Jewel to David. "I thought you should know."

"Take Wrexham with you," David said.

Stephen shook his head. "He said he wouldn't be able to make that long of a journey."

"I'll go," Max said. He wouldn't let Stephen leave him behind one way or another.

Stephen turned his head slowly to meet Max's eyes. "Are you certain you won't be needed to entertain your fiancée?"

Max huffed an impatient breath. "It's not like you to jump to conclusions, Stephen. You know how I feel and you know where I stand."

Stephen dropped his eyes, color splashing across his cheeks. Max could see that he did know and he did understand, but it was too late. The walls had gone up again. It made Max want to punch something.

David drew in a breath, pulling himself to his full height and surveying the storm of emotions and frustrations around him. He settled his glance on Max. "Why do you think Lord Eastleigh is involved in this trafficking ring?"

"He was at Bardess Mansion this morning," Max answered without hesitation, speaking more to Stephen than to David. "He'd arranged my marriage to Lady Bardess before I arrived to question Lady Bardess further about the day of the concert. Not only did my father know where Lord Chisolm and Lord Burbage are, he seemed to have some sort of hold over Lady Bardess." The full implications of that thought hadn't entirely hit him up until that point. There had been too many other things to think about. "She was frightened of him, I'm certain of it."

"It bears investigation," David said with a nod.

"My father has made threats against Stephen and his girls," Max went on, staring hard at Stephen until he glanced up and met Max's eyes. "Threats that worry me deeply," he added with undisguised emotion.

"He made those same threats to me," Stephen said, equally emotional.

It was as if the invisible wall separating them grew in strength to the point of being impenetrable. They both knew what the price of their love would be if they pursued the relationship they wanted. The arrangement with Lady Bardess was nothing to the far more insidious threat of harm to the girls.

When the weight of the silence and misery between Max and Stephen grew almost too heavy to bear, David turned to Stephen and asked, "What evidence specifically did you and Wrexham find in the warehouse that points to Leicestershire?"

Stephen dragged his eyes away from Max as though they were being forcibly torn out of a lovers' embrace. He cleared his throat and said, "A piece of paper with Gretton Mills's address on it and a ticket stub for a journey to London originating in Leicester."

"That doesn't necessarily mean the children were sent there," Lionel said, though he didn't sound happy with his conclusion.

"It doesn't mean we should rule the place out either," David said. He turned to Stephen. "If you're prepared to go there tomorrow, I will help you in any way."

"I'm going with you," Max repeated his offer.

Stephen grimaced as a flood of emotions passed through his expression. "Won't your father stop you?" he asked.

Max took Stephen's failure to immediately forbid him from going as a tiny victory. "The only way he'll be able to stop me is if he physically restrains me. And the only way he can do that is if he finds himself in my presence. Since I have no intention of going within a mile of him until everything is resolved, I don't believe that will happen."

"You're not going home?" Stephen asked, a different sort of color staining his cheeks.

Max shook his head. "That place has never been my home."

"The Brotherhood has several properties where you can stay unobserved," David said with an arch of one eyebrow, glancing between Stephen and Max as though expecting Stephen to offer Max shelter for the night. Stephen kept his mouth shut, staring at the floor.

"Thank you." Max nodded to David, his heart sinking. He felt very much as though a part of him had made the biggest decision of his life and the rest of him was only just catching up to what it all meant.

"While you're busy poking around mills in Leicestershire," Jewel interrupted, "I'm going to pay a visit to a few old friends." He cracked his knuckles and ground his fist into his hand. Max's brow shot up. He never would have imagined the flashy, flamboyantly dressed man with a taste for wearing cosmetics could be so blatantly violent. Even Lionel looked warily at him.

"Do what you have to do," David sighed. "And let me know the results. We will get to the bottom of this."

CHAPTER 17

The journey to Leicester was one of the most uncomfortable of Stephen's life. It began well before dawn, before anyone else in the orphanage was awake, when Max picked him up in a hired carriage bound for St. Pancras Station. It continued as Max paid for a first-class compartment for the two of them to travel north in. Stephen had never traveled in such luxury, but he would have given it up and ridden in the baggage compartment to avoid the awkward silence that hung between him and Max.

"This is intolerable," Max sighed an hour outside of London, as dawn streaked across the passing countryside. "You know me well enough to know I'm not going to marry Lady Bardess simply because my father demands it."

"Do I know you that well?" Stephen asked, fighting the way his gut writhed and his chest squeezed with guilt for being so peevish. "How many weeks have we known each other?"

Max huffed an irritated sigh. "Time is irrelevant, and you know it. My mother and father have known each other for more than thirty years, and they are virtual strangers to each other, whereas I felt as though I'd known you a lifetime from the moment we met."

Stephen remained silent, turning his head to stare out the window. Max was right, of course. Time meant nothing in love, unless it was the time two lovers spent apart. And he was in love with Max. Guilt lashed him for pulling away from Max and it punished him for wanting to embrace him. No matter what he did, it would be the wrong thing.

"I can't stop thinking about how frightened Jane must be," he said, barely above a whisper.

"Neither can I." Max's tone was gentle and compassionate, and he rose from his seat facing Stephen, moving as though he would shift to sit by Stephen's side.

"Don't," Stephen said, holding up his arms to stop him. "I don't want comfort right now. I want you to stay on your side of the compartment."

Max froze mid-movement. His expression pinched, showing how hurt he was. That hurt turned to anger as he fell back into his seat and crossed his arms tightly. "I knew you had it in you to be stalwart," he muttered, glancing out the window himself, "but I had no idea you could be so cruel."

Stephen dragged his gaze away from the countryside,

his eyes widening as he stared at Max. He adjusted his spectacles, but it didn't change the sight in front of him. "I am not cruel," he said, welcoming the anger that boiled up in him. It was easier than feeling guilt and fear.

"Cold then." Max narrowed his eyes. "Without the slightest bit of consideration for what I'm going through."

Affection tainted with shame stung at Stephen's heart. "I'm sorry, I didn't realize this was about you and your hurt feelings. I thought it was about rescuing defenseless children from evil monsters."

Max let out a scornful breath and snapped his eyes away from Stephen. Stephen knew he deserved the reaction, which only added to his maelstrom of emotions. It wasn't like him to be such a horse's arse, but panic did strange things to a man.

Panic. Stephen writhed against the back of his seat, ostensibly stretching his shoulders, but really trying to shake the eerie feeling that word raised in him. He was desperately afraid for Jane, but Max made him panic. Panic because he'd let the man get too close too fast. Panic because he couldn't imagine his life without Max now, and Max was a man from a different world entirely—a world that was attempting to reclaim him. He could protest and claim he wouldn't obey his father's wishes to marry all he wanted, but how long would that last? The upper classes were powerful enough without a man like Lord Eastleigh calling the shots. Stephen didn't think he could bear the heartbreak of watching Max forced into a miserable life. And he couldn't be heartbroken, not with so many young lives depending on him.

"I do care about your life and your feelings," he admitted in a quiet voice after a full fifteen minutes of silence. When Max turned his head to arch one eyebrow doubtfully at him, Stephen went on with, "I care a little too much."

As much as he wanted to say more, to explain himself fully, he felt as though his tongue were stuck to the roof of his mouth. Max said nothing either, merely studied him. Stephen shuddered to think what the man saw. At least his pinched and furious expression softened.

By the time the train arrived in Leicester, Stephen was exhausted and wrung out, as though they'd spent the entire trip in a shouting match. The small city was bustling as they climbed down onto the platform, made their way through the station, and hired a carriage to take them all the way to Gretton Mills. The tension remained between him and Max, though, which made the entire errand seem more miserable than it already was.

Stephen almost gave thanks when they arrived at Gretton Mills. It gave him a chance to think of something else.

"It's a cloth mill," he said as Max paid the driver, then strode up to his side.

"I assumed it would be," Max said, nodding at the building. "Cloth mills need child labor to clean and thread the machines. They always have."

The thought sent a shudder down Stephen's spine.

He'd toured a cloth mill once when its owner had come to the orphanage to recruit young workers. That mill had chilled Stephen to the bone with its noise, dirt, and general feeling of hopelessness. He'd declined to send any of his girls into employment there back then, and one look at Gretton Mills confirmed that he would have refused to send any of his girls there now.

"What do we tell them?" he asked as they approached a corner of the building that looked the most like an office. "Why are we here?"

"To inspect the machinery?" Max suggested.

Stephen shook his head. "The owner and manager probably know who all the inspectors are."

"The press, then," Max said, lowering his voice as a pair of young men in work clothes crossed their path. "Here to do a story on the burgeoning industry of England's heartland."

Stephen glanced to him, sweeping a look over Max's suit. It was apparent by the ill-fitting suit he wore that Max had stayed true to his statement about not going home where his father might confront him. He'd obviously borrowed clothes from someone slightly bigger than he was. Which instantly had Stephen wondering where the shirt he'd loaned Max the week before was.

The thought of Max wearing his shirt led to thoughts of him without a shirt at all, which sent Stephen's thoughts careening off into a thousand places they didn't need to go. He cleared his throat and forced himself to stay focused.

"The press it is, then," he said, reaching for the door and opening it for Max.

He'd guessed correctly. A small office filled with cotton dust stood on the other side of the door. It contained little more than a desk, a few shelves, and a stove in the corner that gave off very little heat. A door stood half open at the other end of the office. Through that, Stephen could hear the rattling din of dozens of weaving machines.

"Good afternoon, sir," Max said with a broad smile, approaching the clerk at the desk with an outstretched hand. "I'm Maxwell Eastleigh with *The Sunday Times*, and this is my colleague, Stephen Siddel."

"How do you do?" Stephen stepped forward to shake the clerk's hand when Max let go. He would have a word with Max about using their real names as soon as they had three seconds alone, but there was nothing he could do about it now.

"Nice to meet you." The clerk glanced anxiously between the two of them. "Er, what are you doing here?"

"We've come to tour the factory, if we might," Max said, exuding charm. "I'm trying to convince my editor here that Gretton Mills is the perfect example of advancement and industry in England. I want to do a profile story about the vital work you all are doing and the excellent quality of English manufacturing. Would you mind if we had a look around so I can prove my point?"

The clerk's jaw dropped, then flapped as he tried to think of an answer. Stephen wasn't impressed with the man's intelligence, but he was ready to bless the dolt all the same when he shrugged and said, "I don't see why not. Let me see if I can find someone to show you around."

The clerk stepped out from behind the desk, heading to the half-opened door. Stephen followed hard on the man's heels, Max right behind him. He wasn't about to wait idly in an office when a door was opened for him, especially if waiting meant they might not be allowed in at all.

They followed the clerk down a short hall into a huge room filled with clattering, noisy machines. Either the clerk didn't notice them right behind him or he didn't care, since he didn't try to stop them from stepping onto the factory floor. The din and whirl of activity was so overwhelming that Stephen was tempted to clap his hands to his ears. White dust filled the air, spinning off the power looms and giant, whirling spools of thread, immediately making it hard for him to draw a deep breath. He could only imagine how frightening the place would seem to a child.

Except that there weren't any children in sight. Slender, stunted men and women, yes, but no children. Few of the workers glanced up to eye Stephen and Max warily as they followed the clerk down a central aisle between machines. Stephen craned his neck, attempting to search under the machines and between moving parts, but he didn't spot a single young face or tiny body anywhere.

A few steps ahead of them, the clerk turned as if

searching for someone. He found Stephen and Max behind him and jumped as though startled. "Oh! I thought you were waiting in the office."

"We thought you meant us to follow you," Stephen said, feeling heat rise to his face.

"What a marvelous establishment you have here," Max said, glancing around as though witnessing one of the wonders of the world. "It is truly a testament to man's ability to harness nature."

Stephen could see in an instant what Max was trying to do by the way his feigned enthusiasm made the clerk smile. Charm and a handsome face could move mountains.

"Yes, er, we are rather proud of it," the clerk said, puffing his chest out as though he had been personally complimented. "But wait right here until I find Mr. Barton."

"Certainly." Max continued to smile. "Take your time."

The clerk nodded to Max, then headed off at a swifter pace.

As soon as the man turned a corner, Max grabbed Stephen's sleeve and tugged him out of the main aisle and down a row of machines. The noise was even more deafening in the heart of the machines, so neither of them spoke, but Max gestured for Stephen to look around.

Stephen didn't need to be told twice. He followed close behind Max as they edged their way down the row of looms, dodging confused and bedraggled workers as they did. As much as Stephen pitied the lot of the factory workers, they were a far cry from being the sort of wretched souls Dickens had written about. None of them looked dangerously malnourished or ill, merely poor.

As far as they traveled and as much of the factory floor as they traversed, Stephen didn't spot a single child. After a few minutes, however, the workers began to take more of a notice of them. Their confused looks turned to curiosity, and then to suspicion as they strode up and down the aisles.

"Who are you?" A burly man with an aura of leadership finally stopped them at the end of one row.

"We're from *The Sunday Times*," Stephen told him, attempting to imitate Max's smile and outwardly warm nature, but knowing he wasn't as good at it. "We're doing a story about—"

"Child labor," Max interrupted, his smile suddenly gone. He'd replaced it with a frank and questioning look, but one that was just as charming as what he'd shown the clerk. Once again, Stephen could see his game. He was attempting to make the burly man see him as an ally.

Unfortunately, the burly man crossed his arms and stared down his nose at Max. "Gretton Mills does not employ children," he said. "Never has, never will."

Several workmen had closed in, as if to see who the newcomers were and what they were about. They nodded along with the burly man. Alarm raced through Stephen. So much so that he grabbed Max's sleeve and tugged it slightly. When Max glanced questioningly at him, Stephen nodded toward the end of the aisle.

"And you should be admired for your moral stance on this matter," Max told the burly man, changing tactics. "Child labor is a blight on England, but Gretton Mills is a shining example of how unnecessary it is to the advancement of industry."

As much as he loved Max, Stephen wanted to roll his eyes. The man needed to learn when to keep his mouth shut.

"Thank you for your time," Stephen said, speaking loudly over the noise of the looms.

He grasped Max's arm tighter and pulled him away, toward the center aisle. The stares they received from workers as they slipped between machines as fast as possible to reach the aisle set the hair on the back of his neck on edge. Something wasn't right, but he couldn't tell if it was merely the noise and the awkwardness of being caught where they shouldn't be or something else.

When they reached the center aisle, they spotted the clerk, along with another, older man in a slightly nicer suit. The two men appeared to be searching for them, and as soon as Stephen and Max stepped out from between the machines, the older man's face dropped into a scowl.

"What is the meaning of this?" the older man growled when he came close enough to be heard, which was almost all the way into Stephen and Max's faces.

"We do not allow visitors on the factory floor. It's too dangerous."

"Yes, we can see that," Stephen replied, attempting to be as authoritative as he could.

"We stepped to the side to inspect one of the looms and got lost," Max added with a laugh.

Stephen was ready to shake his head and assign Max lines to copy on a blackboard—like he did with any of his disobedient girls—for being a fool. Surprisingly, though, the older man's expression dulled to mere annoyance instead of dangerous anger.

"You should have waited in the office," the man said. He turned and gestured for Stephen and Max to follow him.

Part of Stephen felt as though they'd failed, that the entire trip to Gretton Mills had been a mistake. The paper and ticket he and Wrexham had found in the Batcliff Cross warehouse must have come from another shipment of goods that had been stored in the same room as the children. He barely listened, once they were back in the office, as Max spun an unnecessarily elaborate lie about the two of them being reporters hunting down a story. Max came up with questions on the fly for the factory manager, which impressed Stephen even as it made him impatient. By the time they were finally shown the door, Stephen was convinced the manager and the clerk truly did think they were from *The Sunday Times*.

That didn't improve Stephen's mood, though.

"We've wasted an entire day up here," he sighed,

rubbing a hand over his face. It came away covered in fine, white cotton dust. He had to remove his spectacles to clean them as well. Less than an hour in the factory and he and Max were covered in fine dust.

"I wish I could disagree with you," Max said, then fell into a coughing fit.

Stephen paused, waiting for Max to clear his lungs. He would have taken a few deep breaths to clear his own lungs, but the smoke from the chimneys rising above the factory didn't make the outside air any better than that on the factory floor. And there seemed to be quite a few chimneys.

Stephen adjusted his glasses and started counting chimneys in his mind.

"I'll see if I can find us another cab." Max cleared his throat, spitting out cotton dust.

"How large would you say that factory floor was?" Stephen asked, only partially hearing Max's statement.

"Big." Max turned, furrowing his brow as he attempted to see what Stephen was seeing. "I've very little experience with factories, so I wouldn't know—" He stopped.

It was Stephen's turn to follow the line of Max's vision to see what he was looking at. Max had pulled his focus down from the chimneys and was staring at the far corner of the building. A young woman who couldn't have been much older than Beatrice walked to the far edge of the path that wound around the building and tossed a bucket of something that looked vile into a muddy stream. She was too far away to see what exactly was in the bucket or to call out to her. Once her bucket was empty, she dragged herself back around the corner of the building.

"I think there's more to this factory than what we saw," Stephen said, his pulse picking up with a sickening urgency.

"I'm afraid you're right," Max said. He reached out to touch Stephen's hand, then launched himself forward. "Come on. I think we're on to something."

CHAPTER 18

Max couldn't quite catch his breath as he and Stephen hurried around the side of the factory, looking for the young woman, but it wasn't because of the cotton dust he'd breathed in. His heart pounded against his ribs as it became clear to him the dimensions of the building were far greater than what he and Stephen had seen from the inside.

"Do you think—" he started and was instantly silenced as Stephen threw an arm across his chest and pushed both of them up against the side of the building as they neared the corner.

Instantly, Max knew why. Gruff voices were arguing just a few yards away.

"—not to go outside for any reason," a deep, male voice growled.

"But the slop bucket was overflowing," a frightened, young female voice said.

"Any reason," the man repeated, nearly shouting.

"There are children in there," the young woman continued, weeping. "They're hungry, sick."

Max felt Stephen tense beside him. He reached for Stephen's hand only to find it trembling with rage.

"I don't care if they're puking themselves as long as they stay quiet until the wagon gets here," the man growled. "Now get your tarty arse back inside and I'll show you what you're good for."

The young woman whimpered as the sound of footsteps retreated. Max felt sick to his stomach as his imagination filled in what the man meant by his words. Judging by the sound of the woman's voice, she couldn't have been much older than Stephen's girls.

"We have to get in there," Stephen said, his voice thin and his eyes ablaze with fury. "We have to save them."

"I agree," Max said, resting a hand on Stephen's arm in an attempt to settle him. "But we have to be careful. We don't know what we're walking into."

Stephen gulped a few unsteady breaths, still trembling, before nodding his head sharply and shaking out his shoulders. He paused for a moment, eyes closed as if praying, then edged his way to the corner of the building and peeked around.

"There's no one watching," he whispered, pulling back and facing Max. "I can see a door farther along the building."

Max nodded and moved to the corner to get a look for himself. They were lucky in that no one seemed to be patrolling that side of the building, but Max didn't trust the apparent emptiness of the packed, grassless dirt that stretched away from that side of the building at all. If the mill really was some sort of a holding place for kidnapped children, or even if the children had been put to work there, someone had to be guarding that side of the building. There were a few doors along the long back stretch of the building and no telling what waited on the other side.

"We can't just stand here dithering while children are being held captive," Stephen hissed as Max tried to form a plan in his mind. "Jane and the boys could be in there."

Max's heart went out to Stephen, and he stepped back to face him. "They could be," he admitted, taking Stephen's hand and squeezing it. "Which is why I know you would want to proceed as cautiously as possible to bring as little harm to them as we can."

Stephen huffed out a breath and rubbed his free hand over his face, knocking his spectacles askew as he did. "You're right," he said, letting go of Max's hand to fix his spectacles. "But the longer we wait, the more likely we are to be spotted, one way or another."

He had a point. "We have no choice but to do exactly like we did before—we walk in there as though we're supposed to be there."

Stephen winced, proving that he didn't like the plan any more than Max did, but they were out of options. He pulled himself to his full height and walked around the corner of the building as bold as brass, Max following.

When they reached the nearest door, Stephen turned the handle, his hand still shaking.

The world on the other side of the door was a thousand times worse than the noisy, dusty chaos of the front half of the factory. The clatter of power looms and spinning machines made it impossible to think, let alone hear any sounds of conversation that might have been going on in the cavernous space. The same cloud of cotton dust filled the air, but unlike the front of the factory, there was very little light or ventilation. Max spotted windows around the top of the room, but they were all closed.

He was about to point out as much when Stephen clamped a hand on his arm. Max turned to him. His blood chilled when he saw the expression of shock and horror in Stephen's eyes. A moment later, Stephen broke away from him, dashing through the cramped and crowded rows of machinery. Max just barely heard his shout of, "Jane!" over the noise.

She was there, just a few yards away, crouched on the floor with her arm thrust dangerously up into one of the whirring, clacking looms. The expression of terror on her face as she went about whatever insane task she'd been set to do so close to the monstrous machine alone would have been enough to shake Max to his bones, but Jane's ripped and threadbare clothes, her sunken cheeks, and her pale skin had him pulsing with fear and rage that he wasn't sure he would ever get over. And the poor girl been gone less than a week.

"Jane!" Stephen called again, dodging around several

other, hapless and frighteningly young workers to reach her, Max hard on his heels.

Jane must have heard something over the din. She pulled her arm back, shrinking in on herself for a moment before her glassy eyes focused on Stephen. Once they did, she screamed and leapt up from her position, crouched half inside of the thundering machine. The twist of terror and joy in her expression brought tears to Max's eyes as she threw herself at Stephen, wailing, "Sir!"

Stephen caught her, lifting Jane into his arms and hugging her as though he would never let her go. Jane hugged him back, tears streaming down her dirty face. The sight was so dire and tender that Max couldn't breathe.

The workers in that part of the factory were far less disciplined than their fellows in the front of the factory. They sensed at once that Stephen and Max weren't supposed to be there, but unlike the hostility and suspicion they'd been met with before, these workers looked to them as though they were long-awaited saviors.

"Help us," a young, rail-thin lad who couldn't have been more than fourteen gasped, clinging to Max's sleeve. "Help."

"Help us. Save us," an even younger girl pleaded, leaping away from her loom to grab Max's other arm.

Their pleas spread through the factory floor like ripples from a pebble dropped in a pond. The aura of desperation that pervaded the room intensified at an alarming rate until it felt like the air had gone electric with panic.

"Where are the others?" Stephen shouted, still only barely able to be heard over the machinery.

Jane clung to him, wild-eyed and panting, unable to answer his question. Max doubted she'd even heard it.

"Where are the other children?" Max asked the youngsters who had attached themselves to him.

"Everywhere," the young man answered. "Help us, please." Tears now cut trails through the dirt on his face as well.

Rage hardened Max's insides. More and more workers had abandoned their machines to rush toward them, or to stand, trembling, where they were. None of them could have been older than fifteen, and none of them seemed to be steady enough to offer Max and Stephen the kind of help they needed.

"We have to get everyone out of here," Max called to Stephen, hoping Stephen could hear him.

Stephen answered with a nod, but he, too, was so distraught that he merely stood where he was, crushing Jane against his chest, and searching through the increasingly frantic activity of the factory floor.

Max started forward, knowing the only way they would be of any help was if they moved. Already, he swore he could hear loud, deep shouting over the clatter of the machines. He gestured for Stephen and the others to follow him as he backtracked to an aisle between rows of looms and headed in what he hoped was the right direction to take them to one of the doors.

They made it only a few yards before a tough, muscular man stepped into the aisle ahead of him, a cudgel of some sort in his hands. He used it to beat a young man who was trying to dash past him before glancing up and spotting Max, Stephen, and the dozen or so young people who were now following them. The man pointed his cudgel at Max and shouted something before charging forward.

Max reacted before he could think, dropping into an attack stance and rushing to meet the man. He managed to collide with him shoulder first, knocking the man off-balance. The man was bigger and more muscular than Max, but he evidently hadn't expected to be met with any sort of force. Max used surprise against him, throwing a punch across the man's face that splattered blood across the roll of cloth attached to the loom behind him. The man recovered, staggering for a moment, before turning and sprinting off through the machines.

Max turned back to the others, under no illusion that the man was running out of fear. He would be going to fetch help. "We have to get out of here," he shouted above the noise—which was diminishing ominously, as if the machines were being shut down.

"We have to find the boys," Stephen shouted in return.

He was right, but Max was certain it would cost

them. He glanced around, trying to think fast in spite of the edge of panic that he couldn't shake.

His indecision was interrupted as a young woman who looked about fifteen, with dark hair and eyes, her face dolled up with cosmetics, grabbed his wrist. Max met her eyes and nearly shouted in relief to find intelligence and urgency staring back at him instead of mindless panic. The pieces clicked in his mind, and he recognized her as the young woman with the bucket he'd seen outside earlier.

"The youngest children are locked in a cage over there," she said, throwing her free arm out to the side. "The brothel is coming to pick them up within the hour."

Everything about her statement chilled Max, but he nodded to her. "Lead the way."

The young woman nodded back, turned to dash off, and gestured for Max to follow her. She knew exactly how to weave her way between the machines with the least impediment, speeding along to the far end of the room. Max had a harder time following her, since Stephen and the small army of frightened young people who must have seen them as their last hope attempted to follow as well. Stephen seemed unwilling to leave a single one of them behind, and Max couldn't blame him.

The sight that met them at the far end of the room was the most horrific one Max had seen yet. The young woman hadn't been lying when she said the younger children were being kept in a cage. They had obviously sensed something was going on and all stood, pressed against the bars, reaching out and calling for help. The sight was heart wrenching.

"Jerry!" Stephen called, rushing past Max to grab the hand of a tiny, wailing boy who was half crushed against the bars by the others. Max thought he recognized the boy, but it was hard to tell, the way the poor lad was covered in dirt and clearly malnourished.

"How do we get them out?" Max asked the young woman who had led him there.

"The foreman has a key," the young woman told him, a vicious spark in her eyes. "Or at least he did." She drew a key ring with several keys from the pocket of her tattered dress.

Max smiled and took the keys when she handed them to him, but his heart sank as he noticed for the first time how she was dressed. The cut of her cheap gown and the chintzy fabric, combined with the cosmetics she wore, made it clear what she was, even though she was years too young for such a profession. But Max didn't have time to feel pity for her. He lunged toward the cage's door and began attempting to fit the keys into the lock.

"Lily," one of the tiny children in the cage called out. "Lily, help me."

"I'm trying to, love," the young woman, Lily, called back, reaching to squeeze as many hands poking through the bars as she could. "Not long now."

Max finally found the right key and opened the lock, but as he swung the cage door open, a thundering crack filled the air. A moment later, the drone of machinery ground to a stop, filling the air with an ominous, ringing silence.

"Come on," Max urged the children fleeing the cage. "We need to get out of here."

"This way," Stephen shouted as though the looms were still clattering, leading the growing sea of children back through the rows of machines toward the doors.

"You! Stop!" a deep voice shouted at them from the other end of the floor.

"Run," Lily told Max, physically turning him to face the retreating crowd that Stephen led.

"You're coming with us," Max told her, trying to grab her hand.

She pulled away. "I can stop them from following you. Or at least I can try."

"They'll kill you," Max said, grabbing for her again.

"Believe me, they won't," she answered, darkness and steel in her eyes. Before Max could argue with her, she stepped closer to him. "Find my brother," she said. "Tell him it's the man with the lion."

"The what?" Max shook his head at her. "Who's your brother?"

The crack of a gun being fired prevented Lily from answering. Max flinched, which gave Lily enough time to dash past him, heading straight for the men who were barreling closer. One held a smoking gun, but to Max's surprise, one of the others was raging at him as though he'd committed a grave sin. Firing a gun in a cotton mill filled with lint probably wasn't the smartest idea. Max took the distraction as his opportunity to flee and sprinted down the row of looms in the direction Stephen had gone.

He caught up with Stephen and the others as they flooded through tall, broad doors into the dreary, grey of the chilly afternoon. In spite of the slight drizzle and smoke from the chimneys, it was as if the children were seeing light for the first time. Max caught up to Stephen as he gathered the escaping young people, leading them toward the front of the building.

"How do we get them all out of here?" he asked, resting a hand on Stephen's back.

"I have no idea," Stephen said, attempting to keep the children moving. "If we can get them close to the nearest town—"

Stephen stopped, glancing forward with a suddenly shocked expression. Max whirled around to see what he was looking at. His heart nearly dropped to his feet when he saw Lady Bardess striding forward, dressed as though she were going to tea at Buckingham Palace, a pair of grim-faced men in suits flanking her. As soon as she spotted Max, she pulled up short, her mouth dropping in shock.

"Lord Hillsboro." Lady Bardess recovered from her shock first, though she continued to glance around desperately, as though she'd been caught stealing. "What are you doing here?"

"I could ask you the same thing, Lady Bardess," Max said, striding toward her.

"Well, I...that is to say...er...." Lady Bardess's chest rose and fell as though she were close to hyperventilating. She glanced desperately to the men with her.

Another, familiar voice cut into the rising tension of the scene with, "That's them! There they are."

Max glanced past Lady Bardess to see none other than Sister Constance charging toward them. Behind her were at least half a dozen Metropolitan Police officers. Sister Constance's wimple shook with every fierce step she took on her way to Max, Stephen, and the cluster of children.

"Yes, that's them," Lady Bardess echoed, her face suddenly lighting with victory. "Arrest those two men at once."

CHAPTER 19

There were too many wild details for Stephen to process at once in the mad scene in front of him. Sister Constance was the last person he expected to see in Leicestershire. Lady Bardess should have been as well, but he wasn't at all surprised by her presence. The two men with her were clearly thrown by the presence of two men surrounded by dozens of children—numbers that were growing by the second as more young people fled the secret factory floor. Those men seemed even more alarmed by the Metropolitan Police officers, though. Stephen himself was surprised to find such a large contingent of London officers so far from the city, especially after what Wrexham had said about the importance of the investigation in the Met's eyes.

His thoughts happened all within the space of a few seconds before Lady Bardess raised her voice to repeat,

"Arrest those men. They're horrible, perverted kidnappers."

The policemen had already started forward, but their steps slowed when Sister Constance shouted, "No, not them! Arrest...arrest...." She suddenly seemed at a loss, glancing around with a fretful expression as though she wasn't certain who should be arrested.

"If anyone is to be arrested, it should be you, Lady Bardess," Max said, stepping away from Stephen and the children.

The children were loath to let him walk away from them, whimpering and reaching for him as he passed, as though he were their last hope and if he left, they were doomed. The sight broke Stephen's already shattered heart. Calming a growing mob of mistreated and malnourished children was only one of their problems, though. He struggled to set Jane down, prying her hands off his neck.

"Can you keep them calm and organized?" he asked one of the older girls, even though she didn't look calm herself. He glanced on to the painfully thin boy who had begged for Max's help in the factory. "Keep everyone together. Protect the younger ones."

It was enough of an order for the two young people to pull themselves together in an attempt to do as Stephen asked. A few more older children joined the efforts, leaving Stephen free to step away from the children and up to Max's side as the confrontation continued.

"What possible business could you have here, unless

it is connected to your family's activities, Lady Bardess." Max was in the middle of confronting the woman. He glanced to the police officers. "It's no coincidence that this woman's brother was arrested last week in connection with a ring of child kidnappers, or that her father has been implicated as well and gone missing."

"I don't know what you're talking about," Lady Bardess nearly screamed, her voice hysterical. "I...my brother is settling abroad and my father is with him. I merely came here to...to...." She floundered, her face growing redder by the moment.

She was saved by Sister Constance's shout of, "Jerry!" She leapt forward, arms outstretched, as Jerry broke free of the huddle that the older children were trying to organize the youngsters into. Robbie worked his way out of the scrum as well. Both boys rocketed toward Sister Constance, throwing themselves into her arms. "Oh, my darlings, I've been so afraid for you," Sister Constance wailed.

Stephen headed toward her, his instincts prompting him to comfort her if he could. "How did you know they were here?" he asked, slipping an arm around her shoulder.

"My sister showed up on my doorstep this morning and told me where you'd gone," Sister Constance said in a hurry. "She said you might have discovered where the boys and your Jane were. How dare you leave to rescue them without taking me along?"

Her righteous anger was the first thing that felt right

in the entire, mad day they were having. It settled Stephen and filled him with confidence. "We need to get these children to safety," he told the police officers in a commanding tone. "We need to find out where they were each stolen from and return them to—"

"What is the meaning of this?"

Stephen was interrupted by the factory manager and clerk he and Max had encountered earlier charging onto the scene. They had at least a dozen men with them, all of whom looked as though they could win a prize fight. Their arrival meant that even with the police officers, Stephen, Max, and Sister Constance were outnumbered.

It was little consolation that the factory manager's expression pinched into fear that went far beyond ordinary alarm at the sight of the dozens of children huddled together and the police officers. "Who are these children?" he stammered, his face going red.

A surge of energy shot through Stephen. The manager's poor attempt to feign ignorance was all the proof he needed that the man was as guilty as sin. "There's the man that should be arrested," he told the police officers. "Arrested for holding these children against their will. I doubt that forced labor is the only reason they were snatched either." He searched quickly around for the dark-haired young woman who had been dressed up like a tart. She was nowhere to be seen.

"I don't know what you're talking about," the manager said, unable to stay still or look at one person for more than a split-second. "This factory does not employ children. I'll fetch the owner to prove it if you—"

"I don't think I'm needed here," Lady Bardess interrupted, attempting to turn and flee.

Max leapt forward and caught her by the wrist. "You're not going anywhere."

Lady Bardess shrieked and tried her best to pull away. When she saw that Max wasn't going to let her go, she burst into wailing sobs. "I don't have anything to do with it, I swear. I don't know anything."

"Who are these men with you?" Max demanded.

"They're the snatchers," one of the older girls called from the group of children. Her face had gone completely white, and she stared at the two men with hollow, frightened eyes. "They show up, and we never see the ones they take ever again."

"They're solicitors," Lady Bardess contradicted the girl in a high-pitched voice, her eyes wide. "Just my solicitors, that's all."

The two men exchanged anxious looks, twitching and scanning the area as though thinking of running. The police officers all seemed overwhelmed by the scene, glancing between the players as though they had no idea what to make of any of it. Stephen would have given anything for Wrexham to be there among them, but they were out of luck.

"These children need to be taken to safety," Stephen said, grasping for some sense of control.

Before he finished, the factory manager shouted,

"The lot of you need to get off this property before I call in the real police."

"Yes, call the real police." Lady Bardess wrenched away from Max at last, leaping toward the manager. "These men are kidnappers. They've stolen all these children for their nefarious purposes."

"They've done no such thing," Sister Constance snapped. She glared at the police officers. "Don't just stand there, arrest this woman and her accomplices."

The Metropolitan officers didn't move. They gaped at everyone and everything around them like clueless oafs. Every nerve in Stephen's body frayed at the lack of action when it was clear as day to him what needed to be done.

"Enough of this," the manager said at last. He sent the briefest of glances to one of Lady Bardess's accomplices before stepping forward, motioning to the thugs behind him. "Back to work."

Before Stephen could shout in protest, pointing out the contradiction of the manager claiming not to employ children, but then advancing on the poor things, everything erupted into chaos. The thugs hurried toward the crowd of children. The children screamed and wailed, breaking away from the tight knot the older ones had focused them into and scattering in all directions. The manager must have intended for exactly that to happen. He nodded to Lady Bardess's accomplices, who instantly sprinted away from the scene.

"Stop them!" Stephen shouted. But no one listened.

It was complete pandemonium as the toughs from the factory chased the children across the vast expanse of the factory's property. Stephen could see in an instant that none of them were actually trying to catch the children, only frighten them into scattering. The London policemen made a few, halting attempts to chase after the children or the men from the factory, but none of them followed the snatchers.

Max tried to go after them himself, but when Lady Bardess shouted, "Stop that man!" one of the Metropolitan officers lunged after Max, grabbing him and holding him to the spot.

"What are you doing? Let me go." Max struggled and flailed in the man's grasp.

Stephen started toward him, but another of the officers grabbed hold of him and held him to his place. "Get off of me," Stephen shouted, elbowing the man in an attempt to break free.

He only succeeded in angering the officer, who clamped an arm tighter around him.

"Arrest him," Lady Bardess shouted, surging forward. "He's the kidnapper. He's the one who has put these children in danger."

"I have not," Stephen said, struggling in the officer's grip.

"He's...he's a filthy sodomite," Lady Bardess yelped, then clapped her hands over her mouth as though she couldn't believe her own daring.

Stephen felt the tension that suddenly washed over the officer holding him. “A what?” the man barked.

Lady Bardess’s eyes were bright with excitement as she drew her hands away from her mouth and squeaked, “He’s a sodomite. Wicked, filthy, and vile. He...he kidnapped these children to use for his own disgusting reasons. For him and for others like him. He should be hanged for his crimes.”

The officer jerked Stephen so hard he nearly lost his balance. “Is that true?” the man growled.

Deep dread filled Stephen’s gut. He glanced across the tumultuous scene to Max, who was fighting the officer who held him as best he could. No matter how Stephen answered, his fate was sealed. The best he could hope for was that Lady Bardess had even a shred of loyalty for her own class.

“I did not kidnap these children,” Stephen said, ending his struggle.

“I knew it.” Lady Bardess pointed a finger at him as though he’d admitted to everything. “He is the one who should be arrested. He should be locked up where he cannot hurt another child ever again.”

“Are you mad?” Sister Constance stepped forward, Jerry and Robbie clinging to her and impeding her progress. “Stephen Siddel is the kindest, most fatherly man I’ve ever met. He would never harm a hair on a child’s head. He won’t even take the switch to them when they deserve it.”

"He's evil and vile and you know it," Lady Bardess insisted. "You know what he is."

"I...." Sister Constance's jaw worked, but no more words came out. The truth was in her eyes. It was a surprise to Stephen that she knew fully who he was. He could tell by the look of regret she sent his way that she'd known all along, but not once had she said anything to him or called him out for his sins.

"Arrest him," Lady Bardess demanded again. "Take him back to London and lock him away forever."

"What about that one?" The officer holding Stephen gestured with his chin to Max.

"Him?" Lady Bardess's face went pink as she turned toward Max. She wrung her hands and bit her lip as if trying to make up her mind what to do. "Lord Hillsboro is...he's...he should be...."

"What do you think Lord Eastleigh would say if you caused his son to be arrested?" Stephen demanded. When Lady Bardess whipped back to face him, he stared hard into her eyes.

All the color drained from Lady Bardess's face and she gulped. "Lord Hillsboro is my fiancé," she said in a thready voice, looking at Stephen instead of any of the police officers. "I shall deal with him myself."

It was the best Stephen could hope for. At least Max would remain free to continue the fight.

"I am not your fiancé," Max said, breaking away from the officer holding him at last and charging toward Lady Bardess. "I don't care what my father says, I could never marry a bitch like you." He snapped his head toward Stephen. "Stephen is my—"

"Don't be a daft fool, man!" Stephen shouted, more terrified of Max landing himself in as much hot water as he was in, than angry. "Get help."

"That's enough from you," the officer holding Stephen said, jerking him hard enough to yank him off his feet and knock his spectacles off. As if for fun, the officer crunched his heel against the fallen spectacles, shattering one lens.

"Unhand him," Max demanded marching forward.

"This is intolerable." Sister Constance rushed forward as well.

"I'll be all right," Stephen told both of them. He glanced to Max, frustrated by his fuzzy vision. "Go back to London and tell my solicitor what's going on." He trusted that Max would know to contact David Wirth immediately.

"I'll do more than that," Max growled before turning to stride off.

"Where are you going?" Lady Bardess called after him. At least she didn't follow.

"Take care of the children," Stephen told Sister Constance. "Get them to safety."

"Yes," Sister Constance said with a nod, though she sounded deeply uncertain.

"Help the nun with the children," the officer holding Stephen ordered the others. At least the dolt could do one thing right. "I'll get this sorry sod on the road to where he belongs."

The officer yanked Stephen into motion. Without his spectacles, it was hard to tell where exactly he was going. It hardly mattered, though. The man was Met police, meaning he would end up back in London, which was exactly where he wanted to be. It was getting there and what would happen once he was there that made Stephen nervous.

The journey back to London felt interminable for Max. More than anything, he'd wanted to stay by Stephen's side and fight for him. It was agony walking away from the man that he loved more than life itself. And it had taken a tremendous leap of faith to run from the factory with so many of the children they'd tried to rescue scattered and still in danger. As he walked toward Leicester, finally managing to secure a ride with a passing tradesman, and purchased train fare, he had to constantly remind himself that Stephen was right to tell him to seek out David's help and that Sister Constance was strong enough to stop at nothing until all of the children were safe.

All the same, the journey back to London was the most painful Max had had to make in his life. As much as he told himself to take the time to rest as the countryside sped past him, his mind and heart refused to stay still. As soon as the train pulled into St. Pancras Station, he shot off, dodging slower travelers in his haste to reach the street and hire a cab. Once in the cab, however, he did not head straight to the offices of Dandie & Wirth. He had a far more desperate errand to run.

"You are responsible for this," he shouted as he charged into his father's study. He couldn't stay away from the lion's den, not when he knew his father was at least partially behind everything he'd witnessed in Leicestershire. "You unspeakable bastard."

His father glanced up from the desk he sat behind, a banal look on his face. "What drivel are you spouting now, you miserable piece of excrement."

Max pulled up short at the insult. He expected a war of words with his father, but the man's cold look unnerved him. "Gretton Mills," he spat. "I've just been there. I've seen the plight of those children. Don't tell me you aren't as deeply involved in this evil as Lord Chisolm is."

His father didn't reply. He merely stared back at Max with narrowed eyes. The silence was painful.

"I saw with my own eyes what has become of those missing children," Max went on. "I saw the deplorable conditions they are working in, and I saw evidence of other sins they've been thrust into." The image of the girl, Lily—the one who had told him to find her brother and tell him about the man with the lion—was burned in his mind. "If I find out that you've done more than simply mastermind this evil—" He couldn't finish his sentence. His anger was too powerful.

His father put down the pen he'd been rolling between his fingers and narrowed his eyes at Max. "My business ventures are none of your concern," he said.

Max gaped at him. "Children are being starved and abused. That will always be my concern."

"Why?" his father asked with a shrug. "Because you are buggering that fag who fancies himself a father to legions of little girls? He's more of a tart than any of his pitiful charges are."

Rage at the layers of insults burned in Max's stomach. "Stephen is a hundred times the man you are or could ever be."

His father appeared unaffected by the statement. He continued to stare at Max in frosty silence for a few more seconds before sucking in a breath and sitting straighter. "Holmes," he called in a deep, booming voice.

Max tensed, twisting in anticipation of his father's butler striding through the door.

"Holmes," his father called, louder, when the man didn't appear.

"Let me guess." Max faced his father once more. "You're going to sequester me in my room, forbid me to go out in company, and keep me locked away from the man I love."

"No," his father answered with perfect calm. "I'm going to have you arrested and thrown in jail, and then I am going to contact my solicitor to have you stricken from the family rolls and denied any sort of financial benefit that comes with being a part of this family. You are no longer my son, nor are you anything to me. Holmes!"

"Yes, my lord." The butler appeared in the door at last.

Max hissed out a breath, turning to stride out of the room without waiting for the scene that was bound to unfold with Holmes. His father wasn't bluffing, but he didn't care. It was well past time for him to cut ties with all the things that were holding him back and to embrace the future he was destined for. But as much as that filled him with hope and confidence, he knew for absolute certain that he'd made a deadly enemy of his father. He and Stephen would need all the protection they could get, and it might already have been too late.

CHAPTER 20

Stephen wasn't entirely certain where he was, and it unnerved him. Without his glasses, he'd only been able to guess where the police officer who had arrested him dragged him off to once they'd disembarked from the train in London. Wherever it was, it was an unfamiliar part of the city to him. If he had to guess, he'd say he was somewhere north of his usual neighborhood in Limehouse. The jail he'd been thrown in was dim and dreary and smelled of unwashed bodies and hopelessness.

"I demand to speak to my solicitor," he said for what felt like the hundredth time since leaving Leicester as the officer tossed him into a filthy cell. "His name is Mr. David Wirth, and his office is at—"

"You'll speak to the devil before you speak to him," the officer cut him off. Even without his spectacles,

Stephen could see his sneer. "Filth like you should be kept away from decent folks."

The officer shoved him deeper into the cell—so hard Stephen nearly lost his balance—then slammed the cell door shut with a resounding clang.

"What'd he do?" the clerk who had processed his arrival asked the officer with genuine bewilderment in his voice.

"He's a bloody queer," the officer growled, marching back through a door to the front of the building.

One of the two men already in Stephen's cell snorted in derision and stepped to the other side of the cell as though Stephen were contagious. The other stayed where he was but muttered, "Aw, bloody hell," and hunkered in on himself as though Stephen might attack him.

Stephen didn't need glasses to see that his two companions were rough men in mismatched clothes that had obviously come off of a rag pile. Neither had shaved or bathed in what smelled like days, and when he squinted, Stephen could see that one of them was missing more than a few teeth. And yet, they shied away from him, a man in a neat, if not expensive, suit who was only a little worse for wear after a trying day. Added to the mountain of insults that had already been hurled on him that day, their behavior was too much.

"I demand to speak to my solicitor," he shouted, grabbing the cell's bars and shaking them. He knew his efforts would be ignored, but dammit, it felt good to rage and shake and try to take some sort of action.

His outburst got him no attention whatsoever. It didn't matter how loud he shouted or whom he demanded to see, from David to Mrs. Ross. Both his jailors and his cellmates ignored him. Hours passed with no sign of activity from the office at the front of the jail. Stephen eventually sank to a sitting position on the floor, his shoulder propped against the bars, hugging himself. Spending a night in jail was one thing, but the sinking, desperate feeling that he'd been thrown out like so much refuse, shunted aside to be forgotten about, and all because of what he was, wouldn't leave him. Max didn't know where he was. No one knew. He could disappear as certainly as any of the children who had been kidnapped by the ring, and like those children, no one would care or have the slightest idea where he'd gone.

Those thoughts made for a restless and sleepless night. The men in the cell with him dropped into ear-splitting snores as darkness filled the cell. The only light that had been left to them was a sickly, sputtering lantern that burnt itself out somewhere in the middle of the night. That left Stephen completely in the dark, alone with his thoughts and fears, more alone than he had ever been in his life.

"I'm sorry, Max," he whispered, leaning his head against the bars, his heart aching like it'd never ached before. "I'm sorry for pushing you away when you care as much about the girls as I do." Realizing that at such a late hour was bittersweet. Max did care for his girls, which made him so much more than just a distraction. It made him an ally and a partner on so many levels. He was an idiot for not seeing it sooner. "I'm sorry for dragging you into this," he murmured on. "Your life could be so free and easy now if not for—"

He stopped his ramblings, sitting straighter and rolling his shoulders in an attempt to work the knots out. In fact, Max's life wouldn't have been any easier without him. Men like them were condemned to difficult lives, no matter what their fortunes were. He was being held without formal charges, and without his spectacles, for no reason other than whom he loved.

Max's father had to be behind his arrest somehow. That thought filtered through the fuzz in Stephen's brain as the first hint of light crept through the single, small window at the back of the cell. Lord Eastleigh had threatened him directly and through Max, and a man of that stature wasn't the sort to make hollow threats. In the midst of the confusion at the factory, he'd assumed Sister Constance had brought the Metropolitan Police officers with her after learning where he and Max had gone through Mrs. Ross. But the more Stephen thought about it, the less likely it seemed that a single nun from an impoverished orphanage in Limehouse would have the power to convince half a dozen police officers to travel all the way to Leicester. Only someone as powerful and well-connected as a duke could do something like that.

A duke would be able to mastermind a vast kidnapping ring capable of transporting children not just out of London, but out of the country entirely. Details of the entire case as he'd discussed it with David and Lionel came back to him. David and Lionel had stopped a ship from departing Batcliff Cross Docks for the orient. It would take a man of extreme power and connection to organize an international trafficking ring. And if English children were being transported abroad for nefarious reasons, it stood to reason that foreign children might have been kidnapped and brought to European shores. They weren't facing simple kidnappings, they were dealing with crime on an international scale.

Only someone as powerful as Lord Eastleigh would be able to pull something like that off.

But how? And what did Lord Eastleigh stand to gain from it all? Was Max's father the highest rung in the ladder they were trying to bring down or could someone even higher be at the top?

Those questions and more were rattling through Stephen's brain, confusing him more and more, when the door from the office banged open and a harried-looking clerk wandered in with a pitcher of water and several heels of bread that looked like it had seen better days. Stephen pushed himself to his feet, feeling every sore muscle and weary bone in his body, as the young man brought the food to the cell and pushed it through the bars.

"I would like to speak to my solicitor," he told the young man as his two cellmates scrambled to claim the bread and water, leaving none for Stephen. "His name is David Wirth of the offices of Dandie & Wirth. Can you help me reach him?"

The young man backed away, his face pale and his eyes wide, shaking his head.

"Please," Stephen appealed to him, desperation clawing at his insides once more. "I desperately need to speak to him about children who have been kidnapped. I believe I know who is behind it all."

The young man turned tail and ran back to the office, slamming the door and leaving Stephen alone with his thoughts and the two thugs imprisoned with him.

"Children been kidnapped?" one of the thugs asked as he chewed the dry bread.

Stephen clenched his jaw, expecting the worst from the man, and turned toward him. "Yes," he said. He couldn't make out the man's features distinctly across the cell, but he looked less hostile than he had the night before. "Children have gone missing all over the city. Yesterday, my colleague and I found dozens of them being put to work forcibly in a cloth mill in Leicestershire."

The two men stopped chewing and stared at him.

"What happened to 'em?" the other man asked.

Stephen rubbed a hand over his face. "I can only hope that Sister Constance and my friend managed to get them all to safety and can return them to their homes."

"Didn't Bob's boy go missing in the spring?" the second man asked the first.

"He did," the first man said. "Good boy he was too. Not the sort to wander off like that."

"With any luck, he was one of the children we rescued," Stephen said on a sigh.

The two men turned to him. "Hold on," the second one said. "If you rescued 'em like you say, what are you doing locked in here with us?"

"I've been asking the same question since last night."

The statement was made by David Wirth as he marched into the room lined with cells, Mrs. Ross and Annie a few steps behind him. Stephen could have wept for joy at the sight of the man, even if he couldn't make out his features clearly.

"Thank God you found me," he said, turning and grabbing the bars.

"You were not easy to find," David said, arching an eyebrow ominously. "We've been checking every jail in London since Max stormed into The Chameleon Club last night. Not even Jack Craig could tell us where you'd been carted off to." He paused, his mouth pulling into a lopsided grin. "Lionel will be green with envy when he learns I found you first based on Jewel's information."

Stephen was certain he'd see the humor in that situation later, but for the time being, he just wanted his freedom. "Can you get me out of here?" he asked, gripping the bars as though he could rip them from the floor.

"No, he cannot," the officer who had arrested him said, striding over to the cell as though he were the cock of the walk. Stephen hadn't noticed him enter the room.

"This man's here on charges of sodomy. He's to be held until further notice."

"Sodomy?" Annie squeaked. Stephen wasn't close enough to make out her expression clearly, but he winced all the same. Of all the times for Annie to finish putting the pieces together, this was the worst.

"By whose authority have these charges been brought?" David asked, rounding on the man.

David succeeded in intimidating the officer where Stephen had failed. "Um...well...I...."

"He's a dolt if ever I saw one," Mrs. Ross added with a sniff.

"Lord Eastleigh has to be behind this," Stephen said, venom in his voice.

He didn't need to say more. David hummed in agreement, but kept his focus on the officer. "How do you intend to prove the charges?" he asked.

"Prove?" The officer squirmed, glancing Stephen's way. He cleared his throat. "Ain't it obvious, sir?"

Under any other circumstances, Stephen would have smirked at the man's imbecility. He clearly had no idea whom he was talking to as he cowered under David's commanding gaze.

The farce was interrupted yet again as Max flew into the room, two new police officers with him. Stephen squinted, but he couldn't make out who the officers were or decide if they were friend or foe.

"I came as soon as I learned where he was being held," Max said, anxious and out of breath. He rushed toward the cell, reaching for Stephen. Even without his spectacles, Stephen could see the ardent concern painting Max's face.

David stepped between the two of them before Max could reach the cell. "Thank you for your concern, Lord Hillsboro," he said, completely businesslike. "Lord Hillsboro here, a viscount, is patron of Mr. Siddel's orphanage," he explained to the snide officer, who was beginning to look less and less certain of things by the moment. "I assume he has come to post bail."

Annie let out a long, painful, "Oh!"

"Yes," Max said, snapping straight and taking a large step back from the cell. He glanced to Annie with what Stephen hoped was a silencing look. Stephen thanked their lucky stars that Max was clever enough to immediately take his lead from David and not let on how attached they were, and that Annie kept her mouth shut. "Whatever the amount, I'll pay it."

"You got that kind of money?" the snide officer asked, glancing between Max and Stephen with narrowed eyes. "Because what I heard is that you're skint at the moment."

Stephen's gut clenched. The officer clearly knew who Max was and the situation he was in. Which meant he knew Lord Eastleigh. It was proof that his thoughts had traveled down the right path after all.

"Who is in charge of this jail?" he demanded, glancing to David in the hope that he could communicate his realizations to the man. "I am being held under false pretenses in order to satisfy a personal vendetta with Lord Eastleigh."

"I knew it," Max growled.

"You are not," the officer protested, his face splashing with color. "You're here because you're a pervert."

"And what if I wasn't?" Stephen asked, grasping at any straw that might help him.

The officer barked a laugh. "You have the nerve to ask me to prove you're not who we all know you are? Well, why don't you prove you aren't?"

Heat flooded Stephen's face and neck. He should have denied the accusation from the start, as much as it would have hurt his pride. The fact that he'd been silent for so long was damning.

"He's not what you say he is," Annie blurted into the awkward silence that followed. All eyes turned on her. She stepped closer to the cell. "Stephen is my fiancé," she insisted. "We're going to be married."

In spite of the madness of the situation, Stephen grinned. God bless Annie Ross for keeping her head about her when everyone else was losing theirs. "Yes," he said, reaching through the bars for her. "My friends have known the truth all along. Annie and I are to be married. We were just waiting for the time to be right."

"I cannot bear to see you shut away like this, my love," Annie squeaked, rushing the rest of the way to the cell.

Her arms were thin enough that she was able to reach straight through the bars to wrap her arms around him.

She leaned her head against the bars for a moment as she hugged him, then glanced up at him. There was enough heartbreak in her big, round eyes to melt Stephen's heart. She'd finally figured out that she would never get her wish of the two of them being together.

"You are the bravest person I have ever known," he whispered, bringing his face as close to hers as he could. "And you know that if I were able to, I would marry you in an instant."

Annie nodded, her eyes going glassy with tears that brought a lump to Stephen's throat.

"Enough of this nonsense," the snide officer huffed. "I'm under orders to keep this one locked up until...." The man didn't seem to know how to finish his sentence.

"Until when?" David took an intimidating step toward him. "Until your master told you to let him go? Until you were paid off? How do you think your real bosses in the Met Police would react if they knew you were abusing your power to hold innocent men captive?"

"I...I've done no such thing," the officer protested, though it was clear he was on the back foot now.

"Can you prove it?" David demanded, keeping the heat turned up and backing the officer away from the cell and toward the office. "Should I call my friend, Assistant Commissioner Jack Craig, here to settle the matter?"

The officer squealed and stammered, "N-no, sir."

"Then I suggest you release Mr. Siddel at once."

"But he's...." The officer flung his arm toward Stephen, glancing to Max.

Stephen snaked his arms through the bars in an attempt to hug Annie in return. He peeked at Max, who kept his expression carefully neutral. Stephen could feel that Max was fully on board with the ruse, which made it easier for him to commit to it.

"I ask you." David turned to the two policemen who had come in with Max. "Does this man look like the sort of criminal Officer Corrupt says he is?"

"No, sir," one of the policemen answered immediately.

"Not at all," the other agreed, then added, "I've got a mate whose sister died. Mr. Siddel's orphanage took in her girl when no one else in the family would. He's a saint, that one." He nodded to Stephen.

Stephen could have shouted in victory at the sudden twist of good luck.

"He is a saint," Annie said, breaking away from him and turning to stand with her back against the bars, as if she were protecting him. "He's my saint."

"That settles it," David said. "Unlock this cell at once."

The snide officer was forced to do as David said, though when he came close and unlocked the door, he glared at Stephen as though the whole thing were far from over. "You'd better watch your back," the man growled.

"I don't need to watch my back," Stephen muttered in return. "I've got plenty of people watching it for me. People your boss can't touch. You tell him that. Tell him that we're coming for him now and he will be held accountable for what he's done."

The officer looked horrified at the prospect of being the one to deliver that message. Stephen hoped the bastard got everything he feared might be coming to him for being the bearer of bad news.

As soon as the cell door was open, Stephen leapt out, charging right for the front office. "We need to get to the orphanage as soon as possible. We have to see to the safety of the girls before—"

Mrs. Ross stopped him as they all spilled into the front office. "It's not there," she said, her face lined with exhaustion and misery—something Stephen was only just seeing, now that he stood close enough to see her clearly.

"What do you mean, it's not there?" Deep foreboding filled him.

"There was a fire," Max said, stepping up to his side and taking his arm as if he knew Stephen would need steadying. "In the middle of the night. The whole thing burnt to the ground."

Stephen could suddenly smell it—a faint hint of smoke and soot that infused the air around Max, Mrs. Ross, and Annie. Whatever resistance Stephen had to the idea of embracing Max fully as a friend, lover, and partner vanished as it became obvious Max had been there for the fire, had possibly saved precious lives. If not for Max's support, Stephen would have collapsed. "The girls," he said, dreading the answer. "What about the girls?"

"They're all safe," David told him, rushing their group through the office and out to the street. "Max came to me as soon as he returned from Leicestershire. He told me all about the threats his father made and what happened at Gretton Mills."

"I knew my father would retaliate swiftly," Max continued the story. "Sister Constance was the one who suggested getting all of the girls out of the orphanage and moving them to the Sisters of Perpetual Sorrow as fast as possible. When the arsonists arrived, the building was empty but for the three of us." He nodded to Mrs. Ross and Annie.

"We saved as much as we could before...." Mrs. Ross burst into a sob.

"So none of the girls were hurt?" Stephen asked, his voice weak and rough.

"Not a hair on any of their heads," David said, giving Stephen a reassuring pat on the back before pushing him into a carriage that was waiting on the curb. "The building is a loss, though. But unless I'm mistaken, it was insured."

"Insured?" Stephen's head spun as they all squeezed into the carriage.

"I took the liberty of insuring my investment almost immediately after it was made," Max said with a broad grin, grasping Stephen's hand once they were seated side-by-side and twining their fingers together.

"But why?" Stephen asked.

"Because I know my father," Max answered grimly.

It was all the answer he gave, all the answer Stephen needed. Buildings were mere afterthoughts. As long as his girls were all safe, he could consider it a victory over Lord Eastleigh. "Where are we going to go?" he asked his next thought aloud.

"Don't worry," David said with a triumphant grin. "The Brotherhood has that covered."

Stephen could only imagine what the man meant. He was grateful to The Brotherhood in more ways than he could count and eager to discover what they would do next.

CHAPTER 21

ne month later…

GIGGLES AND SCREAMS RANG THROUGH THE HALLS of the newly-relocated Briar Street Orphanage. Stephen glanced up from the seemingly endless paperwork connected to his insurance claim on the old, Briar Street building and the purchase of the new property in Earl's Court. Not that he needed to worry about their new home in the least. The property was one of many owned by Mr. Daniel Long, and the man was selling it for a song. He'd allowed Stephen, Max, and the girls, along with Mrs. Ross and Annie, to move in immediately, well before the sale was final. The building also had the advantage of being located in a square where nearly every house was owned or occupied by members of The Brotherhood.

Lord Eastleigh could try his best to rain terror down on Stephen and Max for what he saw as defiance of his supreme authority, but they and the girls were protected in ways the bastard couldn't imagine.

Another giddy shriek kept Stephen from returning to his work, and the smiling, rosy-cheeked figure of Jane streaked past the door to his office. Stephen caught a flash of something shiny in her hands.

"Jane, sweetheart, for the last time, please don't run with scissors," Max called out, dashing past Stephen's doorway in chase of her.

Stephen grinned before he could stop himself, his heart feeling far too large for his chest. Jane was home and happy. She still had nightmares, and Stephen suspected she would have them for the rest of her life, but he was confident she felt safe under his roof. Under his and Max's roof. There had been no question at all that Max would move into the new Briar Street Orphanage, move into a room and a bed with Stephen as well. Not even Annie had questioned that when the arrangements were made.

Stephen stood, tossing his pen on the unfinished paperwork, and walking around the corner of the desk to the hall to see what the commotion was. The new orphanage was slightly larger than the old one, but it felt more crowded and noisier than the old one ever had. That was due, in part, to the constant stream of visitors, several of whom were gathered in the great hall, enjoying supper with the girls.

"Sir, look, look!" Beatrice leapt up from the table nearest to the door as Stephen entered the room. Instead of two, long tables, the new great hall contained a dozen round tables, most of which were draped with crisp cloths and adorned with flowers—gifts from Mr. Nigel Merriweather, who owned a flower shop on Cromwell Road. "Mr. Tarleton taught me how to style my hair like the ladies at the opera."

Stephen couldn't keep his smile in check. Beatrice's mass of brown hair was piled artfully atop her head. James Tarleton applauded as Beatrice spun once to give Stephen the full impression. If anyone was qualified to teach Beatrice how to style her hair, it was Tarleton, who regularly styled his own hair, or at least a wig, in a similar fashion when he performed as a supernumerary at the Royal Opera House.

"Oh, Sir, you must see this," Ginny flagged Stephen down from a table deeper into the room. "Mr. Cristofori is helping me write a play."

"Is that so?" Stephen gave Beatrice an encouraging squeeze of her shoulder before moving on to see what Ginny and the renowned playwright, Niall Cristofori, were working on.

"I hope you don't mind," Cristofori said with an apologetic look as Stephen reached their table. "Most fathers wouldn't approve of their impressionable young daughters developing an interest in any aspect of the theater."

Stephen laughed aloud. "Look around," he said, glancing across the room himself. "I think the list of things most fathers would disapprove of that are considered normal here is pretty long."

In fact, the orphanage had become the pet project of more than a few of the members of The Brotherhood who lived on the square. A constant parade of guests were in and out of the house all day, bringing gifts of food, clothing, and toys, offering to teach classes, and bringing as much love and affection to the girls as it was clear the men desperately needed themselves. They were all outcasts, whether they were unwanted orphans or society's castaways. It filled Stephen with immense pride to see all the ways his girls and the community around them were able to help each other. And the more men there were in the house, men with a vested interest in the girls' well-being, the greater the protection his girls would have.

"Mr. Siddel, there you are," Annie said, glancing up from the rectangular table at the front of the room, where the adults took their meals. "You haven't eaten supper yet. I've tried to keep it warm for you."

"You're too kind, Annie." Stephen nodded to Cristofori and started toward the head table, a slight blush heating his face. In spite of Annie apologizing for being such a fool where he was concerned after the incident at the jail and her insistence that she didn't have any lingering feelings for him, Stephen continued to feel awkward around the young woman. Perhaps it was because she never quite looked him in the eye anymore and seemed a little sad when he and Max were at their happiest together.

"That kind Mr. Arnold brought us four simply gigantic geese," Annie went on, ushering him to his spot at the table. "I would say they'd feed us for a week, but he insisted that he'd bring us an entire suckling pig on Sunday and that we shouldn't try to ration out the geese. Can you imagine?"

Stephen took his seat at the table with a laugh. "It seems the Briar Street Orphanage has gone from having to sing for our supper to having more patrons than we know what to do with."

"I'll say." Annie removed a covering from the plate in front of Stephen and poured him a glass of weak ale from the pitcher on the table. "It's the most curious thing I've ever seen. Although I'd be lying if I said I wasn't just a bit concerned about all these men spending so much time with our girls," she added in a quiet, suspicious voice.

Stephen laughed as he took up his cutlery. "Believe me, there is no danger at all in having them here. We're much safer for it."

Annie hummed in thought and moved away, beginning to clear the places of the girls who had finished their meals and were completing the last of their schoolwork or entertaining their guests. A young man who Stephen knew for a fact had escaped a pitiful life of prostitution on London's docks jumped up to help her clear. Stephen was considering hiring the man full-time, but wanted to consult with Max first.

He made it halfway through his meal before Jane came flying into the room, still giggling and wielding scissors, Max still chasing her.

"Jane, for the love of—" Max finally caught her, scooping an arm around her waist and lifting her into the air. He pried the scissors from her hand and continued carrying her all the way up to the table where Stephen sat. "I'm not sure whether to set this one up as an apprentice to a butcher or a seamstress, or to send her off to darkest Africa to fight the Boers," he told Stephen.

"Oh, let me fight the Boers," Jane gasped and wriggled out of Max's arms, landing on her feet. "I would make such a good soldier."

"I believe you would," Stephen told her with a smile. "But until you prove that you can behave and keep yourself safe by not running with scissors, you are forbidden from handling any sharp objects for a month."

"Oh." Jane deflated, her shoulders sagging. "What am I supposed to do, then?"

"Eat your supper, for one," Max told her. "Everyone else is already finished."

"But eat it with a spoon," Stephen called after her as she slunk her way to the one table where girls were still eating. Annie left what she was doing to make sure Jane was served.

Max grinned after her for a moment before walking

around the table to take a seat next to Stephen. "If you had told me two months ago that I would be chasing rapscallion orphan girls through undoubtedly the most unconventional orphanage in all of London, stopping them from doing themselves harm by running with scissors, I never would have believed you." He reached for Stephen's hand as he scooted his chair in, squeezing it briefly before removing the lid Annie had placed over his plate.

"If you had told me I'd be sitting down to supper with the man I love and gazing adoringly at him without anyone in the overcrowded room thinking twice about it, I never would have believed you either," Stephen said.

Max glanced at him, and Stephen treated him to his most adoring look to prove his point. He must have looked as treacly as he felt, because Max burst into a chuckle. He then leaned in and stole a kiss from Stephen's lips.

"Take that, Father," Max said with a wink before returning to his food.

The statement of defiance sobered Stephen, and he sat straighter. "Is he still spreading the rumor about town that we've run off together to live in sin?"

"Of course," Max answered before taking a bite of goose. "And he and George are still parading around as though they are morally superior in every way, in spite of Lady Bardess naming the two of them in connection to the Manchester brothel."

Stephen snorted in disgust. In spite of the fact that

they'd rescued nearly three dozen young people from slave labor at Gretton Mills, and in spite of the connection that had been uncovered with a brothel in Manchester, absolutely nothing had been done to take action against the noblemen that Stephen and Max knew were involved. Lesser men had been blamed—the manager of Gretton Mills, for one. And even though Lady Bardess had cracked under pressure and named her father and brother, along with Max's father and brother, as accomplices in the kidnapping ring, she had been declared mentally unfit and sent away to live with relatives in Italy as a rest cure.

The injustice of it all rankled at Stephen, putting him off the rest of his supper. He threw his fork down and leaned back in his chair to rub his hands over his face, knocking his spectacles askew. The one good thing that had come out of the entire fiasco—aside from the new and decidedly better orphanage and its neighbors—was Stephen's new pair of spectacles. They were a surprising improvement over his old pair and allowed him to see things much more clearly. It was a blatant metaphor for his improved grasp of the situation they all found themselves in.

Max stopped eating for a moment to grasp Stephen's hand once he rested it on the table. "Rome wasn't built in a day," he said. "Yes, the bastards got away for the time being, but their days are numbered."

"I pray you're right," Stephen said, twisting his hand in Max's so that he could thread their fingers together.

"With so many people working on the investigation, they're bound to be caught in time."

"Precisely," Max said, attempting to continue eating with one hand. "David's sent a man to the continent to find Joe Logan and to ask him what his sister meant by 'the man with the lion', after all."

Stephen's pulse sped. As soon as Max had told him about the girl, Lily, and her message, David had known exactly who Lily was. Apparently, Joe Logan had been searching for his sister for almost a year, which was troubling in itself. Stephen couldn't shake the image of the girl and the certain knowledge of her fate from his mind. She hadn't been at the Manchester brothel when it was raided and shut down. He only hoped they would be able to find her again and break the ring as soon as possible.

"You're doing everything you can do," Max reminded him. "And you're not doing it alone anymore."

Stephen smiled at him, his heart warming and filling him with the deepest affection he'd ever known. "Your father gave me the greatest gift imaginable by disowning you," he said, raising Max's hand to his lips to kiss it.

Max barked a laugh. "Not the result he was hoping for, I'm sure."

"No." Stephen laughed along with him, letting go of Max's hand and returning to his supper.

He was close to finished when the entire room suddenly erupted into a flurry of excitement. Girls leapt up from their seats and rushed to the great hall's door.

Stephen could see in an instant what had his girls squealing for joy. Lionel Mercer had entered the room.

"Hello, my lovely little hellions," he announced himself in a loud and cheerful voice. "Don't you all look beautiful and devilish tonight."

Stephen rolled his eyes and sent a sideways grin to Max.

Max put down his fork and shook his head, muttering an oath under his breath before saying, "That man is worse than Everett Jewel when he has the right audience."

"I suspect Lionel is attempting to outdo Jewel when it comes to adoring admirers," Stephen laughed.

"What did I bring for you all this evening?" Lionel went on, reaching into the small, purple velvet sack he carried with him as David stepped around him, shaking his head, and strode toward Stephen and Max at the front of the room. Lionel drew a fistful of brightly-colored lollipops from the sack with a flourish and a, "Ta da!"

The girls burst into shouts of delight, giggling and falling all over themselves in their efforts to be the first to snatch one from Lionel's hands. Lionel, for his part, beamed as if he were Father Christmas—albeit Father Christmas dressed in an impeccably-tailored mauve suite without a hair out of place—as he handed them out and accepted hugs as payment.

"I'm convinced he only comes here to bask in the glow of his adoring public," David said as he reached the table. He turned to lean against it and watch Lionel, arms crossed. He could pretend impatience with Lionel all he wanted, but there was a little too much enjoyment in his eyes and a shade too much pink to his cheeks.

"The girls do adore him," Stephen pointed out. He abandoned the rest of his supper to walk around the table and stand by David's side. Max shoved a last few mouthfuls down, then got up to join them.

"I never would have guessed it, but Lionel is a natural with children," Max said.

"That's because he's still a child at heart, no matter how adult most of his life has been," David said, a fair amount of wistfulness in his voice.

"What are you doing, you daft man?" Mrs. Ross shouted at Lionel as she entered the great hall, still wearing the apron that indicated she'd been busy in the kitchen with the new cook and maid they'd hired. "What sort of fool gives children sweets right before bedtime?"

"The very best kind," Ursula chirped as she took a particularly big lolly from Lionel.

"There you have it." Lionel grinned at Mrs. Ross. "I am the very best kind of fool."

A few of the girls who were old enough to grasp his joke laughed. The younger ones beamed at him. Ursula latched herself to his side, looking as though she had no intention of letting go.

"Well, on your head be it," Mrs. Ross scolded. "And as punishment for riling them up at such a late hour, I am charging you with reading them a bedtime story."

The girls rippled with excitement all over again.

"Yes, please, Lionel."

"Read us a fairy tale."

"You do the best voices."

The girls jumped up and down in their excitement. Several of the gentlemen guests laughed and looked just as excited about the prospect of being tucked into bed by Lionel.

"Very well," Lionel said as though they'd twisted his arm, though it was clear he'd come for a visit at such a late hour expressly so he could read to the girls. "But only after you're all scrubbed and in your nightgowns and ready for bed."

The girls leapt into action as fast as if it were a race and Lionel had fired the starter's pistol. They rushed from the room, each one trying to beat the others up the stairs to the dormitories. Their footsteps were thunderous on the stairs even from the great hall. Lionel nodded toward Stephen and Max before following them. As he left, the majority of the gentlemen guests got up to head home as well, though a few stayed behind to help clean up.

"It baffles me how popular this place has become," Stephen said, leaning against the table. When Max slid up next to him, Stephen rested an arm around his back as casual as could be.

David shrugged. "You should know as well as anyone how starved for affection our kind can be. It was no accident I suggested you reopen the orphanage here. These men need it."

Stephen hummed sagely, his confidence growing as David confirmed the very thoughts he'd been having earlier.

A moment later, that confidence hardened into business as David's expression darkened.

"We've located Joe and Alistair on the continent," David said. "They were in Spain, but they're on their way home now."

"Any word on who the man with the lion is or what that even means?" Max asked, tensing as he leaned into Stephen's side.

David shook his head, rubbing his chin. "Jewel claims he knows, or thinks he knows. He says it's only a matter of time before he finds what he's looking for."

"And what is he looking for?" Stephen asked.

David let out an irritated breath. "He won't say." He paused, then added, "Lionel might be on to something when it comes to Jewel's penchant for dramatics and self-aggrandizement."

"He is an actor, after all," Max agreed.

"He's also one of the cleverest people I know," David said. "When he applies himself."

Stephen knew exactly what he was talking about. In his ten years of raising and teaching young children, he'd encountered more than a few who were stunningly brilliant but lacked the ability to focus, and who were therefore considered stupid by those who didn't know better.

"What about my father?" Max asked. "Has he made any moves lately?"

"None that we can detect," David said, shaking his head. "But something is clearly afoot. The number of reported kidnappings has remained steady instead of going down, as we had hoped it would after Gretton Mills. Which means the ring is still active."

"Are Sister Constance and her children safe?" Stephen asked, troubled at the mere idea that they wouldn't be.

David sighed again. "She refuses to let us relocate her orphanage. Though if you ask me, it's the Church that doesn't want to relocate, not her. I'll give the woman this much, she's loyal to the things she believes in."

"She always has been," Stephen agreed.

"At least we've got a team of men guarding her orphanage night and day." David paused. "I was honestly surprised by how many men volunteered for that duty."

"I'm not," Max said. When Stephen and David both looked at him, he went on with, "Who would say no when given the opportunity to finally stand up and do something to protect those who are being unfairly mistreated? Standing up for them is standing up for ourselves, the same as any of the fellows who spend their time braiding hair, doing lessons, and reading stories to the girls here. We can finally do something instead of feeling impotent."

"Well said." Stephen rested a hand on Max's shoulder, his heart swelling with affection.

Max glanced to him with a fire in his eyes that was

anything but impotent. It stirred Stephen in every sort of delicious way.

"With that," David said, standing straight, mischief in his eyes. "I'd better go see what new trouble Lionel is getting himself into." He winked at Stephen and Max, then turned and strode out of the great hall.

"Oh, Mr. Wirth, I've been meaning to ask you about...about something legal." Annie jumped away from the table she was clearing to walk by David's side. She stared at him with the same starry expression she'd always worn with Stephen, clearly besotted. "Seeing as you're so smart and handsome and commanding and all," she finished, her face going pink as the two of them turned the corner and left the great hall.

"God preserve us," Stephen said, shaking his head. "And here I thought the poor thing had learned the ways of the world."

"Not enough, or so it would seem," Max laughed. "She's such a dear thing."

"A little too dear sometimes." Stephen sent him a soft look. "If only there were a man in her life whom she could really love." He slid his hand into Max's

Max grinned at their entwined fingers. "I think it's about time the two of us put ourselves to bed as well," he said in a low voice, leaning close to Stephen's ear.

Stephen blushed in spite of himself, doubly when Max let go of his hand to stroke his thigh. "With the house so full of people?" he asked, his breath catching in his throat as Max's hand ventured into tempting territory.

"What better time?" Max asked in a whisper. "Everyone will be distracted."

"Good point."

Stephen pushed away from the table, taking Max's hand as he cut his way through the empty tables and the discarded dishes and projects they held.

Unlike his bedroom in the old orphanage, Stephen had chosen a room for him and Max on the second floor, at the front of the house. It was far enough from the dormitories and Mrs. Ross and Annie's room that they could carry on without fear of disturbing anyone, but close enough to the stairs and the front of the house that they would always have a clear line of sight for everything going on in the building. They heard Lionel reading aloud in a colorful voice on the first floor as they slipped up, but thankfully, no one saw them pass.

As soon as their bedroom door was shut, Max pivoted to press Stephen's back against the door, turning the lock with one hand and planting the other beside Stephen's head. "I've been waiting all day to get you alone," he said in a tempting voice, staring at Stephen's lips for a moment before leaning in to kiss him.

It was heaven to be able to give in to his love for Max so easily. Stephen made quick work of the buttons of Max's waistcoat, glad he wasn't wearing a jacket, since they were at home, and tugged his shirt out of his trousers. He let out a sound of satisfaction as he smoothed his hands along the lean lines of Max's sides, loving the feel of his skin. Max growled in approval and went straight to unfastening Stephen's trousers as their mouths continued to meld together. In the relatively short time they'd been together, they'd managed to learn exactly what the other liked while still feeling the flames as though they were new.

"We must be the luckiest men in London," Stephen sighed as the intensity of their efforts to undress each other increased. He pushed away from the door, backing Max toward the bed even as they both shed clothes.

"Because we found each other at precisely the right moment?" Max asked as the back of his legs bumped against the side of the bed.

"Because we found a way to be together, in spite of your father's threats and society's judgements," Stephen said. He pushed Max just enough to send him spilling across the bed, then bent to lift one of his legs so that he could untie Max's shoes.

"I doubt society or the law would turn a blind eye if they took a closer look at this orphanage," Max said, chuckling in spite of his seriousness. He wriggled out of his suspenders and pulled off his shirt as Stephen removed his other shoe.

"We've the same protection that we've always had," Stephen reasoned, bending to take off his own shoes once Max's were taken care of. "Ignorance is bliss. And I have faith in The Brotherhood and the men of this neighborhood to keep everyone around us in the dark."

"It's amazing how discreet even the biggest queens can be when discretion is the difference between life and death," Max agreed. He unfastened his trousers and kicked them off, leaving him gloriously naked and waiting for Stephen, his cock already hard. "Once we help David and Lionel defeat this horrific trafficking ring, I dare say we'll have the most charmed life anyone of our kind has ever had the luck to live."

The need that pulsed through Stephen as he tore off the rest of his clothes while gazing hungrily at Max's waiting body made the seriousness of Max's statement ring discordantly in his head. "I don't want to think about the darkness," he said climbing onto the bed and balancing himself over top of Max. "I know it's there, but when I'm with you like this, I can't think of anything but how good you taste and how much it drives me wild to be inside you."

"God, you're irresistible when you're worked up," Max sighed. He plucked the spectacles from Stephen's face and reached to set them on the bedside table before grabbing Stephen's face and bringing it down for a kiss.

They'd learned so much about each other in the short months they'd been together, but Stephen was eager to learn more. He raked his hands along Max's body, his breath catching at the heat of his skin and the firmness of his muscles. Max couldn't seem to get enough of him either. Their hands were greedy as they explored each other. Stephen broke away from Max's mouth to kiss his way across his neck and shoulder. He'd intended to travel as far south as he could and to sheathe Max's cock deep in his mouth, but already he could sense that Max wouldn't last that long.

"If I had known you were so hungry for this I would have skipped supper altogether," he laughed, shifting to the side so that he could open the drawer in his bedside table and take out the jar of ointment they kept there.

Max pushed to his knees as well, plucking the jar from Stephen's hands with a glint in his eyes. "If I had known it would be so easy to convince you to go to bed early tonight I would have lured you up here earlier."

Max slipped an arm around Stephen's waist and leaned in for a searing kiss. He was commanding and passionate, leaving Stephen in no doubt of what he wanted that evening. And Stephen was all too happy to give it to him. That in itself surprised him. Max had broken through every protective wall he'd put up over the years, in spite of his resistance, and proved that he was devoted and true. Nothing Stephen could possibly imagine was as arousing as Max's faithfulness.

"Remember," Max said with a teasing grin as he unscrewed the lid of the jar and helped himself to a generous amount of its contents. "Lionel is just downstairs, and if anyone in London is capable of hearing and distinguishing the slightest sounds, it's him."

"Are you warning me not to scream?" Stephen asked coyly over his shoulder as he bent forward, drawing a thick pillow to his stomach for balance. "Because I can't promise anything."

"Minx," Max laughed, then brushed his fingers over the cleft of Stephen's arse.

The jolt of cool ointment against his hot flesh had Stephen sucking in a breath in anticipation. Max moved closer, stroking and spreading him in preparation. He reached around Stephen's side to close a hand around his cock, working him with an insistence that had Stephen sighing with pleasure and arching his hips for more. It was one thing to take the lead with Max when they were together, but opening himself up that way, surrendering all of his desperately needed control, all because he loved Max beyond anything he would have imagined was possible, meant the world to him.

"You are irresistible," Max sighed, repositioning himself. He leaned forward to kiss Stephen's shoulder before driving himself home.

Stephen let out a long, low moan of pleasure, adjusting his body to accommodate Max's delicious invasion. Some men needed a lifetime to learn how to be with another in a way that brought the most pleasure to them both, but he and Max had found their rhythm astoundingly fast. Their joining was erotic and emotional, and so pleasurable it blurred Stephen's vision. Max knew just how to thrust in him to hit the perfect spot, heightening his pleasure to an unbelievable degree.

Max's thrusts sped up quickly, and Stephen knew he wasn't going to last long. He wanted more than anything to fly into oblivion along with Max, so he grabbed Max's hand and brought it to his aching cock, their fingers entwined. It was exactly what he needed to speed toward the edge himself, and as Max's heavy breaths turned into desperate gasps of pleasure, and then a long, sharp cry, Stephen let himself go as well. The pleasure that shot through him, sending his seed spilling across their joined hands and the sheets, was too much for him to keep silent, as Max had warned. He cried out for joy, feeling as though his soul and Max's were one.

Exhaustion overtook both of them, and within seconds they'd collapsed and rolled into each other's arms, overheated, sweaty, and panting.

"You are my everything," Stephen said, stroking Max's damp, curling hair away from his forehead.

"I'm the luckiest man alive," Max sighed, lifting his leg over Stephen's hip and snuggling closer to him. "And I swear, I will stand by you for the rest of our lives, no matter what is thrown our way."

Stephen kissed him with all the ardor in his heart that words simply couldn't express. They would be together forever, and together, they would be strong enough to defeat even the most daunting of foes.

EPILOGUE

David Wirth paced the length of his office, his mind whirring with all of the new developments that had happened in the kidnapping ring in the last few weeks. Two groups of children had been rescued, but reports of even more going missing kept pouring in. He felt as though he were the proverbial Dutch boy, attempting to plug more and more holes in a dam and running out of hands.

The worst part was that they knew exactly who was involved in the ring, but those men were untouchable. He wanted to kick the waste bin sitting at the corner of his desk as he paced out of sheer frustration. Men like Lord Chisolm and Lord Eastleigh believed they could get away with murder, because more often than not, they could.

"There has to be a way to expose them and bring them to justice," he grumbled to himself as he turned at the far corner of his room and started back again.

"There are plenty of ways to expose men like that," Lionel said from the doorway. "If you're willing to pay the price of bringing them down."

David jumped. He hadn't noticed Lionel sauntering into the doorway. The way Lionel leaned against the frame, arms crossed, watching David with an otherworldly fire in his eyes was unnerving, to say the least. Lionel's stance said he'd been watching for a while, and his eyes said he'd enjoyed what he was seeing a little too much.

"Good men shouldn't have to sacrifice anything to bring down evil," David muttered, continuing his pacing. "Justice should triumph over fortune and title."

"Should," Lionel agreed with a nod of his head. "But you and I both know it rarely happens that way."

David huffed a humorless laugh. "I still don't believe either Chisolm or Eastleigh are the masterminds behind this whole thing," he said. "Deeply involved, yes. Financing the ring's activity, also yes. But masterminding it?" He shook his head. "Someone higher must be involved."

"Higher than a duke?" Lionel arched a perfectly-manicured eyebrow and whistled.

"Perhaps not in rank," David went on, scowling as he racked his brain for answers. "There's always an inner hierarchy in circles like that one."

"Just like there is an inner hierarchy in The Brotherhood?" Lionel suggested.

David sent a wry grin his way. They both knew

exactly how that particular hierarchy stood. "Whoever is at the top might not be a duke or higher."

"They might even be the son of lower level gentry." Lionel smirked, buffing his nails against the lapels of his midnight blue suit jacket.

David laughed. "You're adorable when you give yourself delusions of grandeur."

"And how would you know that they're delusions?" Lionel straightened in mock offense.

"You're precious, darling, but not to that degree," David said with a grin.

"I'll let you continue to believe that, if you'd like." Lionel pushed away from the doorway, stepping into the path of David's pacing. David was inches away from him, their eyes locked and their lips just a breath away before he was aware of it. "Seeing as I like you and all," Lionel finished in a low purr.

A swooping rush filled David's gut and tightened his groin. Lionel stared at him as if daring him to lean in for a kiss. David stared right back, refusing to give in. It was a battle of wills they'd fought before and would fight again and again until one of them buckled.

The sound of the outer office door opening and closing cut through the vibrating tension between them.

"Hello?" a deep voice asked from the main room.

Lionel turned toward the door, keeping his eyes locked on David's until the very last moment. He broke away, strode into the main part of the office, and said, "Why, hello, Officer Wrexham."

David sucked in a breath, fighting to compose himself. Patrick Wrexham was exactly the man he needed to speak with, but he would trip all over himself and stammer like an idiot if he didn't shake off the spell Lionel had come so close to putting him under.

"Is David in?" Wrexham asked as David rolled his shoulders and took a few more deep breaths in preparation for greeting him. "He'll want to hear what I've uncovered."

That was enough to ground David firmly in the issue at hand once more. "What have you uncovered?" he asked, striding into the main part of the office.

Lionel was already fixing tea for Wrexham as though nothing at all were out of the ordinary. Wrexham's shoulders relaxed and his worried expression turned more confident as he stepped around one of the room's sofas to shake David's hand.

"I've had reports that Chisolm is back in England," Wrexham said. "Though I haven't been able to locate exactly where he is yet."

"That's more than we knew about the man yesterday," David said, encouraged by the news. "By any chance have Joe Logan and Alistair Bevan returned as well?"

"Not yet," Lionel answered, bringing a steaming cup of tea to Wrexham. "It seems there were some difficulties along the border between France and Spain."

David could only imagine what those were. "If they can't get home that way, they need to find another," he said. "The sooner we talk to Joe about his sister, the sooner we'll be able to unravel another part of this mystery."

"About the man with the lion?" Wrexham asked.

"Precisely." David nodded. "I can't help but think that the man with the lion, whoever or whatever that is, holds the key to unraveling this whole thing."

"And nobody else has a clue who the man with the lion is?" Wrexham asked.

"Nobody," Lionel answered, brow furrowed in frustration.

"That's not true." They all snapped to face the door as Everett Jewel swept into the room, making an entrance as grand as any he might make on the stage. "I know who the man with the lion is."

I hope you've enjoyed Stephen and Max's story! I have to confess that the character of Stephen is, in part, based on one of my teachers when I was about Jane's age. It was a terrible time in my life, my parents had just divorced, my beloved grandfather had died, everything was a mess, and by some wonderful stroke of destiny, I was assigned to this man's class. The kindness and care he showed me helped me through an impossibly painful time. It was only years later that he came out, but he is one of the reasons that I find gay men to be such a comfort and why they make me feel safe.

. . .

But I bet you're dying to know how the hunt for the masterminds behind the kidnapping ring continues! What insider information has superstar Everett Jewel uncovered, what are his connections to the underworld, and what deeper pain is he hiding? Will he and Officer Patrick Wrexham be able to get to the bottom of things, or will the irresistible attraction between them cause more problems than it solves? And where does Lionel Mercer fall into this equation? Find out soon in *Just a Little Danger*, available for pre-order now! Keep clicking to get started reading Chapter One...

If you enjoyed this book and would like to hear more from me, please sign up for my newsletter! When you sign up, you'll get a free, full-length novella, *A Passionate Deception*. Victorian identity theft has never been so exciting in this story of hope, tricks, and starting over. Part of my *West Meets East* series, *A Passionate Deception* can be read as a stand-alone. Pick up your free copy today by signing up to receive my newsletter (which I only send out when I have a new release)!

Sign up here: http://eepurl.com/cbaVMH

. . .

Are you on social media? I am! Come and join the fun on Facebook: http://www.facebook.com/merryfarmerreaders

I'm also a huge fan of Instagram and post lots of original content there: https://www.instagram.com/merryfarmer/

AND NOW, GET STARTED ON JUST A LITTLE DANGER...

Chapter One

London – May, 1890

London in the summer was one of the most miserable places Metropolitan Police officer Patrick Wrexham could think to be, but it was where he, and countless others, were forced to stay while the loftier members of British society, the toffs and the nobs, buggered off to the country for the summer. There were still a few weeks of balmier weather to go before the heat and the stink set in, but as Patrick strode from Whitehall, across Trafalgar Square, and on to The City, he spotted more than a few carriages laden with baggage carrying relieved ladies away from the most miserable place on earth.

It was just his luck that the most miserable place on earth was his home, and had been for his whole life. Though that didn't mean that a single soul who he passed on his journey knew who he was. His fellow pedestrians barely saw him, in spite of his crisp, clean uniform. Few men bothered to step out of his way, in spite of his burly build and above average height. Patrick stepped out of their way instead, wanting nothing more than to reach his destination as quickly as possible without drawing attention.

The sooner he reached the law offices of Dandie & Wirth, the better. For the last few weeks, Patrick had been involved with the indomitable team of David Wirth and Lionel Mercer as they investigated a child kidnapping and human trafficking ring. The very thought of the ring turned Patrick's stomach and had him clenching his jaw. It was horrific enough that anyone would kidnap children and sell them into slavery, both at home and abroad, if the information David and Lionel had been able to collect was right. It was worse that the kidnappers preyed on the poorest strata of society, children who no one cared about and whose lives were miserable enough already. Patrick knew that kind of misery all too well. It had been a part of him for as long as he could remember.

He rested a hand instinctively on the small pouch

attached to his belt, as if it contained a hoard of precious jewels. In fact, it held half a sausage and a heel of bread, but as far as Patrick was concerned, that was worth more than the crown jewels. He knew what it was like to be a starving child, so desperate for the tiniest morsel of food that he would have done anything, gone with anyone, just to ease the gnawing in his belly. He had no doubt that whoever was luring the most vulnerable children of London into a life of horror barely had to lift a finger to carry out their evil deeds. The callousness of the kidnappers made their deeds even blacker in Patrick's mind.

The worst part of all was that the more information had been uncovered about the kidnapping ring—by David and Lionel, but also by orphanage owner Stephen Siddel and his partner, Lord Hillsboro, with help from Lord Alistair Farnham and his valet, Joe Logan, whose sister, Lily, was one of the children who had been taken—the more apparent it was that the ringleaders of the entire, sordid operation were noblemen. Not just any noblemen, but those with titles that put set them far above even their peers.

In short, the men responsible for the destruction of young and innocent lives were untouchable. All the same, Patrick was determined to bring them to justice.

Whether it was the inner heat of his fury or the way his thoughts had him scowling like a dragon about to breathe fire, more than a few of his fellow pedestrians suddenly seemed to notice him and jump out of his way. A pair of well-born ladies even gasped and dashed quickly to the other side of the street as though he would eat them alive. Their reaction only depressed Patrick, dampening his fierce expression as he walked on. The ladies likely feared for their virtue in the face of a man of his size, but they had less than nothing to worry about. Patrick had never been interested in women of any sort a day in his life, aside from having them as friend. If growing up in the orphanage hadn't destroyed any possibility of him trusting another soul, he would have banded together with the gang of older girls who always seemed to get the better of the tyrants who ran the place. But no, he'd learned early on it was better to trust no one and to fend for himself.

He reached for his pouch of food once again, then jerked his hand away as soon as he realized what he'd done. Shame twisted his gut. He had to remind himself that he had a steady job making decent money, that he hadn't gone hungry for years, and that even if something catastrophic did happen to him, he could rely on The Brotherhood to help him out. Not that he could ever bring himself to set foot inside The Chameleon Club—the central social location of most Brotherhood activity—let alone ask anyone for help. It was a miracle he'd let David Wirth convince him to join The Brotherhood in the first place. The organization was for men who loved other men. Patrick didn't consider himself capable of loving anyone.

He was saved from the downward spiral of his thoughts as he reached the building that housed the law offices of Dandie & Wirth. Concentrating on vile kidnappers and corrupters of the innocent was far more palatable to him than dwelling on the darkness in his own soul.

The main room of the office was empty when he stepped in. Something about the place always set Patrick at ease, in spite of the intensity of the sort of work David and Lionel did. It was decorated in calming shades of lavender, with rich, warm wooden shelves lining three walls, a large mahogany desk directly opposite the door, and curtains that would have been more at home in a lady's boudoir than a law office. Two leather sofas sat facing each other in the center of the room over an oriental carpet. The room always smelled of tea and cakes, as well as some sort of spicy cologne that fired Patrick's blood, no matter how hard he tried to deny the carnal side of his nature.

"Hello?" he asked glancing around.

A moment later, Lionel Mercer strode out of the back office. "Why, hello, Officer Wrexham," he greeted Patrick with a smile, thrusting out his hand as he approached.

Patrick cleared his throat, feeling himself flush, as he took Lionel's hand. The man was unnerving. He had a lithe, almost delicate build, but one handshake was enough to prove to anyone that he had more power in his little finger than even Patrick, with all his muscle, had in his entire body. Lionel was dressed like a fashion plate in a blue waistcoat that set off the vibrant blue of his eyes. His lips were soft and sensual, and almost always curved into a secret smile. Not a hair on his head was out of place, which made Patrick feel like a hulk by comparison.

"Tea?" Lionel asked, walking past Patrick to the stove in the corner of the room.

Patrick cleared his throat, swiped his hat from his head, and asked, "Is David in?" He cursed his voice for cracking and rushed on with, "He'll want to hear what I've uncovered."

David came out of his office. "What have you uncovered?" Patrick noted that he was flushed and had a somewhat distracted air about him. It was enough to make him wonder what he and Lionel had been doing in the office moments before, but seeing as that was none of his business, he pushed the thought out of his mind.

Patrick shook David's hand once he approached. It was far less unnerving than greeting Lionel, which shifted him back to business.

"I've had reports that Chisolm is back in England," he said. "Though I haven't been able to locate exactly where he is yet."

"That's more than we knew about the man yesterday." David smiled encouragingly. "By any chance have Joe Logan and Alistair Bevan returned as well?" he asked Lionel.

"Not yet," Lionel answered, bringing Patrick a steaming cup of tea. "It seems there were some difficulties along the border between France and Spain."

Patrick's brow inched up as he took the offered tea. He had forgotten Lord Farnham and his valet had left for a holiday in Spain when Farnham's father, Lord Winslow, who was reportedly quite ill, had left with his wife and other son for their country estate.

"If they can't get home that way, they need to find another," David said. "The sooner we talk to Joe about his sister, the sooner we'll be able to unravel another part of this mystery."

"About the man with the lion?" Patrick asked.

As part of their mission to a cotton mill in Leicestershire, Stephen Siddel and Lord Hillsboro had stumbled across Lily Logan. The poor girl had been sold into prostitution, but she was present at the mill when it was raided and a great many children were rescued. Lily had disappeared again before she could be freed, but not before conveying the cryptic message that "the man with the lion" was responsible for the entire trafficking ring. She'd been confident that her brother would know who she was talking about. Unfortunately, the rest of them didn't.

"Precisely." David nodded. "I can't help but think that the man with the lion, whoever or whatever that is, holds the key to unraveling this whole thing."

"And nobody else has a clue who the man with the lion is?" Patrick asked, his heart sinking. Every new revelation in the investigation brought them one step closer to solving the whole thing while pushing them two steps back.

"Nobody," Lionel answered, brow furrowed in frustration.

"That's not true."

They all snapped to face the door as none other than Everett Jewel, the famous actor, swept into the room, making an entrance as grand as any he might make on the stage. Patrick's heart dropped into a whirlpool of butterflies in his stomach, and his cock jumped as though it would stand up to give the glorious man a standing ovation. The reaction was so sudden and so visceral that he nearly dropped his tea. He did the only thing he could think of to hide his sudden attack of nerves and the flush he was certain painted his face by taking a long drink of tea, even though it was so hot it scalded his tongue. The pain might help him control his body's reaction to Jewel, but probably not.

"I know who the man with the lion is," Jewel said, marching to stand in the center of the room, his back straight and his eyes ablaze with intrigue.

He wore a suit every bit as fashionable as Lionel's and every bit as eccentric, except where Lionel wore muted, pastel tones that blended with his naturally pale coloring, Jewel wore a maroon jacket and vivid green tie that practically screamed for attention. Jewel's eyes were outlined with kohl, as though he'd forgotten to remove his stage make-up, that accentuated eyes so blue they were nearly violet. They were a stunning contrast to his black hair and would almost have made him seem feminine, if not for his carefully trimmed beard and moustache.

Rather than breezing on to reveal who the man with the lion was, Jewel turned to Patrick. His eyes narrowed mischievously, and he broke into a grin that showed off his surprisingly straight and white teeth. "Hello," he practically purred, inching closer to Patrick and extending a hand. "I don't believe we've met. Everett Jewel. And you are?"

Patrick's mouth dropped open, but not a sound came out. He knew good and well who Jewel was. He'd spent far more than he wanted to admit to on tickets to the theater to watch Jewel perform night after night. He'd skulked in the back of the crowd at The Cock and Bear pub, where Jewel often went after shows to continue entertaining a certain type of crowd with ribald songs and other theatrics after shows, more times than he could count. His face heated even more at the inconvenient memory of how many nights he'd lain awake in bed, stroking himself like a madman, while imagining what Jewel must look like naked.

Lionel's derisive snort spared Patrick from the embarrassment of attempting to form words to reply to his idol. "Is it impossible for you to walk into a room without demanding every man drop to their knees to suck your cock?"

"Lionel!" David glowered at him.

Jewel merely turned his saucy grin on Lionel. "Wishful thinking, eh, Lionel?" He sauntered closer to Lionel, arched one eyebrow, and grabbed the bulge in his trousers. "I'm always ready to go when you are." Lionel sniffed and turned away, but before he could say anything, Jewel continued with, "Oh, that's right. You're out of the game at the moment." Jewel glanced back to Patrick as though they were best of friends. "More like sour grapes because he couldn't get what he wanted, if you ask me."

"I could have, and I *have* had, any man I want," Lionel snapped, far less composed than Patrick had ever seen the enigmatic man.

"Except me," Jewel answered with a shrug. He shifted to stand by Patrick's side. "He's still bitter about that," he said with off-handed arrogance.

"You always were a delusional ass." Lionel crossed his arms and tilted his chin up, but his pale cheeks were flushed scarlet.

David cleared his throat, sending a withering look to both Jewel and Lionel. "There's no time for the two of you to play Who Has the Bigger Dick, and no one cares anyhow."

"We both know who would win in any case," Jewel commented to Patrick in a low, teasing voice.

Patrick nearly choked on his tea. His trousers were uncommonly tight.

David held up a hand to both Jewel and Lionel, as though they'd both made a ribald comment and needed to be stopped. "Children are being snatched from the streets and sold into slavery, but by all means, if the two of you believe your pitiful rivalry is more important...."

Lionel lowered his chin by a fraction, a stony look of contrition hardening his features. "Fine. If you believe you know who the man with the lion is, then by all means, enlighten us."

WANT TO READ MORE?
PREORDER JUST A LITTLE DANGER TODAY!

Click here for a complete list of other works by Merry Farmer.

ABOUT THE AUTHOR

I hope you have enjoyed *Just a Little Temptation.* If you'd like to be the first to learn about when new books in the series come out and more, please sign up for my newsletter here: http://eepurl.com/cbaVMH And remember, Read it, Review it, Share it! For a complete list of works by Merry Farmer with links, please visit http://wp.me/P5ttjb-14F.

Merry Farmer is an award-winning novelist who lives in suburban Philadelphia with her cats, Torpedo, her grumpy old man, and Justine, her hyperactive new baby. She has been writing since she was ten years old and realized one day that she didn't have to wait for the teacher to assign a creative writing project to write something. It was the best day of her life. She then went on to earn not one but two degrees in History so that she would always have something to write about. Her books have reached the Top 100 at Amazon, iBooks, and Barnes & Noble, and have been named finalists in the prestigious RONE and Rom Com Reader's Crown awards.

ACKNOWLEDGMENTS

I owe a huge debt of gratitude to my awesome beta-readers, Caroline Lee and Jolene Stewart, for their suggestions and advice. And double thanks to Julie Tague, for being a truly excellent editor and assistant!

Click here for a complete list of other works by Merry Farmer.

Printed in Great Britain
by Amazon